LACEY SILKS

MyLit Publishing

To those whose love stood the test of time.

"You're mine as I'm yours. And if we die, we die. But first, we'll live." – Ygritte, Game of Thrones

CHAPTER 1

"I'll show you mine if you show me yours."

Who could have known that a stupid game of skipping stones would be the beginning of a lifelong friendship? I sat on a grass patch by the shore, holding my hands behind my back, squeezing the flat rock with my fingers, praying that this was the gem I'd been searching for.

"I bet you mine is bigger," Nick teased. "I'll get at least ten skips."

My curiosity spiked, and I wondered whether he did have a better stone than I had. But I wouldn't accept defeat that easily. The flat one I'd found a half hour earlier and stuffed into my pocket was definitely a winner.

"Impossible. Not with this one." Though I wished I could see just how big his was, though, and so I tried to see what he was hiding in his hands.

"No cheating, Jo. You know the rules."

We'd spent the last hour walking up and down the cliffs of Hope Bay, looking for the perfect stones. The challenge to find the best one, an Olympic gold medal-winning flat rock, the one that would skip the furthest, highest, and most often, was on. We each would have one chance to skim our stones over the blue water of Stone Lake, and this sunny and windless July day couldn't have turned out better for our little competition.

The winner would get the dibs on choosing our lookout point for the night – my roof or Nick's roof – because the night sky was not only full of surprises but also full of falling stars you could wish upon. I had so many wishes I could barely keep them all in my head, and my rooftop was waiting for that special day when I was a winner and I could share my view of the sky with my best friend. Separated by only a few feet, his was to the west, mine to the east.

Given that I'd never won this challenge before, I figured my chances were somewhere close to those of seeing an asteroid hit the atmosphere and land on top of my head: pretty much a miracle. That was until I found the perfectly round, flat rock, without any sharp edges or flaws. I expected at least fifteen skips on this one. With good eight years of practice behind me — that's when Nick and I began our friendly feud in grade one — and a strong arm, unless he'd found his rock on Mars and it had special anti-gravity hovering powers, my hope to win just once was renewed.

"Ladies first."

"Are you afraid I'll win?" I asked.

"Not a chance."

"We'll see. Feast your eyes on this." I held my stone up between my fingers, displaying it as if it were gold. To me, it was way more than gold. It would give me bragging rights for the rest of the summer, at least. His eyes went wide for a moment before that calmness he was so good at carrying around him at all times returned to his face.

He gestured with his hand for me to take my place.

With my head held high, I cranked my neck to the side and stepped closer to the shore. There was no wind in Hope Bay today, as if Mother Nature knew that I needed this win. I prepped my arm, going through the motion of throwing three times before the rock left my palm, and I counted.

Five, seven, ten, twelve, fourteen...

"Did you see that? That was fifteen and a half." I jumped, trying to outdo gravity, the way my stone had.

"A half?"

"Yes, I saw it. It was almost sixteen."

"Like I can't beat a half." He rolled his eyes.

"Fifteen and a half. I just beat my record, and you haven't hit a fifteen in... well, it's been a while. I'm pretty sure that I'll be the winner this time."

I braced my hands on my hips, waiting patiently, and then Nick pulled his rock from behind his back and my mouth dropped open. If I thought that my rock was perfect, then his was flawless, crafted over thousands of years in the caressing waves of Stone Lake, until it was meant to be found by him.

I felt my heart pound in my chest.

He winked and gave me that smile full of confidence before his arm flew back like a pitcher's, pulling all the strength from his shoulder and forcing it to his fingertips, right into the rock. The whizz of air was enough for me to doubt my perfect fifteen and a half skips.

I watched the rock glide over the calm water as if in slow motion, counting each long leap. My heart raced as the jumps lost their height and shortened, quickening their graceful journey.

Eight, ten, twelve, fourteen, sixteen... no!

"That last one was a half! It's a tie." I pointed toward the ripples in the water.

"Are you going to be a sore loser again, Jo?"

"I. Am not. A sore loser."

"Said a sore loser."

"You know this challenge isn't fair. Men have stronger arms."

"Then why do you challenge me to do this every week?"

"Because...well, if you had an older brother, he'd teach you how to treat girls."

"What are you talking about?"

How was I supposed to explain to him that sometimes guys were supposed to let the woman win? They were supposed to make the woman feel special; at least that's what my father had done with me. He'd let me cast the first fishing rod into a river when we fished, waited for me at the car with the door open, and stood at the table, patiently waiting to take his seat, until I was sitting. Was Nick treating me this way because I wasn't a woman yet? If that was the reason, then I still had a few years of waiting until Nick grew up and acted like a real man.

"Never mind." I waved my hand. "You'll never get it."

"Is it because I'm a guy?"

"Well, yes."

He coughed *sore loser* into his hand and I threw him a dirty look.

"One day I'll beat you. You'll see."

"And that will be the day that I also land on Mars."

"Shut up." I frowned. "What time is it?"

He looked at his watch — the only one between the two of us – so that we could be back in town by ten in the morning. In the summertime, when school was out, my father needed my help at his bakery, and Nick helped his mom with decorating the cakes at her place. He was really good at it, too, though he only agreed to do the job if she didn't tell anyone. Our stores were next to each other, with the three-bedroom apartments right above, on the outskirts of our town, a fifteen-minute walk to the other end closed off by a fire station. My bedroom window was only a foot away from Nick's; that's how we'd become friends before school even started, because we'd both lived in those houses since birth. So technically, I'd known him my entire life.

"Jo, it's quarter to. We gotta run."

The lake wasn't that far away, but we chose an area no one ever came to because of all the rocks – Pebble Beach they called it – and that was a good eight-minute run back home.

I took off first, but Nick soon caught up. Obviously, as a boy, he was always a faster runner, but since I'd been secretly practicing every morning, I could keep up with his pace. We pushed our feet to the max, running through the forest and back to town. The side of my leg scraped against a branch, but I didn't stop. Helping Dad was important, and I wouldn't ever let him down, especially since summer time was the only time he could get somewhat of a break when I helped.

"Rooftop this evening?" he asked, before dashing through the door of his bakery.

"Yours or mine?"

Was it possible that he'd consider mine for a change?

"Mine, of course."

Yeah, I didn't think so. I sighed, making a promise to myself to go to my rooftop afterward so that I could wish upon a falling star. Why wouldn't Nick believe me that we got more comets on the east side?

"I'll see you after the sun goes down." I waved, and we both pushed open the doors to our respective stores.

"Hi, Daddy!" I ran to my father and hugged him tightly.

"You're cutting it pretty close, aren't you, sweetheart?"

"Still on time, though."

"Yes, you are. You know what to do."

I went to the back of the store, where I would spend the remainder of my day mixing and kneading dough, cutting it into even parts for the buns and larger ones for the breads, before they were set aside to rise. My father did the first run of breads and buns at four in the morning, and I helped him with the afternoon batch, before the customers rushed in after work. See, my father wasn't just any baker - he was the best baker in the world, and his breads and buns were known all over West Virginia. Trucks lined up early in the morning for pick-up so that they could distribute his fresh goods to the larger cities. The aroma of freshly baked breads drifted through town each day, advertising his delicious goods. During school months, he hired Mrs. Gladstone, who lived close to the fire station with her three cows and a bull, so that I could concentrate on my homework, and on being a kid. And since I was going into eighth grade, the first year of junior high school this September, I wasn't expecting to have much time for work.

"Make sure you get a good education and good grades, so that you can make something of yourself," he'd always said. "It's what your mother would have wanted."

About an hour into my work, I heard the bell of the front door ring and looked at the clock on the wall. It was too early for the first customers. Living in a small town, everybody knew where everyone else was at all times. That's why I liked to get away with Nick in the mornings. I wondered who it could be.

"Hello, Walter." I heard Marge, Nick's mom, say, and I wondered whether he'd come in with her, but I doubted it. He was probably stuck decorating the cakes.

"Hello, Marge. What can I do for you today?"

"One loaf, please."

Ever since I could remember, our parents had always acted weird when they were around each other. Unless you got a couple of glasses of wine in Mrs. Tuscan, and a handful of beers into my father, despite knowing each other their entire lives, they always remained formal.

I heard him ring her up, but they didn't exchange another word. When I peeked through the small window in the back door, I saw Mrs. Tuscan standing on her tiptoes, lip-locked with my father.

"Oh, my God," I breathed out, and crouched down so that they wouldn't see me.

Nick. Where was Nick? I had to tell him. But he was working now.

What did it all mean? How long had this been going on, and why hadn't my father told me anything? Okay, so maybe an adult conversation wasn't that appropriate with a twelve-year-old, but I was almost a teen, and so was Nick. That was like a stone's throw from adulthood, wasn't it?

Nick and I shared the same birthday. Our moms had delivered us within minutes of one another, making me older and wiser than Nick by three hundred and thirty seconds, to be exact. Three hundred and thirty seconds sounded much longer than five and a half minutes — something I liked to remind him about when he acted like the all-mighty stone-skipper.

I went back to work, putting what I'd seen out of my mind, at least for now, and decided not to mention anything to my father, who seemed to be running the store in an uplifted mood.

When I climbed from my room to Nick's that evening, he had already opened the door to his balcony for me. Maybe there was hope for him to be a gentleman, after all? I climbed up the ladder to the roof and lay back on the blanket spread over the shingles. The angle here wasn't that steep, exactly the same as on my roof, and it afforded the perfect rest spot to watch the night sky.

I sighed.

"What's the matter?" he asked. "Are you still upset about the loss? I won fair and square, and I was teasing you, you know."

"No, I'm not upset about that."

"What is it, then?"

"Did you know that my dad and your mom have a thing for each other?"

"What?"

I flipped over on my stomach and looked into his eyes, which were reflecting the stars above. They were just like his mother's: a beautiful green that drew everyone's attention from far away.

"I saw them kissing today."

"What? Our parents?"

"Yeah."

"That's gross."

"Why is it gross?"

"I don't know; because he's your dad, I guess. I never thought about my mom being with someone else."

"I never thought about my dad being with anyone else either, but maybe this is a good thing. I mean, they need someone to love, don't they?"

"They've got us."

"Don't be stupid, Nick. I meant real love between a man and a woman. Oh, my God, do you think they'll get married?"

"Why would you even ask that? It was just a kiss. They should date first. And if my mom's gonna marry, I have to approve."

"Are you saying that you wouldn't approve of my father?"

"No, but I'm the man of the house now."

"You're only twelve."

"Almost thirteen."

"If they got married, that would make you my step-brother." I flipped again onto my back to look at the stars. I didn't like that idea. I preferred that we remained friends, instead being of step-siblings.

"Jo, it was just a kiss, okay? Besides, my mother's not over my father yet."

"Nick, it's been five years."

"I know, but I can still hear her cry at night."

"Maybe she's crying because she thinks her son is an asshat who doesn't know how to treat women."

"Jo! How many times do I have to tell you that you're not a woman?"

"Well, you're not a man."

"I know that!"

"Argh!" I hated when we fought. Ever since Nick's father died while serving in the navy, he hadn't been the same. I remembered his dad as a brave man. We went to New York when we were in first grade, and Nick's father ended up securing a man wearing a suicide vest. We later found out the guy was a religious extremist. That experience was one of the reasons I loved living in a small town, one which led to nowhere because it was cut off by the mountains on one side a lake on the other and farms to the west. Unless you were lost, no one ever came here. This wasn't a drive-through town.

Mr. Tuscan had saved a lot of lives that day, including mine. We were lucky, and Nick was always proud of the fact that his father was a hero. He wanted to be just like him. I'd never forget the day a police officer came knocking on his door with the news of his father's death while serving our country. I was there at the bakery. Nick was never the same after the funeral. He wanted to protect his family, especially his mother.

"I think both our parents need a change. They need something good in their lives."

"I think your brain is doing that girl thing again."

"What girl thing?"

"Where you fantasize about boys, heroes, and happy endings. There are no happy endings. My mom's alone, and so is your dad. They lost their loved ones and will never have them again."

"But we're happy, aren't we?"

"Yeah, but we're just kids.

"Well, they still kissed, so I think that made them happy."

"A kiss doesn't mean anything, Jo."

I shook my head and sighed. He was such a boy.

"Have you kissed a girl before?" I asked, knowing very well that he hadn't; because if he had, he would have told me. And if he didn't tell me, I would have found out from one of the girls at school, and there weren't that many of us there. Eight in our class, to be exact.

"Why are you asking? Have you kissed a boy?"

"No. I'm not letting a boy kiss me until I know we're in love."

"That's stupid."

"You're stupid. It doesn't make sense to do it earlier."

"What if you fall in love and he ends up being a bad kisser?"

I hadn't thought about it that way. "Then I'll have to teach him how to kiss."

"A man who has to be taught how to kiss is not a man."

"When did you become an expert at kissing?"

"I'm not. That's just the way it is. It should be natural. Why are we talking about spit-swapping anyway? Our parents are old enough to know what they're doing."

I hoped they were, because when it came to the matters of the heart, I felt like I was getting more confused with each passing month — especially when I talked to Nick about it.

"Now, what are you doing on your birthday? It's in one week," he asked.

"Nothing, I guess. Do you have any plans?"

"Nope. Want to celebrate them together?"

It was a silly question because I couldn't even remember one birthday that we hadn't spent together.

"Sure. Hey, look at that one. Is that a comet or a satellite?" I pointed to the night sky sprinkled with white dots.

"Satellite. It's too steady to be a comet."

"I wish we could do this on my roof. I bet you we'd see more falling stars than here."

"Well, maybe if you learn how to skip stones better, we can," he teased. I hated him when he did that. Maybe we were already more like siblings than friends?

I shook the thought away, because I didn't want Nick to be my brother. Despite him being an ass-hat sometimes, I liked him as my friend.

CHAPTER 2

"Good morning, sunshine. Happy birthday. You're officially a teenager now."

My father stood in the doorway to my room with a wide smile on his face. I hadn't asked him about the kiss I'd seen last week, but I hadn't seen Nick's mom come around more than once a day to get her bread, so I wondered whether it was a one-time thing, or if perhaps they'd had a fight.

"Thank you."

"Any special plans for today, or are you doing the usual dinner and movies with Nick?"

"The usual. I wish you could come," I pouted, knowing very well how much my father's heart broke when I did that.

"Me too, baby. But you know I have to run the store. I'll have a surprise for you when you come back, though."

"You don't need to give me anything, Daddy. I have everything I need."

"And I have the most thoughtful daughter in the world. How about a piggyback ride to the front door?" he asked.

"Dad, I'm thirteen now. I think I may be a little old for that."

He pouted. Now I knew where I'd gotten that skill from. "Okay, one last time." I hopped on his back, and he treaded toward the front door before setting me down.

"You're sure you don't need me this afternoon?" I asked.

"I always need you, but today is special." He took me into his arms, folding me in a tight hug. I could feel all the emotions rolling off him and onto me, and I knew that his thoughts were running to the past again. "If your mother could see you now, she'd be so proud. You are the best daughter a father could ask for."

My mom had died at my birth, so my only memories of her were from the photographs my father had saved from before they had me. I didn't own a single photograph of the two of us together, and the only female figure in my life was Nick's mom next door, who was a pastry chef. Marge's store smelled ten times better than ours did, but that was because of all the frostings, fruits, and sugar creations she used to decorate her cakes, muffins, cupcakes, and cookies. Still, I bet having my mom would have been a million times better.

"I love you too, Dad. See you tonight?"

"Yes, I'll see you tonight." He pulled a few bills out of his pocket and handed them to me. "Have a great time at the movies."

"Thanks!" I grabbed my backpack with the bathing suit and ran out the door. We were planning to go for a swim at the beach later on. Outside, I turned right and ran back up the three steps that led to Marge's bakery.

"Hi, Mrs. Tuscan."

"Happy birthday, Joelle." She came out from behind the counter where she'd been shelving a new batch of cookies and hugged me tight. I loved it when she hugged me, especially the sweet way she always smelled, like a mother.

"Thank you. Is Nick ready?" I started heading for the door to the back where I hoped to find my best friend.

"Oh, you can't go in there, Joelle." Her eyes went wide with fear.

I stopped. "Has something happened?"

"No, it's just that..."

"It's okay, Mom. I'm done." Nick came out from behind the swinging back door. At the front of the house, the Tuscans had the store; at the back, a ginormous kitchen that took up the rest of the downstairs. There was a small sitting area with a door out to the patio, just like at our house, that they called a dining room. It was just a table with four chairs in the back of the kitchen. One day, when I had a job, I dreamed of buying my father a real house with a fireplace, a family room, a proper dining room, and a way smaller kitchen than the one we had now.

"Done with what?" I asked, swiping the buttercream frosting off his shirt pocket.

"I'll tell you after the movies. Ready?"

I nodded, and we hopped out the door. We were meeting a few friends from school at the theater and were going to go out for pizza later on. Although our town was small, we did have a movie theater. There was only one screen, but at least it was there. I'd heard theaters in large cities had several screens, but I was sure that ours was much more intimate. Different movies were scheduled at various times during the weekends, and the theater was closed during the week — except during the summertime when kids were off school, and they held camps and acting classes. I hadn't heard of anyone from our town becoming a famous actor, so I wasn't too sure about the quality of those classes. Perhaps it was just another activity to pass the time.

"Be careful." Marge waved us goodbye and we ran out the door.

"Which guys are coming?" I asked, once we were on our way.

"Andrew and Carter."

"You three are inseparable."

"I could say the same thing about you, Molly, and Daisy. That's who you invited, isn't it?"

"Yes," I laughed. "Why are you wearing your swim shorts already?"

"Because they're a two in one. They're shorts – and you can swim in them. What's the point of carrying both around?"

"What about a towel?"

"Did you see the sun outside? They'll air dry."

"You're such a boy." I shook my head.

"So?"

"So nothing. Let's just go."

He pulled out a granola bar from his pocket and chewed it. One thing about Nick was that he always had something to eat in his pockets.

We walked along the side road, not talking to each other, which was very odd. Any other day, it'd be difficult to get one of us to shut up so that the other could speak. I saw Nick sneak a look at me once every few minutes, but I pretended not to notice it. I wasn't sure what it was about today that irked me, but something was off.

The heat wave the past two weeks had dried up the grass, road, and anything else the sun had touched. Each time a car passed us, yellow dirt rose up, swallowing us in its cloud. By the time we got to the theater, I could taste it in my mouth and shake it off the curls of my hair.

We walked up to the concession stand. The aroma of melting butter and popcorn filled the air.

"The usual?" Nick asked, heading for the line.

"I'll have a water instead of a coke today."

"Why?"

"Because it's less calories."

"Since when do you worry about that stuff? You're like a toothpick, no matter how many cookies my mom tries to stuff in you."

"Since I've seen the way Carter looks at Daisy. She's skinnier. I have to watch what I eat. I can feel my body changing."

Was I really talking to Nick about my body? It just sort of slipped out, but I'd caught him sneaking a peek at my growing boobs on several occasions, so I knew that he'd noticed.

Nick stopped and pulled on my hand, "Don't do that, Jo. Don't let anyone else question how beautiful you are. Daisy's a toothpick. You're... you're perfect."

I felt my cheeks heat. If it were any other day, Nick's compliment wouldn't have affected me, but it did today, and I didn't know why.

"Thanks."

"I mean it, Jo. I never want to hear you talking about your weight again."

Who was this boy? Even though I didn't want to admit it, Nick was right. When I didn't think about how other girls looked, I felt much prettier.

"Maybe I'll have a root beer, then. After all, it's our birthday, right?"

The drink was one of my and Nick's favorite's.

"That's more like it!"

Once we got our popcorn and drinks, we went inside the theater where the others were already seated. I followed Nick down the aisle. The first seat was empty. I found it odd that our friends hadn't filled the beginning of the row, and then there was another one between Carter and Molly.

"You sit here." Daisy pulled on Nick's hand so that he'd take the first empty seat, and I felt my face heat with anger.

Nick and I always sat together at the movies, especially on our birthdays. Why did Daisy have to separate us?

"Wouldn't you rather sit with the guys?" I asked.

Nick shrugged, which again rubbed me the wrong way. As Nick took his spot, I frowned and moved over to the only other seat available and plopped down between two of my friends.

"Hey, cupcake girl." Carter looked at me in a dreamy way before leaning in for a hug. "Happy Birthday."

Carter had always called me cupcake. It just so happened that I'd dropped one in a school hallway once and then slipped on it, falling flat on my ass, and the nickname had stuck. He'd had a crush on me for a long time, but I never saw anything more in him than a friend. Besides, I was only thirteen, and my dad always told me that I'd have plenty of time to think about boys in my life after I finished school. That's why he was so proud of my friendship with Nick. We looked out for each other like best friends should. When I leaned over and saw Daisy tickle Nick's hand with her finger, I felt a shiver of jealousy hit me, so I leaned into Carter and held him for a bit longer than usual.

"Thanks, Carter. You must be excited about the movie."

So was I, but we all knew that Carter was the biggest Transformers fan ever.

"I'm gonna see it again with my brother tomorrow."

"But you don't even know if you'll like it."

"Oh, I know I'll love it. There's no way this movie will fail."

"Happy Birthday, Joelle," Molly said from my other side. "Thanks for inviting us over."

"You're welcome. How's your little brother?"

Molly's mom just had a baby a month ago, so she'd been spending a lot of time outside the house to avoid the colicky cries.

"He's gotten bigger, and Momma says that his tummy should settle soon and he'll stop crying. She's tried everything, I tell ya, but then we found this trick of turning on a hair dryer. He stops crying and listens to the buzzing as if it was the most fascinating sound in the world. Babies, I tell ya. I'm not sure I'll ever want kids."

"Well, you're lucky you have a sibling."

This was coming from a child who had always wished for a large family. But I always had my father, and that made me a very lucky girl because there were enough foster kids and orphans in the world.

"It doesn't feel like luck right now," she sighed.

"It will get better."

"I hope so."

I got another peek at Daisy putting her hand into Nick's popcorn bag – as if she didn't have her own – and fluttering her lashes. Didn't he see that she was flirting? Why lead her on?

"Hey, pay attention. It's about to start." Andrew, another Transformers fan, called Daisy out. If I were brave enough, I'd have kissed him right then and there.

The credits began rolling, and we all turned our attention to the screen. I wished I could concentrate as much on the movie as I did on Daisy, who every so often leaned into Nick to whisper something in his ear; maybe I would have enjoyed it much more. When it was over, pulsing with excitement, the boys couldn't stop talking about it. Instead of going to the lake for a swim, we ended up hiking through the forest. Daisy twisted her ankle, or at least she was good at pretending that she did, and hung onto Nick's arm for the remainder of the hike. That's why we didn't go swimming at Pebble Beach in the end – because of Daisy's supposedly twisted ankle.

We passed old Mr. Grafton's house. The rumor was that it was haunted, yet it was still the best place to trick-or-treat. He always put up the spookiest decorations, although with the way his yard was kept, that really wasn't too difficult to do.

Next was Mrs. Gladstone's ranch. We all stopped by the fence, staring at all the activity as Betty Sue, one of her cows, was calving.

"Is it time, Mrs. Gladstone?" Andrew asked.

"It sure is. Probably another hour or so and we'll have a brand new calf."

"What are you going to name it?"

"Well, if it's female, Betsy, after her mother. If it's male, Duke, after his father."

"Good luck!" I yelled out.

"Thank you. And happy birthday, Joelle and Nicholas!"

"Thanks!" We waved.

"I bet you it will be Duke," Carter said with pride.

"I'm betting on Betsy," Molly countered.

"How do you know?"

"Girl's intuition." She shrugged.

"Feminine intuition is fiction," Carter laughed.

"That's bull," Molly argued.

"It's not. It's ridiculous. You girls justify everything with intuition, even when it's the most illogical scenario, so long as it suits you."

"And I see you still haven't learned when to keep your mouth shut."

"I'm just saying how it is."

Molly just shook her head. Those two always argued, and their minds worked at the opposite sides of the spectrum.

As soon as we passed the farm, Nick and Daisy fell behind, and I joined Molly, Carter, and Andrew ahead. We found the sweetest blueberries and blackberries near the cliffs. Carter had a knack for finding the best ones, which he gave to me. Soon enough my stomach was full of berries, and my mouth and tongue were stained purple.

Once I forgot about Nick and Daisy behind us, my mood lifted.

"I can't wait until high school," Molly sighed.

"Why?" I asked.

"Because Carter's older brother goes there," Andrew teased.

"Shut up. That's not the only reason."

"Yeah, but it's the main one. Who wants high school? All that homework and long classes. *This* is the life!" He looked down, swinging his legs back and forth.

We were sitting on the high beam of an abandoned barn. The town often held parties and carnivals there. It was smack in the middle of town, just beyond the forest, and a stone's throw away from the lake. Andrew passed me the last slice of pizza from one of the two boxes we'd brought. The air was dense, swirling with visible heat waves. Part of me wished for a swim to cool off, but that would mean I'd need to get into my bathing suit, which in the heat felt like a hassle. Besides, I could have used a few more minutes in the sun to tend to my summer tan. My skin was already brown, and while my freckles were waiting to pepper my nose and cheeks, Molly's were more prominent than ever. The sound of thunder rolled behind us.

"We better get out of here if we don't want to get wet. Nick, can I have your shirt if it starts raining?"

I felt my nose wrinkle up. Nick only shrugged, obviously confused by Daisy's request.

"It's time for cake, anyways," I said. "Let's go." I jumped off the beam, right down onto the stage below.

"Jo, are you crazy?" Nick yelled out.

"What?"

"You could have broken a leg."

"It's not that high."

"But I'd get in trouble. I don't want your father to think that I wasn't looking out for you."

"He wouldn't."

He shook his head in disapproval, as if he were my father. Sometimes I didn't understand boys, but other times I wanted to, a lot.

Nick's mom was baking us special cakes, the way she did every year. We gathered our knapsacks and hurried through the woods. Miraculously, Daisy's sprained ankle was feeling much better. I bet she didn't want her perfect hair to get wet, and so she managed to hurry along with us.

Once we hit the road, the thunderstorm had passed to the south. The few drops that caught us were barely a teasing sprinkle, and I wished it had rained more so that I could have seen Daisy's hairdo frizzle up. Her curls and rain didn't exactly mesh.

On the way back home, Nick draped his arm around me. No one else, except for Daisy and Carter, seemed to notice or care, yet the gesture still made me feel very special. For the first time since we left our house, I felt like we were ourselves again, or at least I was. I just didn't feel complete without Nick. He was my best friend and my partner in crime. We stayed a few good feet behind the group, and I knew that they were out of earshot.

"So, how does it feel to be thirteen?"

"The same way as it felt to be twelve." I shrugged his arm off my shoulder.

"You're upset."

"Am not."

"Why are you upset?"

"I always thought that having our birthdays together was special. This was supposed to be our day, and Daisy ruined it. But you know what the worst part is? That you didn't do anything to stop it."

"Jo, I have no clue what you're talking about."

"At the movies. Why didn't you ask her to move? She clearly wanted to separate us."

"Because it would have been rude?"

"So it was better to be rude to me?"

"How was I rude to you?"

"You didn't sit beside me."

I wasn't sure why that made me so angry today. We often went out with our friends, and I never cared who Nick talked to or sat beside at the movies. But today was different, and I was pretty sure that I would have preferred to have gone to the movies just with him.

"Jo, it wasn't my fault. And I thought you were rude too, but I didn't want to ruin your birthday by mentioning it."

"What did I do?"

"You couldn't stop talking to Carter about the movie."

"So?"

"So, we always talk about it together, on the rooftop."

"But Carter was right there, and when we were hiking, you were with Daisy." I rolled my eyes. He hated when I did that, but at this moment, I didn't care. "You're being weird about Carter."

"Well, you're being weird about Daisy."

"So we're both being weird?"

"I guess." He paused for a moment, staring at the ground. "I'm sorry if it bothered you. Next time I'll ask her to move."

"Thank you. You know it's because you're my best friend, and our birthdays are special."

"I know."

By the time we finished our conversation, our friends had reached the bakery and were waiting for us on the front steps.

"Ready?" Molly asked, stepping from one foot to the other. Having our cakes revealed was always the best part of our birthday, and I wondered about the theme Marge had chosen to decorate the cakes with this year.

When we entered the bakery, my dad was there, smiling, and everyone started singing "Happy Birthday." I took Nick's hand without a thought and held it for the entire song. As they finished and I looked on the table: there was only one cake, and it must have been Nick's because it was in the shape of a yellow Camaro.

Bumblebee, I thought.

Nick let go of my hand, saying, "Wait here." A moment later he rolled out a cart with a box on top and a big red bow.

"I thought you said no gifts. We're saving money for the high school camping trip."

"This only cost me my time, and I really wanted to do this for you."

I sighed, pulling out the square box from my backpack before he got a chance to call me a hypocrite. "Happy birthday, Nick. I hope you like it."

"What is this?"

"Open it."

He tore the wrapping paper apart and gasped when he saw the rock in his hand. I had carved in the letter "N" on its flat surface.

"Joelle, where did you find this?"

He didn't call me by my full name unless he wanted my attention.

"Pebble Beach. Do you like it?"

"You know you'll never win against this, don't you?"

"I know. But I'd rather see you skip it and beat your own record."

He threw his arms around me and said, "Thank you so much."

"You're welcome."

"Now open yours."

Excited, I pulled on the red bow, lifted the square box cover off, and there it was: an absolutely beautiful cake. I pulled in a sniffle and covered my mouth with one hand while pointing with the other.

"It's us." I finally lowered my hand. "Skipping stones on the lake. Nick, this is beautiful. You did this?"

He nodded.

"Thank you. It's the best gift ever!" I hugged him tightly.

We cut the cakes and shared them with our parents, friends, and a few of Mrs. Tuscan's customers who happened to stop by. And everything between me and Nick was well again. He had surprised me with a birthday gift that was as thoughtful as it was lovely, and that was how I knew that our friendship was forever.

CHAPTER 3

Three years later

"Hey, Jo." Carter's voice echoed through the forest as he jogged toward me. "Wanna go get more wood for tonight?"

There it was: that signature *I wanna show you I like you* look on his face. I scanned the forest clearing for Nick, who usually managed to save me from Carter's advances, but he was nowhere to be found. It wasn't that I didn't like Carter; he was not only a good friend but also a very handsome and buff young man, and all the girls squealed when he walked into the room. I just wasn't interested. He'd always be just a friend.

"Ahm, sure, I guess."

I took one of the handles of the basket he'd brought while he gripped the other. We'd been waiting for our end-of-year high school trip ever since we found out that it existed, back in elementary school. Our class would stay away from home for three nights and four days. We had set up our tents about an hour before, girls on one side of the clearing and boys on the other, and now everyone was taking a break. There were only eighteen of us, for a total of four tents, plus two teachers: Mr. Simmons and Ms. Goodfield, who happened to be a married couple and would occupy the last two tents, smack in the middle.

We headed out into the woods, picking up dry sticks and twigs that would make perfect kindling for tonight and tossing them into the basket. As the sounds behind us quieted, shivers prickled up my arms. It was one thing to be out in the woods with a large group, and another to be just a pair, walking further and further out — especially with bears inhabiting these forests. We weren't supposed to venture further than earshot, and I was beginning to have trouble hearing our classmates' voices.

I stopped and asked, "Have you seen Nick?"

"I think Daisy was showing him a bird's nest she found." Carter pulled on the handle to continue, and I followed him.

Of course she was!

I liked Daisy. She was a good friend – one of my best friends, in fact – but she was just not right for Nick. I knew them both so well that I couldn't see them as a couple. They wouldn't mesh. I mean, she was a vegetarian, and Nick was a meat man. There. And that was just a pit stop on the No Way José highway.

Why wouldn't she just stop trying? What bugged me even more was that he seemed to be enjoying all the attention she was giving him and didn't even try to ignore her. Why was he leading her on, when I knew that he'd never actually go out with her?

"So, what's up with you and Nick?" Carter brought me out of my daze, and I stopped.

"What do you mean?"

"Are you two gonna date? Because everyone thinks you are."

"Why would we date?" I shook my head. "No, that'd be weird. We're just friends."

Had I thought about dating? Yes, of course I had. But dating Nick? No! He was like a brother to me; though truthfully, I wasn't interested in anyone else, either. I was too young and having way too much fun to be dating.

"So you're saying that if Daisy asked him out, you'd be okay with it?"

"Why? Do you think she will?"

"That wasn't my question."

"Daisy can do whatever she wants." I looked around the darkening forest. "I think we've gone too far."

Carter stopped. Which way had we come from? It took one circular turn for me to get lost. The trees and shrubs all looked the same.

"Oh my—"

"Shh!"

"Can you hear them?" I asked.

"Barely. You need to stay quiet. That way." He pointed in a direction I would have definitely not chosen. After a moment of walking, our classmates' voices became clearer, and I let go of the breath I'd been holding.

"What if someone asked you out?" Carter asked.

"Like who?"

"Me."

"Are you asking me out?"

"Only if you say yes."

"I don't know, Carter. My life's pretty busy. I've been helping Marge with cookies and cupcakes, and my father's bun requisitions are piling up. Dating means a commitment to go out and stuff. I don't think I have time to date."

"That's not what dating should feel like, Jo. You date because you want to get to know that person better. Because you can't stop thinking about them day and night."

"Well, then it's not for me, for sure. My mind and time are both filled with baking."

"So, there's no one you think about all the time?"

"I don't know. I think about a lot of people. Doesn't mean I'm dating them all."

He laughed. "It's because you're already closer to Nick than you think. You two are dating without even knowing."

"I don't think so. I've known Nick my entire life, and we live next door to each other. That's all there is to it." I shrugged it off. Besides, if Nick were interested, he needed to be the one to make a move, not me. Wasn't that how it was supposed to work? No, it wouldn't work. I knew him too well and too intimately. For Pete's sake, we used to swap our pacifiers and share a potty trainer.

"Okay, so how much time do you two spend together?"

"Well, we walk to school together, sit in the same class, walk back home, do our homework, bake, stock up the bakeries…"

His mouth was curving up higher the more I spoke. Was he trying to make a point? Good thing I didn't tell him about our rooftop star gazing each evening the weather permitted. So what if we spent a lot of time together? Our houses were separated by only a foot, our parents had known each other forever, and Nick was a very good friend. How many times did I have to repeat it for people to stop asking whether we were an item?

"He's your boyfriend."

"I'd say more like a brother."

"Hmm. If you say so." He shook his head. "But there's this theory I'd like to test."

"What theory?"

He let go of the basket. My fingers gave out under the full weight, and the wood spilled to the forest floor. As I looked down at the mess of twigs, I felt Carter lift my chin with his fingers. The next thing I knew, I was in Carter's arms as he pressed his lips to mine. Shocked, I froze and kept my eyes wide open and mouth tight as his lips tenderly kissed mine, and then I pulled away.

Okay, so I might have closed my eyes for a split second to enjoy the moment. Hey, YOLO, right? Besides, I'd never been kissed before, and practicing against my bedroom mirror was definitely not the same.

I took a step back and touched my fingers to my lips. "Why did you do that?"

"Because I wanted to check if you felt anything. Well?"

Oh, I definitely felt something, but the thief of my first kiss would not know his power.

"You shouldn't have done that!" I punched him in his arm.

"Why?" He rubbed the limb as if he'd been hit by an MMA fighter.

"Because it's wrong, and you're a friend, and... I don't want to date."

"You don't want to date, or you don't want to date anyone other than Nick?"

"Why does it matter to you?"

"Molly's never gonna put out, and you're involved with a guy who doesn't even know it. And neither do you!"

"Carter, that's mean!" I punched him in his arm again. He grasped my fist into his full hand, his fingers overlapping mine, and growled, causing my body to stiffen upright at the sound, ready for another one of his surprises.

What was happening to me?

"Why would you say that about Molly? She's awesome."

"And she's wearing a chastity belt."

"So? What's wrong with waiting for the right guy?"

"Nothing. Just that the 'right guy' doesn't exist. No matter who you date or whom you choose or end up with, no one will ever be right because you're two different people. You'll have issues with each other no matter what."

"That's called compromise. And acceptance of each other is part of the deal."

His brows scrunched, and I knew that he knew that I was right.

"If you want to have a chance with Molly, then you'll wait for her and give her as much time as she needs." I crouched down and began collecting the spilled twigs back into the basket. Carter joined my effort.

"And you'll respect her the way any girl should be because no one kisses a girl without her permission!" I felt my face heat with anger again. How dare he steal that kiss from me! It wasn't his to take.

"You mean, I should have asked you first?"

"Yes, of course."

"But you would have said no."

"Exactly my point."

The *duh* look on his face was beginning to shine some light on what it meant to fully respect a woman.

"Okay, I get it."

We stood up, but neither one of us moved.

"I'm sorry, Jo. I didn't meant to disrespect you."

"Apology accepted. Now let's get the wood back to the site before they wonder where we are."

"Wait." Carter bent down to the ground again and picked up a piece of broken glass. "Whoever was here before us is a pig. If the sun strikes it at the right angle, the grass could catch fire," he explained. Being the Captain's son came with the territory of knowing everything about fires. Carter's father had been a firefighter our entire lives.

The basket was almost full, and the clearing where our tents had been set up was visible. As we approached, I stopped for a moment and said, "And if you truly have any respect for me whatsoever, you will not mention what happened back there to anyone. Got it?"

"You mean, our kiss?"

"Shh! I said, no mentioning it."

"You just don't want Nick to find out."

"If you value having any future children, you will not say anything. If you do, I promise that Nick won't be the one kicking you in your balls."

He gave me a crooked grin as if I'd said something that intrigued him. We finally reached the campground and set the basket of wood near the fire pit in the center.

"Where have you been? I was worried." Nick almost knocked me over when he ran to me from the boys' side of the clearing where the tents had been set up.

"We were getting wood."

"You went out far enough not to hear us, didn't you?"

His fiery gaze flew from me to Carter and back. His hands rested on his hips, making his shoulders appear wider. What was wrong with him? Why was he fuming?

"Why are you being so weird, Nick? We didn't get lost. I'm very capable of getting wood and not getting lost."

"She got lost." Carter coughed into his hand and I threw him a dirty look — the kind that could kill. Why wasn't he falling down the way I imagined?

"I'll leave you two lovebirds alone." Carter chuckled and walked away.

"Why did he call us lovebirds?" I asked. "Did you say something to him? He was asking weird questions."

"Because that's what everyone calls us." Nick had another weird look on his face. I would be very glad when this puberty thing with boys was over, because the continued testosterone war between the guys in our class was beginning to drive me crazy.

"Well, then you need to stop them." I pulled on his arm to get him out of earshot.

"Why me?"

"Because you're the man, and you have to protect my honor," I whispered loudly.

"I think your father has been reading too many fairytales to you. That's old-fashioned."

"Maybe sometimes girls like it when you're old-fashioned."

This time it was Nick who pulled on my arm, lowering his voice to a whisper. "Did he try to kiss you?"

I made a grossed out face. "No, he didn't. Why would you even ask that?"

If the 'becoming a teacher' dream didn't work out, I could always be an actress. And the only reason teaching was a dream was because my first grade teacher had praised me for my patience and good habits. She'd said I would make an amazing teacher.

"Because Andrew said that Carter said he was going to try to kiss you on this camping trip. I tried to find you two, but you were gone."

By this time we'd reached the outer edge of the campground and were slowly walking away. There was no way that I wanted anyone to hear one of our crazy conversations. Enough people already thought my relationship with Nick was odd because we lived adjacent to each other, and I didn't need any new stares or rumors flying around our school. And there was no way that I wanted Carter to hear the word *kissing* out of my or Nick's mouths for at least the remainder of our high school careers.

Somewhere along the way, Nick had grabbed another basket. I took hold of the other handle and we walked a few steps into the woods, picking up more sticks for the fire.

"You know, I'm disappointed that you think I couldn't handle myself," I said.

Okay, maybe I was pushing this, but I had backed away when Carter kissed me. And I'd given him a good dose of Jo's medicine, I was sure, which included a stern warning about how to treat women.

"I know you can handle yourself. But you never know with guys."

"What do you mean, you never know with guys?"

"They always have a hidden agenda."

"Do you?" I asked.

"No, of course not."

Why did I get the feeling that he wasn't being truthful?

"So, see any birds' nests today?" I picked up a handful of twigs.

"One. It had fledglings. Daisy was really excited about it. She said being here made her feel alive."

I was excited to be here as well, yet Nick didn't seem to care.

"You know she has the hots for you, right?" I bit my lip, wondering to myself what kind of answer I wanted to hear from him.

"She does? So, what do you think I should do?"

Not that one. "Nothing. Ignore her." I shrugged

"Why?" He bent over and grabbed a few of the larger pieces of dried wood.

"Because she's not right for you. She's been trying to get your attention for years, but you don't like clingy girls."

"How do you know that?"

"I just do. She's not your type."

"Who is my type, then?"

"I think someone witty and smart would be better. Not school smart, although that's a bonus, but life smart. Someone who can survive anything and will have your back, no matter what." I paused, thinking for a moment. "And someone who can definitely bake."

"Someone like you?" he asked.

I stopped, surprised at his question. A patch of light shone through the canopy above, lighting his face. He looked handsome today and in his element. Nick had a few good layers of summer tan, and the humidity not only made him sweat like a pig, but also curled his hair into frizzy waves. They looked kind of nice. Maybe even a little sexy. He reached for the elastic around his wrist and tied it up.

Yes, that was definitely one of his sexier looks.

"I can't bake."

"Sure you can. I've seen you."

"Yeah, but not like you."

"That's because my mom's a pastry chef and your dad's a bread baker. I bet if she gave you instructions on how to bake a cake you'd be awesome."

"Maybe, but I could never decorate it the way you do."

He was lost in deep thought for a moment, and I wondered what he was thinking.

"What if I showed you how?"

"To decorate?"

"Yes. It'd take some practice, but it'd be fun." His smile stretched so wide that it forced my mouth to curve as well.

"I think I'd like that."

"When we get back home, then?"

"It's a date. Well, not a *date*. You know what I mean. Just knock on my window, and I'll be there. You know where I live." I winked.

Why did I just wink at him? And what was it with my heart beating so fast that I could barely catch a full breath of air?

He stopped, yanking at the basket, forcing me to look back at him.

"Do you hear anything?"

I listened to the sounds of the forest. The only noise I could catch was the one of ruffling leaves above us.

"No."

"Exactly."

Wait, what?

I looked around the forest… and all the trees, shrubs, and brushes appeared the same.

"Please tell me that you know the way back," I said.

"I thought you said you'd never get lost."

"That was before you distracted me."

Nick's shoulders stiffened, and he was looking at something behind me.

"Jo, I think finding our way back is the least of our problems." He brought his finger to his lips, indicating that I shouldn't talk, and then pointed in the direction I thought we'd come from.

I strained my eyes, trying to see what he was looking at, but the dense trees were pretty much it. That was, until something crunched in the distance, and I concentrated harder. My gaze flew from Nick's wide eyes and shocked face back toward where he was looking, and then I saw it: a black bear, about a hundred feet from us.

CHAPTER 4

We slowly lowered the basket of wood. Nick took my hand and we started backing away, toward the clearing we saw. I prayed inside that it led to a road, so we could wave someone down, or maybe it signaled a house in the forest we could hide out in. Anything other than the bear's habitat would be welcome. Why hadn't I taken my bear spray? Why hadn't Nick?

So far, the bear was oblivious to our presence; that is, until I stepped on a larger branch and it snapped, and the bear's attention turned our way.

"Whatever you do, don't run, Jo."

"Easy to say, hard to do," I whispered, but kept backing away, a bit more quickly than before. The bear stood on its hinds, stretching his full length up to the sky. That thing looked like it had undergone some sort of a growth mutation. "Holy shit. I think it thinks it's found dinner."

"Don't say that. Keep walking and make noise, lots of noise. If it gets closer, curl into a ball! Cover your head and neck with your arms!"

"I don't think it wants to play ball." I heard the vibrations in my voice, clearly remembering the same instructions we'd been given by our teachers and the park guide. My legs were trembling and my heart — was it even there? It was beating so quickly I couldn't even count the thumps in my chest.

"It's for your safety."

The bear growled, inspiring the hairs on my arms to stand tall. Now with my whole body on high alert, I was afraid I'd have no control over my legs if it turned out that they wanted to run. I could already picture the bear's teeth sinking into my skin like a hot knife through butter.

"Nick, if you get us out of here alive, I will kiss you."

"Well, that gives me all the reason I need to make sure we get safely back to camp, then."

Was he saying that he wanted to kiss me? It didn't matter now, and I had no mind to think about what he'd said, because the bear set its front feet down on the ground and stomped in the same spot a few times, challenging our invasion.

"Get out of here!" Nick yelled.

"I'm not tasty!" I screamed.

"Tasty?"

"Yes, I don't taste good. You wouldn't want us for dinner!"

"I don't think he can understand, Jo!"

We both kept yelling out our conversation, but the bear didn't appear to be fazed; in fact, it seemed more interested than before.

"It doesn't matter what we do, Nick! I think he's getting ready to charge!"

The bear let out another growl and headed straight for us.

'Don't run,' they said? Well, whoever said that wasn't being chased by a bear. Fortunately the clearing we'd seen earlier was just behind a stretch of bushes a few feet away. We pushed through the mesh of leaves and branches. Thorns scraped the sides of my arms and my legs, but I didn't stop until I got through to the other side where our situation became even more daunting than before. Couldn't a girl ever get a break?

We were standing at the edge of a cliff. Below, it looked like there was nothing but space. Strike that. There was a river far, far, far, far away; barely visible. Or maybe it was the sweat that was blurring my vision. The sound I thought I'd heard earlier, of passing cars, was actually raging whitewater. I turned to see Nick's reaction, asking with my eyes what we should do next. He had a cut just above his left brow, which was bleeding down his cheek, staining his shirt red. The way the blood was streaming down, you'd think someone had slit his throat.

Get that image out of your mind, Jo!

The bear's roar behind us shook the trembles out of my body.

Holy shit! If there was one thing I was certain of, it was that the bear was now closer than before.

"Come on, climb down."

"Where?"

"Doesn't matter, just down."

"He won't get through the shrubs, will he?"

"Wanna take the chance that he will?"

Nick lowered his body and took a few calculated steps down, slowly making his way to a thin ledge. He reached up, saying, "Come on, Jo. You can do it. Quick."

I followed the steps he'd taken to get down, but my foot slipped. I felt my body grind against the rock, until it was free falling. This was it. This was how I'd die. Not exactly the best way to go. I had pictured myself as an old woman when I died, hopefully with someone like Nick at my side, not as a sixteen-year-old girl who only got kissed for the first time earlier in the day. Was that all I'd experience? A kiss that I pushed away from?

Then I stopped falling and dangled in the air as Nick held my hand. I looked up. "Don't let go!"

"I'll never let you go. I promise." He must have used all the strength he had to pull me up. His face was red, his jaw was tense, and sweat poured down his face in streams, falling right on me. But if there was anything that I didn't mind, it was Nick sweating when he was saving my life. Halfway up, he grabbed me by my torso, right under the ribcage, then by my ass, to make sure I was secure, and brought me close, flat against his body. We pressed against each other on the narrow ledge above the water. I was now wedged between him and the cliff. A quarter of his feet dangled over the ledge.

"Here, put one of your legs between mine and the other on the side."

He shifted, firming his stance. It was only moments later that the bear found a way around the shrubs and started pacing back and forth along the cliff's edge, looking down at us and growling.

"Holy shit, that was close." I leaned my head back against the rock.

"Way too close."

My arms and legs were shaking; in fact, my whole body was shaking.

"Jo, you're okay. Calm down."

"I... I don't think I can. I think I saw my life flash before my eyes."

Actually, I hadn't, because there'd been no time for it to flash, but that was what people said when they faced certain death, wasn't it?

"Everything's going to be fine, Joelle. I'll take care of you."

On a normal day, I would have told him that I could take care of myself, but today, I really wanted to rely on Nick, because I had no clue how we'd get out of here if the bear didn't leave. Even if it did, I was afraid I couldn't climb back up.

I looked up, almost straight into the bear's open jaw. Saliva dripped off its teeth and I could smell its nasty breath. That, and wet fur. Gross. If the stupid bear was going to keep this up, my gag reflex would definitely be tested today. Thankfully we were low enough that he couldn't reach us.

"He's not giving up, Nick."

"Let's give it some time, okay?" He smoothed my cheek with the back of his hand, which felt very comforting. I couldn't stop looking in his eyes. They were not only calming, but mesmerizing, with their green depth lightened by the perfectly sunny day.

"Yeah, okay. So, what's up?" I asked.

"A bear."

I burst out laughing, spitting right in his face.

"I'm so sorry. I couldn't hold it in."

"It's okay. Now I can officially say that we swapped spit."

"But you haven't spat at me."

"Not yet. You should be grateful. I had garlic bread for lunch."

"Is that what that smell is?" I teased.

Nick only smiled, keeping my attention on him instead of the bear.

"Technically, we swapped spit when you stole my pacifier," I accused.

"Anything I can't remember, I won't admit to, so you could be making this up."

"It's a story my father told me."

"Yeah, you're right. I've heard that one from my mother as well."

I took a deep breath in and felt my heart rate slowly begin to settle.

"Well, at least the view from up here is nice." The scenery past the forest of rolling hills and little towns in between was postcard-worthy. It stretched for miles beyond us, and despite the bear above, I couldn't wait to tell my father about the scenic landscape. Although if we got out of here alive, I was pretty sure I'd get an earful about how we'd gone out into the forest without bear spray.

I heard a deep sigh from Nick and lifted my head. He had apparently been looking at me this entire time. "You're a beautiful girl, Joelle. You deserve someone better than Carter."

I felt my cheeks heat. "Thank you. I mean that."

"You're welcome."

"How long do you think he'll keep this up?" Did the bear think we would climb up and introduce ourselves? It didn't look like he was anywhere near giving up.

"Until we come back up and serve him dinner?" Nick shrugged, his wide shoulders rising. Standing so close to him, I noticed for the first time just how wide they were. Lifting those bags of flour at his mom's bakery had definitely paid off. His body was composed of muscles on top of muscles. I'd seen him work out in his room in the mornings sometimes, but I didn't tell him that.

"That's not very encouraging."

"Or we could leave this place right now."

"The only other way is down."

"Exactly."

I looked into the frothing waters below. "Nick, that's gotta be more than twenty feet down. Broken bones guaranteed."

We'd jumped off rocks into a lake plenty of times before, but never from this height. Both of us knew how much it hurt when you hit the water, pancake style.

"Not if we jump the right way. There," he said, pointing, "see that black spot? It's gotta be deep there. It's our best shot."

I hunched over just a bit and felt the world spin. Then I pressed myself harder against Nick, who grasped me by my waist and held me close to his body.

"I'm not sure I can do this."

"Jo, you can do anything you put your mind to. I know that. I believe in you."

I looked up and down again, and then back at Nick. His eyes held enough confidence for the both of us.

"Are we really going to do this?" I asked.

Nick looked up again. The bear's muzzle shrank back, his expression as fierce as before.

"I don't think we have a choice, Jo." He took another look below, determination rolling through his body. "Okay, you're going to cross your legs and keep your arms over your chest. Point your toes to go straight in. Just slice through that water. Got it?"

I nodded. I still couldn't believe this was happening, but once Nick made a decision, I knew he'd go through with it. He was as brave as his father. Nick carefully shifted so that his back was against the cliff beside me, and took my hand.

"Wait, what are we going to do after we jump?"

"Swim."

"No, I mean, swim where?"

"There's a town down the river. But I'm not sure how far down."

I took three deep breaths, trying to control the sudden rush of nerves running through my body. If there was anyone I trusted, it was Nick.

"Okay, I think I'm ready."

"On three?"

I nodded.

"One, two—"

"Wait! Nick, if I die, I just want you to know that you're the best friend I've ever had. And you're hot and you deserve someone much better than Daisy, so please, don't go out with her."

"First of all, don't talk like that. You're not going to die. And second... did you just say I'm hot?" He looked at me with a perplexed expression as if he'd just discovered a new galaxy.

"That's what you got out of that?"

"Well, yeah. And by the way, Jo, Daisy's got nothing on you."

I smiled. At least if I died, I knew now that Nick liked me more than he liked Daisy, and while I'd deny that little fact was important to me, it gave me that much more will to survive this jump.

"Ready?" he asked again.

"You get me out of this alive and I promise to kiss you. Please grab my arm once we're in the water."

"Wouldn't have it any other way. One, two, three!"

We pushed off the cliff together. I crossed my legs and arms, pointed my toes, and took a deep breath. Perpendicular to the river, I went in like a sword, cutting through the water.

I did it!

Well, not quite. There was still the task of getting back up to the surface. I kicked my feet as hard as I could, moving my arms in large circles, looking up, but no matter how hard I tried, I just couldn't get closer. A strong current pulled me sideways, and I panicked, opening my mouth. My lungs burned instantly as I took in the water and seconds later, I lost consciousness.

CHAPTER 5

Water fountained out of my lungs, and my body was forced to the side so I could spit it out. My lower half was still in the water as I braced myself on my elbows against a rock.

"Thank God," I heard from beside me, where Nick was holding me by my hips, making sure that I didn't flip back over, smoothing his hand over my arm. I heaved fresh air in and out, desperate for it to replace the fluids in my lungs, but that only catapulted more water out. I braced my body on my hands, crawling out of the river and slowly got up on my knees, my lungs and veins still desperate for oxygen. After a couple of minutes, my pulse somewhat steadied as I regained control of my breathing.

Nick sat on a rock beside me and wiped what looked like worry off his forehead.

"What happened?"

"You took water on like the *Titanic*. I had to dive to get you."

"Thank you. The current... it was strong." It was still difficult to breathe, and my heart didn't seem to want to slow down.

"Take your time, Jo. I can't believe you jumped."

"You told me to."

"Yeah, but I still can't believe you did it. You're badass."

"Where's the bear?"

He pointed to the cliff across the river where the beast was still pacing back and forth.

"Nick, we gotta find help and alert the campground. That thing doesn't give up, and we weren't that far off."

"I know. I know." He looked around the area, somewhat worried. "But I'm hoping the larger group will scare it off."

His head was still turning one way, then another.

"What is it?"

"Nothing."

"You're lying."

"Hey, now we definitely swapped spit," he winked.

I leaned my head to the side. Was he trying to distract me?

"I had to give you mouth to mouth to get that water out."

I wished I remembered that part.

"How are you feeling?" he asked.

"Okay, I think. Thank you for saving me."

"I need you alive so that I can claim the kiss you promised me." He winked.

You tell a boy you'll kiss him and he'll do anything to make sure he'll get it, including saving your life. Not that I minded, of course.

"We're not out of the woods yet, literally."

"But we will be." He touched the side of his shorts. "Shoot, I must have lost my granola bar in the water."

"There goes dinner," I joked, and actually made Nick chuckle.

"Come on – are you ready to head downstream?"

"Yeah, I think so."

I reached up to his offered hand, which he didn't let go of until we had to climb over a few piles of rock. I followed his carefully chosen steps, wary of my surroundings. After all, didn't bears come to the river when they were thirsty? I had never joined the Girl Scouts, but I hoped that staying on the move was a better idea than remaining in the same spot, waiting to be rescued. There were more clouds in the sky, and the sun was way past the noon point. Anytime a cool breeze blew, I shivered. Nick, on the other hand, given that he always wore a pair of swim shorts when camping even when he wasn't going swimming, was nice and dry from the waist down. Well, except for his soaked sneakers.

What if we were making a mistake by heading down the river? Wasn't it better to stay closer to where camp was and get a fire going? Then the rescue party our teachers had probably sent out could see the smoke.

"Nick, are you sure this is a good idea?" I asked.

"No, I'm not, but I'm doing the best I can."

"I know. It's just getting a little cold, and you're hurt."
I reached to his face, gently touching the cut he had over
his left brow. "You're going to have a scar."

"Cool."

Boys!

I shivered again. It had been just over an hour walking,
and I didn't want to complain, but I wanted to make sure
that our chances of survival weren't slipping.

He stopped and looked me over. "Okay, let's take a
break and try to get your clothes dry."

"How?"

"Take your shirt and shorts off and put them on that
rock. It should still be hot from the sun."

"But I'm not wearing a bathing suit like you."

"Jo, it's nothing I haven't seen before."

"What do you mean?"

"The windows to our rooms are a foot apart."

"Peeping Tom."

"Hey, if you want privacy, shut your drapes. Otherwise,
I can't help it." He shrugged. "Now undress. This is about
staying warm, nothing else. Besides, I'm sure your pink bra
looks just like a bathing suit."

"How did you know it's pink?"

"Because I can see through your wet shirt."

Oh! I made a note to shut my drapes in the morning.
He couldn't have seen a lot because I usually got dressed in
the bathroom, but yes, there had been times that I'd been
in a hurry and might have run around my room in my
undergarments.

"Wait for me on the rocks, and I'll see if I can find something to eat."

"No, you can't leave me. We'll go together, and then dry the clothes."

He sighed. "Okay, come on. But the shirt and your shorts stay on the rocks."

He turned around and removed his shirt, then splayed it out flat on the hot surface. "I won't look, I promise."

I imagined how nice the dry clothing would feel on my body and finally gave in. Once undressed, we turned right, into the woods. Fortunately there weren't any hungry mosquitos around, but I was afraid that once dusk came, they'd descend upon us. It only took a few steps before the blueberry shrubs appeared. We stuffed our faces until we couldn't eat any more. When Nick grinned, his teeth were purple. I stuck my colored tongue out and he laughed.

"These are delicious."

Nick looked around the forest. "This place looks like a good rest stop. Maybe we should start a fire and wait it out. I have a feeling the day will pass before we reach that town."

"You think we'll have to spend the night here?"

"Possible. But don't worry. I won't let anything happen to you. I've got your back, Jo."

"I know. Thank you."

"You rest. I'm going to make a fire."

"I'll help you."

"No, it's okay. You're better off there." He pointed to the rock where our shirts were drying. Nick was acting all macho and totally weird.

"Why?"

"Because." His jaw was tense and his eyes kept on darting from me to a random spot. My gaze slid down his body, to where his excitement was tenting his shorts. "Ahm, never mind. I'll be on the rock."

I whipped my body around, praying that he hadn't seen embarrassment shade my cheeks. And if he had, he was probably as embarrassed by the situation himself. I propped myself up on the rock. It was still warm from the sun, and my frozen limbs needed the heat. I removed my running shoes and socks and set them by our clothes as well.

The water flowed steadily, shimmering where the sun touched it when the clouds let it through every so often. Downstream, the river swerved to the side, forming a small pond of almost still water where I thought I saw something move. Slowly, I made my way down and stepped barefoot into the river, shifting marginally toward the small pond. A few feet away, Nick had set up some kindling of dried leaves and twigs as well as larger pieces of wood, and was rubbing one stick against another.

"What are you doing?" he asked.

"Shh! You better get that fire going if you want to have dinner."

He resumed the movement of his hands, back and forth, once in a while sneaking a peek at me. I concentrated on the healthy trout as inch by inch, I made my way closer. My father was a good fisherman, and I knew that this piece of fish would be enough for the two of us – if I managed to catch it, that was.

I crouched in slow motion, cupped my hands together, and patiently lowered them into the water. The trout had no idea that I was even there. I let my feet and hands blend in with the surroundings, slowly making them part of the trout's world. Then in one swift scoop I pushed the trout up and out of the little pond. It landed near Nick, whose mouth almost dropped to the forest floor.

"What the hell?"

"I did it! I caught dinner."

The fish flopped around near Nick, who stood up, looking at it as if it had fallen from the sky.

"Yeah, but it's alive. What are we supposed to do with it?"

"You know, sometimes for a handy guy, you surprise me. Have you never gutted a fish?"

"No, and I'm not sure that I want to."

"Keep rubbing then and watch a pro. Unless we get a fire going, that fish will be a waste."

"Sushi?"

"Gross! It's wild, and I'm pretty sure it has worms in it."

"How do you know this stuff? Oh, your father."

"Yup."

I found a sharper rock near the shore and used it to cut the fish open and remove its insides. As soon as it was clean, the first smell of wood wafted toward me, and Nick's kindling lit. We hurried to build a larger and larger fire, eventually surrounding three healthy logs with stones so that it wouldn't spread to the forest.

While Nick set up a frame of criss-crossed branches above the fire to fully dry our clothes and sneakers, I placed the fish on a rock near the heat. Half an hour later, when I was sure that it was cooked through, we dug in.

"This is the best fish I've ever had. Even if it has worms."

"That's just extra protein," I said.

"Just when I thought I knew everything about you." He shook his head in disbelief, smiling. "Your shirt should be dry by now, if you'd like to put it on."

"Is it going to make you more comfortable?"

He lowered his gaze to his straining shorts. "Definitely. I'm sorry about this."

"Don't be. You're a guy. It's harder to hide, excuse the pun, when you're... turned on."

"Just so you know, this would have happened with any girl in her bra and panties."

"I know."

"With you it just happens quicker."

"Really?"

"Well, you're beautiful and sexy."

"You think I'm sexy?" I looked down on my cleavage. My boobs were a healthy size, if I compared them to those of other girls in our class, but I was sure they weren't mature yet.

"Hell, yeah."

My cheeks heated. Actually, my whole body heated. "Thanks, Nick. You're a very handsome guy too."

It didn't seem right to call him a man or a boy; Nick was at that in between stage. The hours he'd spent helping his mom at the bakery definitely showed in his muscles and wide shoulders. Nick was one of the most defined boys in our school, although not many people saw all his assets because he normally wore a shirt. Today, seeing him in only his shorts sparked an interest inside of me that I didn't know I had.

"You're welcome. My arms are sore from rubbing the wood."

I chuckled.

"Wait, that sounds wrong." Nick startled with embarrassment, and I couldn't stop giggling.

"But your stomach is full, isn't it?"

"I could eat another one."

"That will have to hold us over until they find us. They will find us, won't they?" I looked around the darkening forest. We were right by the river on our left, but to the right, I couldn't see much past a dozen feet except for trees and bushes. This place was as wild as it got.

"Yeah, I hope so."

"You *hope* so?"

"They will. Let's get more wood for the fire. Maybe they'll see the smoke."

We put on our dry clothes and gathered enough wood to last us through the night. Nick moved the fire pit over to a spot where the smoke could escape through the canopy. I gathered more blueberries and found a few wild strawberries as well, and then sat down beside Nick, against the trunk of a tree. He had spread evergreen branches at the foot of the tree and covered them with leaves for more comfort.

"I really don't want to spend the night here." I sighed.

"It's not that bad, is it? I bet you the night sky looks the same as from our rooftops."

"I guess you're right. If there was anyone I'd want to be lost with, it's you."

"Not Carter?"

"No way. He acts all brave, but he would have peed his pants the moment he saw that bear. You were calm and got us out of trouble."

"Carter's strong. Very strong."

"But you're... *you*."

How could I explain to Nick that I could never feel as comfortable around anyone other than him, without him taking it the wrong way? So I changed the subject instead. "Who taught you to make a fire so quickly?"

"My father. It was one of the last things I remembered him teaching me before he was deployed."

"That must have been hard, you know, losing him in battle. You're brave. He would have been proud of you."

He gave me that grateful smile. But it was true. Nick had inherited the best parts of both his parents. He was as patient and talented with pastries as his mother and as strong and courageous as his father who'd served our country and died for our freedom.

"You were brave too, Jo. I don't think anyone else would have jumped off that cliff."

"It was only because I was with you."

"I don't think so. You're the strongest woman I know."

He thought of me as a woman? Maybe this was the right time to bring up what Carter had mentioned before. "Can I ask you a stupid question? I mean, I know we're friends – actually, make that best friends – but have you ever thought about dating?"

"Dating you?"

Maybe I shouldn't have asked. I didn't want to ruin the best part of us — our friendship. Nick reached for another log and added it to the fire along with two handfuls of dried leaves we'd collected. If there was anyone nearby, there was no way they could miss the billowing black smoke.

"Ahm, yes. Like, would I be the kind of girl you date?"

"No." He shook his head, making me regret my question.

"What?"

"You're the kind of girl someone like me would want to marry."

I sucked in a sharp breath. "But you have to date before you marry... you know, to get to know each other."

"Jo, I don't think anyone else in this world, other than my mother, knows me as well as you do. In fact, I'm pretty sure that you know me better."

"But dating—"

"I always felt like you were mine, anyways," he stated.

"Yours?" That statement made me feel alive inside. I didn't understand the feeling, but it was a good one, despite Nick's alpha posturing.

"That's why I don't like seeing you with Carter." He turned his body toward me. His eyes were dreamy; or maybe it was just me, imagining them to be so. Their green depths held compassion — Nick didn't usually speak so seriously about our friendship. "I'm afraid if we dated, it'd be weird, and I wouldn't want to do anything to ruin our friendship."

We were sitting beside each other, our arms touching. And maybe it was just me, or perhaps being secluded and away from everyone was messing with my mind, but I could feel the heat of his skin rise with each minute.

"But we wouldn't know unless we tried, Nick. Sometimes you have to take that leap in life. And if there's anyone I'd jump off a cliff with, it's you."

Was I actually justifying why we should date? He was like a brother to me. But looking at him today, spending this time with him, made me wonder whether that was just an excuse I'd been keeping in the back of my mind.

He leaned in closer, looking straight into my eyes. "I wouldn't want to hurt you."

His voice was low, almost a whisper, and I didn't understand what it meant or why it made me feel all these weird things on the inside. This was the first time ever that I noticed Nick's freckle underneath his lower lip. His mouth was plump and very inviting.

"You have no idea how badly I want to kiss you now."

"Then do it." I leaned forward with permission, feeling my eyes slowly close instinctively, and then it happened. Our first kiss. A real kiss that I couldn't have known just how much I wanted. The river stopped flowing and the wind stilled. The birds were no longer chirping above and trees paused their swaying motion. The world around us ceased to exist. It was just me and him. His warm mouth on mine as his tongue slipped in gently between my lips. I opened my mouth with a moan, then held my breath as his tongue played with mine. When he pulled away, I couldn't believe what had just happened. This kiss was nothing like the one Carter had stolen from me earlier in the day. It was delicate, full of emotions, reciprocated and real. It took my breath away, filled my stomach with butterflies and prickled my skin with excitement. It was everything I'd always imagined a first kiss to be, and so much more. It was perfect.

I lifted my hand to my mouth, drawing my fingers over the delicate skin he had just kissed.

"You okay?" he whispered.

"I think so. That was... really good, Nick."

His mouth curved on one side with confidence and then he grabbed my face between his hands and kissed me harder. This time his tongue dove deeper into my mouth and I felt my chest rise. I drew my hands up his arms, for the first time feeling the strength of his muscles. I could have kissed him like this for hours, if not days. Heck, I wanted to kiss him for days, but if I didn't pull away my heart would rip out of my chest.

Where had he learned how to kiss like that? Yeah, I definitely would never think of Nick as a brother again.

"That was—"

"Good?" he asked.

"Very good." I brought my hand to my trembling lips, trying to think about what the kiss meant.

"What does this mean?"

"I'm not sure. I mean, obviously I like you. Actually, I like you a lot, but you already knew that."

Please don't let there be a *but*. I wanted us to try to make it work, like other couples did. Go to the movies as a couple, hold hands as a couple, and date like the rest of the teenagers did. This was it. This was what I'd been waiting for, and I didn't even know I'd been waiting for him.

"But I think everyone will treat us differently. I mean, do you think your dad and my mom will let us go up on the rooftop together, without peeking through the window every five minutes to see what we're doing?"

"I... I don't know. I haven't thought about it that way."

"Well, I have."

"You have?"

"Every guy fantasizes about a special girl." He shrugged.

He fantasized about me? I was still in a daze from our kiss, and I was afraid it would take some time for me to snap out of it.

"Okay, let me put it this way: if your father knew that I was kissing you on that rooftop, he'd never let us go up together, even if we just wanted to enjoy the stars."

"I think you're right."

"And our friends are going to tease us. They're not dating, and I don't want them to push us aside. We wouldn't be a group anymore."

I could already see them excluding us from movie nights or swimming at the lake. It had happened before. I remembered when the seniors in our high school started dating and their friends made immature lip-smacking sounds. I didn't want anyone knowing that we had kissed, or that we liked each other. I didn't want them to treat us any differently; especially since I'd always been so close to Nick. Was it possible we could keep this a secret? The thought of dating in secret was exciting and I felt my heart skip a beat.

"And all this time, I'll be thinking about your pink lips and how much I want to kiss them again."

I gasped.

"I've wanted to kiss you for a long time, Jo."

"I think I've wanted you to kiss me for a long time too. I want you to kiss me again." I leaned my forehead against his, the anticipation of touching his lips to mine again growing with every second.

"When we get back home, I will kiss you every day, Jo. It will be our secret, yours and mine."

"I think I'd really like that."

He gently touched his lips to mine again and held them there. I never knew that so much elation could soar through my heart because of one kiss – well, three as of now, if anyone was counting – but I felt like I was floating. A distinct echo in the distance drew our gazes up to the sky. Although I couldn't see it yet, I knew it was a helicopter.

Talk about bad timing.

We pulled apart, staring at each other for longer than we probably should have, and then shot off the forest floor and ran to the large rock by the river, climbing up and waving our arms back and forth.

"We're here!" we screamed.

As happy as I should have been that we were being rescued, I wished I had more alone time with Nick. Thankfully, now that we had our little secret, I knew that he'd kiss me again soon. His lips were mine, and mine were his.

CHAPTER 6

He was the first person I saw in the morning and the last person I saw at night. I shot out of my bed as soon as my alarm went off, waving to him. He'd wink and blow me a kiss before getting ready for school.

We'd go about our day as usual, walking to school together, spending lunch at the same table, and then walking back home. It took an enormous amount of restraint not to touch him or kiss him when we were alone, even on the side road, but I kept my distance. The last thing I wanted was for a neighbor to sneak a peek through a window and tell our parents on us. In a town this small, keeping a secret was definitely a challenge. So we reserved our make-out sessions for the weekends, when we met up on the rooftop. And no one was the wiser.

In the evenings, when Nick wasn't looking and his lights were turned on, I'd sometimes peek through the window when he changed. If my lights were off, even if he looked my way, he wouldn't be able to see me in the darkness. Part of me felt like a pervert, but I was pretty sure that he knew I was watching. Every few days he put on a little show for me, doing push-ups on the floor in his low-hanging sweat pants, lunging forward and then back, before changing into his pajamas. He always turned the light off when it was time to get out of his underwear, which was a good thing because I wasn't ready to see him without them.

It took six months of playing Peeping Tom for me to work up the nerve to tease Nick the way he'd been teasing me. I wore my nicest bra and panties that day, with a tank top and a t-shirt over top, as well as a sweater. I hoped the extra few layers I'd need to remove would give me enough courage to show myself in the see-through undergarments.

As soon as my light flicked on that evening, Nick's turned off, and I knew that he was watching me. Taking the sweater off was easy. I folded it on my bed and then placed it on the highest shelf in my closet, causing my shirt to rise and mid-drift to be exposed. Next came the t-shirt. That part wasn't so bad either, but when I got ready to remove my leggings, with my backside toward the window, I took in a deep breath. There would be nothing left to the imagination once those were off.

Anticipating this evening, I had bought them a month ago when I went to the city with Daisy and Molly. I snuck out of the bookstore for a few minutes and used a good amount of my savings to purchase the matching ensemble.

Slowly, I slid the leggings off, bending lower and lower until they were at my ankles, wishing I could see Nick's reaction. Dressed in my panties, bra, and the tank top, I then slowly turned around and grasped the hem of my tank, pulling it over my head. A cool breeze blew through my room as Nick jumped from his window to mine. He took two confident steps toward me, cupped my face between his hands, and kissed me hard. It all happened so quickly that I didn't get a chance to think about the possible consequences. My knees bent as I backed onto my bed. Nick lowered me slowly to the mattress and, supporting most of his weight, laid on top of me. We'd made out this way up on the rooftop nearly every weekend, but never in our rooms, on our beds, nearly naked.

Nick had already changed into his pajama bottoms, and his shirt was off. The skin-to-skin contact stirred up a new wave of emotion I wasn't familiar with. My hands slid up his back, feeling the muscles and his ribs, then back down to his narrow waist and his ass. I'd never felt his ass before, and its firmness surprised me. One of his hands cupped my breast, and I pushed my chest higher into it. My hips thrust against his leg while I rubbed myself on him as I got lost in us. When he finally pulled away, his breaths were inconsistent, and I was glad that I still remembered how to breathe.

"You don't know what you're doing to me, Jo."

From the way his erection was hard against my stomach, I had a pretty good idea. "I want to touch you...

everywhere." He kissed me again, this time harder. A loud bang sounded as my lamp fell to the floor. Nick had inadvertently knocked it off my side-table.

"Jo?" we heard from downstairs.

"Shit, Nick. You gotta go."

There was no way that I wanted to take a chance my father would come upstairs and find us nearly naked in my room.

Nick shot off my bed, but that's when the lights in his room turned on – his mom was looking for him. I quickly pulled the curtains over my window before she saw us.

"Joelle, is everything okay?" My father knocked on my door.

"Everything's fine, Dad." I turned to Nick. "Quick, the balcony," I loud-whispered, shoving him outside before I grabbed my robe off a hook on the door.

"May I come in?" my dad asked. "There's something I need to talk to you about."

"One sec."

I closed the balcony door and saw Nick climbing up the ladder to my roof. I could hear him leap off my roof and land on his. I peeked through my curtain just as Nick entered his room through his balcony door, no doubt telling his mom that he'd been on the rooftop.

With a big sigh of relief, I opened the door for my father.

"Are you okay? I heard a loud noise," he explained.

"I accidentally knocked the lamp off my desk. I'm sorry for disturbing you."

"No, it's fine. But there's something I want to talk to you about."

He sounded serious. "Well, you're seventeen now, and I thought that maybe we should have a chat about boys; I mean, men."

No, no, no. I didn't want to talk to him about sex.

"Honey, you're going to grow more curious about—"

"Dad, is this about sex?"

"Ahm, I was going to start with dating, but yeah, I guess that leads to sex."

"We had sex ed in seventh grade."

"You did?"

I nodded.

"So, you're safe?"

"Yes. I mean no."

"No?"

"Yes, it's a no because I'm not having sex."

"Oh, okay. Good. Well, not good, but I'm glad that you're being smart." He rubbed the stubble on his face with his hand.

"Dad, if you feel this is uncomfortable for you, then it's a hundred times as uncomfortable for me. But I'm fine. My sex life, or lack of it, is fine too."

"But if you had questions, would you come to me?"

"Well, yes, I guess. It'd be easier if you were a woman. But really, there's no need."

"You can talk to Marge, if that makes you feel better."

There was no way I would talk to Nick's mom about my sex life, ever. It'd be weird.

"I know. And I will if I need to. I promise."

"Good. The last thing I'd want is to be a grandfather before you're ready."

"I promise no grand-babies any time soon."

"So, is there anyone special in your life? Have you thought about dating?"

"Nope. I like staying friends with everyone. And dating's overrated."

"Even Nick? I know you two have been close all your lives."

"Dad, Nick's like a brother to me," I lied. But this was the most believable lie yet, because that was the way I'd explained our relationship to myself before our kiss in the woods.

My father let out a breath of relief. "Good. I'm glad you two have remained friends."

"How about you?" I asked.

"What about me?"

"Anyone special in your life? You know, I never told you, but I saw you kissing Marge a few years ago."

"You did?" His cheeks took on a brighter shade of red.

"In the store. She came to get some bread. Were you dating?"

"We were trying to, but we didn't want to confuse you and Nick."

"So, you didn't because of us?"

He nodded.

Well, that was funny. Because that was one of the reasons Nick and I had decided to keep our dating life a secret.

"Dad, you and Marge deserve to be happy. I'd have nothing against you two being together."

"Do you think Nick would mind?"

"I don't know. You'd have to ask him, but Nick's cool. I think he'd want his mom happy as well."

He looked at me adoringly. "You remind me of your mother so much, Joelle. She would have been proud of the young woman you grew up to be."

"Thanks, Dad. It's because of you. You did a good job raising me."

"No, honey. Sometimes I feel like you grew up all on your own. Sometimes I don't know what I've done in life to deserve you."

I felt my eyes well up, and I threw my arms around him, "I love you too, Dad."

My father had raised a daughter from the first day I was born. He'd changed diapers on his own, got up in the middle of the night when I had nightmares, and learned how to braid my hair. My father had given up his life for me, and there was never enough love I could give him back.

For the first time since I'd started dating Nick in secret, I felt guilty, wondering whether we were doing the right thing by hiding.

As soon as my father left for his room, I turned off the light and hurried to my window. Nick was already waiting for me on the other side.

"You okay?" he asked.

"Yeah, but that was close. I can't believe you jumped the roofs."

"They're not that far apart."

"Far enough. Sometimes I think you like playing with danger."

"You getting undressed like that is playing with danger."

My whole body heated just thinking about the lack of clothing underneath my robe and the fact that Nick had not only seen it all but also touched a good portion of it. What scared me even more was that I wanted him to touch me that way again.

"So... did you like the lace?"

"What lace?" he winked, making me heat again. "You keep that up, Jo, and I'm going to do something illegal."

"What if I want you to do something illegal?"

"Joelle, you better close your window right now." His voice was stern, and I knew that his warning was serious – which made me want to crawl over to his room that much more.

I saw his hand lower beneath the window ledge and I wondered whether he was feeling himself. The thought made me want to check the status of my sheer panties to determine if I'd need to change them before bed time. Actually, I was pretty sure that they were laundry ready.

He proceeded to close his window when I stopped him. "Wait. I think my dad and your mom still have something for each other. He said they never dated because they didn't want us to be uncomfortable."

"Hmm. You may be right. She asked me the other day if I'd be okay if she went out. I thought she meant with a friend, but I didn't realize she might have meant your father."

"Let's fix them up. This weekend we can set up a dinner for them in the back yard. Oh, and we can bake a cake together."

"You want to bake?"

"I've been meaning to try a cake for a while now. You know that."

"So, it'd be like a secret date?"

"Sure, if you want to call it that. So? Are we gonna do it?"

"Anything to make you happy, Jo."

He then gestured with his finger in a come-hither motion. I leaned over the window and kissed Nick's waiting lips. That night was the first night I'd ever had a wet dream.

CHAPTER 7

Friday night, ready with my hairnet, I met Nick in the back of the store. His serious expression made me want to giggle, but I kept it inside. If there was anything Nick didn't joke about, it was baking.

"What are you two up to?" Marge joined us in the back.

"It's Jo's first cake. Want to meet us in the back yard tomorrow night to try it out?"

We'd made a plan to ask my father to do the same, and then we'd leave them alone with a bottle of wine for the evening.

"Sure, but why tomorrow night?"

"Because there won't be time to try it tonight. It won't be ready."

Her brows scrunched. Marge lowered her hands to her hips. "Should I be worried?"

"No," we replied at the same time, and looked at each other surreptitiously.

"Okay, holler if you need anything. I closed the store up, Nick. I'm going out for a walk."

"Thanks, Mom."

As soon as she closed the door, I turned to Nick. "I knew it! My father said he was going on a walk too."

"How long do you think this has been going on?" he asked.

"I don't know. Years? It must have been a while. I mean, we've been sneaking around for almost a year and a half, and no one has a clue."

"Oh, the irony." He laughed. "One day, when our kids are old, we'll tell our parents the truth about what's been going on, and they'll have a heart attack."

I froze. "You think about us that way?" I asked.

"Yeah, don't you?"

"I do too."

We were standing facing each other. I could smell his sweet chocolate breath mixed with his cologne and lifted my hands to his chest, slowly sliding them over his pecs, over his shoulders, and around his neck. When we were like this, just the two of us, nothing else mattered. I could have remained in his arms forever, sharing the same space and breathing the same air.

"There's no one else I'd rather be with, Nick."

"Tell me you're mine," he breathed, and a need for something deep I couldn't understand rolled off his body.

"I'm yours, Nick."

His mouth lowered to mine. Rising higher on my toes, I tasted the sweetness of chocolate on his tongue. There was a sense of danger kissing him in the back of his mother's bakery – she could walk in any time – yet I couldn't pull my lips away. When we finally parted, I straightened my apron, and Nick shifted his pants. I wondered whether he was hard underneath his apron.

He took me by my hips and lifted me up to the counter. Our height was now even. Our gazes locked, and his hands slid over my jeans and up my thighs. He slowly lowered his gaze down my body, right over my swelling breasts. I was pretty sure that I stopped breathing at one point; that is, until his concentration zoomed in on my zipper and his nails scratched over the fabric there, sending delectable vibrations right to my crotch. I felt that swelling sensation build between my legs, the same way it did at night when I touched myself thinking about Nick.

"Tell me to stop," he whispered. "Please."

I didn't want to. I wanted him to keep going. I wanted to see how far he'd go and how far I'd let him go. He was testing my patience.

"No."

"Jo, you have to. Otherwise..."

"I want to have sex with you," I blurted.

He withdrew his hand from my crotch. His expression became angrier as he stepped away.

"Do you not want that?" I felt my eyes swell, my heart cry, and my body shudder with disappointment. What if I wasn't enough for him?

"Of course I do, Jo. I mean, look at me." He pulled away his apron and pointed to the bulge in his pants. "But not now. Not here where anyone can walk in."

"When?" I jumped off the counter, stepping closer to him. He finally took me by my hips, bringing me up against his body, removing my doubts and making everything right again with one touch.

"Soon, baby. I want it to be perfect and special because you deserve... everything."

I stole a quick kiss, smiling, hoping I'd have enough patience to wait for that right moment.

"So, red velvet is your favorite, right?"

"Right. But we should probably make your mom's favorite, black forest."

"Black forest it is, then."

We started measuring, sifting, melting, and pouring, then mixing the batter together. I followed all of Nick's instructions, combining the wet and dry ingredients separately before mixing them all together. It was closer to making bread dough than I had thought. With my experience at Dad's bakery and a detailed recipe, baking cakes wasn't that much different. In fact, you didn't have to wait for the dough to rise. Seeing all the masterpieces in Marge's bakery had always felt magical to me, and now Nick was explaining that magic to me one step at a time.

Once the cake was in the oven, Nick prepped another batch of ingredients but didn't tell me what he was mixing. When I saw the burgundy dough, I knew he'd made a red velvet cake for me. My heart was full to bursting. Not for the cake — but for this man who'd found a way of cherishing me with the smallest of gestures.

"Are you going to be a baker like your mom?" I asked, as he removed the chocolate cake from the oven to cool and put in the red velvet.

"I don't know. I may, one day. But there's other stuff I want to do before that."

"Like what?"

"I've been thinking about joining the navy."

"What? Where did this come from?"

"My father went into the navy."

"And that's where he died, Nick."

"I know. But look at how many people he saved. I want to make sure I live up to his expectations."

"You know that he would have been proud of you, don't you?"

"For baking cakes?"

"Nick, there's more to you than being a baker. Wait, please tell me that you'll be applying to college."

"I did, but I'm not sure if I'll go."

"Nick…"

"Jo… I've been thinking about this for a long time. I really want to do this."

"But—" I felt my eyes fill with tears. He wouldn't leave me, would he? I mean, I'd always secretly hoped that we'd end up at the same college. That was the way life was supposed to be, wasn't it? I knew there was a chance we'd end up apart for a few years, but I'd assumed he'd be safe at another school, waiting for me, not fighting a war thousands of miles away, where I wouldn't know whether he was alive for weeks or months.

"Don't get upset, Jo. I haven't made a decision yet. But even if I don't go into the navy, I'm not a college person."

"So, what will you do?"

"Be a fireman?"

I burst out laughing.

"What?"

"A fireman? Since when?"

He lifted the bag full of cream, pointing at me.

"You keep this up and you'll be decorating on your own."

"Of all people Nick, I know you can take a joke."

"Can you?" He reached out and plopped a large finger-scoop of buttercream on my nose.

"Hey!" I dipped my finger into the cream as well, but before I got a chance to get it on his face, he grasped my wrist and brought my finger to his lips. He licked and sucked it clean and I just stood there, with my mouth open and my nose dirty. Nick proceeded to step closer and licked the excess cream off my nose. I felt my heart pick up and chest swell. That was unbelievably sexy.

We stood only a foot away, staring into each other's eyes, and for that moment I forgot that he was thinking of joining the navy, and everything was perfect again.

"Is there anything I can do to persuade you?" I asked.

"Probably, but I wouldn't want us caught making out right here on this floor."

My body heated. If there were any cream left on my face, it would have melted.

"Jo, remember Washington and how my father saved us? I want to be able to do that for you — for us. If I do this, if I go away, it's because I need to. I'm doing this for you and for me. For our future. And I can't do it without your support. I won't leave unless I have your blessing."

"All I want is for you to be happy. I'd do anything for you, Nick. You know that. Even if I have to wait for you for years."

That was partially true, because now that I knew of his plans, I also knew that I had a year left to change his mind. A life without Nick was not worth living. It would take special kind of persuasion to keep him in Hope Bay. And if I failed, my heart would go into hibernation while he was gone.

We proceeded to layer the black forest cake, scooping in the cherry filling and then smoothing the cake all the way around with buttercream. Nick showed me how to swirl around the edges, and then how to make buttercream roses. My first one didn't come out so well, so I started over. The second and third were a little better, and by the time I got to the fourth, it was perfect.

And all this time, in between me decorating and him instructing, Nick worked on the red velvet as if it were just another day. By the time I was done with the black forest cake, he was done with his cake as well. I had no idea that baking cakes, decorating and then seeing the final product would bring so much satisfaction.

"I think I found a new hobby," I grinned.

He spun the cake on its turntable, examining it from every angle. "Jo, you're better at this than I am. You sure this is your first cake?"

"Yes, I'm sure."

"Well, then let me be the first one to congratulate you, baby." He lifted me up into his arms, twirled me around, pressing his lips to mine, and then set me down on the counter. "I could get used to this, you know."

"What?"

"Having you in my kitchen all the time."

That predatory look in his eyes rolled over my body as I pictured myself with long, bushy and unkempt hair, in the middle of a Neanderthal cave, watching my man build a fire. Hopefully he'd drag me onto the sabre tooth skins laid out in the back of the cave, after we ate the meat he caught earlier in the day, for a nice make-out session. Although I was sure that as Neanderthals, we'd be much wilder than I was ready to be.

"I didn't know you were so alpha."

He laughed, sliding his hands over my knees and up to my thighs. Just then, the bell to the store rang, Nick's hands flew down to his sides, and I jumped off the counter as if it were a freshly lit stove. Nick hurried to cover the surprise cake, and his mom walked in.

"You guys done already?" she asked.

"Jo's a pro. If you're ever busy and need help, you know who to call."

Why would Nick say that? He was always here to help, and he was the pro. Was he preparing me for when he'd leave for the navy? I shook the thought away because for now, I'd rather pretend that he'd never leave me. My heart would break if he did.

That Saturday night, when our parents met us in the back yard and we sliced my first black forest cake, I practically glowed with pride. We set up a table with candles and brought out a bottle of wine for the two of them to enjoy, and then turned around to leave.

"Aren't you guys joining us for the cake?" My father asked.

"No – we thought the two of you could use some time alone without sneaking around."

Marge shifted from one foot to another, stealing a glance at my father.

"It's okay, Mom. We know you guys are seeing each other. We just don't understand all the sneaking around," Nick explained.

Oh, the irony!

"We didn't want to make you uncomfortable." For the first time, my father took a step closer to Marge.

"You're not. And we're happy for you guys," I said. "Enjoy the cake."

We turned around and left to go to the rooftop. Having our parents busy with each other meant less attention on the two of us, so that we could make out under the star lit sky on Nick's rooftop.

CHAPTER 8

Dating in secret wasn't exactly easy. It had been almost two years since our first secret kiss, stranded by the river, and we never spoke about it again. No one was the wiser that we'd been kissing almost every day since then. But now that we were older I wanted to kiss him anytime I felt like it. I wanted to twine my fingers with his, and show all the girls that he was mine and I was his. The need to roam my hands over his chest, feeling his muscles twitch underneath my palms, was growing, and curiosity of how it would feel if Nick put his hands on me like a man was reaching its breaking point.

But the reward for keeping our secret was worth it. Every time we went up onto the rooftop, we made out until our mouths were sore. The past year, Nick had also begun working out, so his body had changed since our camping trip, and my hands definitely felt the difference. Touching his abs, bulging arms, and biceps felt like a new adventure every week. Lying on top of his body, his leg between mine, and feeling the strong muscle of his thigh against my nether regions was exhilarating. I thought about our first time together, which had yet to come, more often than I probably should have. We hadn't broached the subject, but I had a feeling that losing our virginity was on his mind as much as it was on mine. After that night in my bedroom when I'd tried to tease him with my sexy lingerie, we pushed the boundaries further and further. He'd cup my sex through my jeans and I'd feel his excitement by curving my hand over him.

As months and days passed, I could feel my patience waning. He had morphed from a healthy boy to a young man, and the girls at our school were certainly taking notice. As for me, well, my hips had grown a little and so had my boobs, which Nick seemed to appreciate when he cupped them through my bra underneath my shirt, because he'd always get hard. I'd take the opportunity to feel his erection, massaging him through his jeans. But no matter how much we kissed, or how much we made out, it was never enough.

And no one, including our parents, was the wiser. No one knew we were together, but as we got closer to graduation, I wanted to make our relationship public. I wanted the world to know how much Nick meant to me.

I threw another rock over the water and it gave me fifteen solid skips. Nick's throws were reaching the twenty-five mark more often now. His right arm was much stronger than when we were kids, though he hadn't used the stone I gave him for his thirteenth birthday just yet. I had a feeling that he was waiting for the perfect time.

It was Saturday morning and we'd stopped by the lake to rest from our routine jog every other day.

"It feels wrong to keep us a secret," I said.

"School's over in a month. We can do it then. And we'll be able to start our lives as adults. No one will judge us or tell us what to do."

"Daisy will be upset. She's been waiting for you for a while."

"So will Carter. He's been waiting for you."

"We're so going to hurt them."

"I don't think so. I have a feeling they've been secretly rooting for us to get together."

"If that's true, then all the more reason to come out with the secret."

Nick seemed lost in thought, as if contemplating a decision I wasn't privy to.

"Carter's been asking me if I'm taking you to the prom," he said, out of nowhere.

"What did you tell him?"

"Nothing. I wanted to ask you about it first."

I couldn't help but feel disappointed. While the sneaking around had its advantages, I was proud to be Nick's girlfriend, and no one even knew about it.

"I think we should break it gently to them. I don't want to see Carter or Daisy moping around for the next two weeks before the prom, disappointed that we didn't say yes." I kicked a rock forward and watched it ripple the water on the flat lake ahead.

"I can see the wheels turning in your head." Nick stepped in front of me, took me by my hips, and brought me closer to his body which at this moment, all sweaty and hot from our run, felt too distracting. "What are you thinking, Jo?"

"What if we each agree to go to the prom with them, then fix them up there? I'll tell Carter how Daisy's been asking about him but was too shy to say anything, and you can do the same with Daisy. Nick, they're perfect for each other, and they don't even know it."

"Blindside them? This could turn ugly."

"Or it could be the perfect set up. Daisy's a good friend. She'll understand and so will Carter."

"All I know, is that at the end of that night, I want you in my arms, like this." He lowered his mouth to mine, kissing me deeply. I stepped up on my toes and snaked my hands around his neck, plastering myself against him. No amount of sweat could have kept me away from Nick. I could stay in this moment forever.

He pulled away nervously. "There's something I should tell you, Jo."

For the past three months, I'd noticed that Nick was struggling with internal demons more and more. He'd talked about his father more often. He got upset when he saw the news of terrorism, bombs going off at airports and at concerts. I knew he wanted to make a difference, but I was afraid of what that meant. I hadn't brought up the fact that he'd mentioned the navy earlier in the year, hoping that it was only a phase he'd been going through, but deep in my heart, I was afraid Nick was making decisions without saying a word, in fear of upsetting me. Up until now, I pretended that decision was still far away in the future. After all, he had applied to college.

"You're making me nervous," I whispered.

He led us to the rocks on the side and pulled my hand to sit down. Instead of joining me, he opted to sit behind me. His legs rested at the sides of mine, and his arms hugged my body from behind. Nick kissed the back of my head, took in a deep breath, and released it. I looked out over the lake, watching the waves silently lap against the rocky shore, afraid of what he was about to say.

"I've been avoiding this subject for a while now, but I can't much longer, and I'd rather it wasn't a shock."

"I'm not going to like this, am I?"

"I'm sure you remember I mentioned that I might not be going to college."

I pushed his arms to the side and turned around so that he could face me. Whatever devastating reason he had for this decision, I wanted him to say it to my face. But deep inside, I was afraid that I already knew the reason.

"I decided to be a SEAL — join the Navy, just like my father."

"I was hoping you'd decide to make a difference in other ways. Like be a firefighter. Didn't you say you wanted to be a fireman, Nick?"

He didn't, but I was desperate, and we both knew it.

"I just got a letter notifying me that I passed my medical screening. My physical screening test is next week. If I get high scores, I'll be able to skip right on to boot camp."

I didn't want to tell him that I didn't understand half of what he was saying, because I didn't want to understand.

"When did this happen?"

"I didn't tell you because I didn't want you worried."

"Well, now I'm officially worried."

"Jo, it won't be that bad. It's less than a year of training. Eighty percent of people who go through the training and tests either give up or fail, so I might even be back sooner."

But I knew that Nick wasn't a quitter. I knew that if he left, he'd succeed.

"Then why even try and waste all this time away from me?"

"I... I just have to do it. I want to try to be the man that my father was."

"Nick, your father died in combat."

"I know."

"I don't want you to die."

"It's just training, Jo."

"But this would lead you to be in combat one day, wouldn't it?"

"You won't change my mind, Jo. And it would feel so much better knowing I had your support."

Was that why he'd been working out so hard?

"That's like asking me to pull a trigger on you. Don't you see that if I support you in this, I'll be responsible for what happens to you? No, Nick! I'm not going to send you to your death."

"I'm sorry you feel that way."

He lowered his head. If he thought making me feel guilty about his stupid decision would work, then he had another thing coming.

"You're joking, Nick. Right? Please tell me you're joking."

He didn't say anything.

"You've already decided, haven't you? Without talking to me about the decision? When did this happen?"

"Three months ago. I'm set to leave a week after graduation."

My heart was squeezing so hard that I had a difficult time breathing. At the time when I thought we'd finally start our lives together, he'd leave me. He would actually leave me.

"And you somehow forgot to tell me earlier?"

"Jo, I am telling you earlier. We have another month together."

"A month? I was expecting a lifetime with you, and now I get a month?"

"A year will pass quicker than you think."

"What about after?"

"Don't worry about the after yet. Whatever happens, I promise to come back home."

"Nick, I can't stand being two days away from you. Remember when you caught the flu last winter? I was afraid my father would tie me down. If I couldn't see you through that window, I would have died."

"It will be hard, I know, but if there's anyone that can do this, it's us. What we have... it's unbreakable. If I stay,

I'm afraid I won't be able to find myself at the bakery or as a firefighter… or anywhere else, as a matter of fact."

The funny thing was that I couldn't picture Nick anywhere else. While he had told me that he'd leave, it hadn't registered in my mind. I didn't want to believe that he'd actually leave our little town to go and train as a SEAL.

"Oh, my God, your mom must have flipped when you told her."

He took a deep breath and then let go of the tension in one long exhale.

"You haven't told her yet, have you?"

Which made my day so much better now. There was no way she'd let him go, and once Nick saw her tears and heard her begging not to leave her, he'd stay. Marge had lost her husband in a battle, and she'd do anything to prevent the same from happening to her son – I was sure of that.

"No. I was hoping to do it right after the prom."

"Nick, you can't. She'll kill you if you give her only a week's notice."

"I don't want her crying over it for the next month."

"She'll cry regardless. You just want your feelings spared. You're afraid to see her puffy eyes, aren't you? So it's better to leave and let her cry while you're away? That's a cowardly way to leave, Nick, and I know that you're not a coward."

"It's different with my mom. I don't want to see her hurting."

"You have to tell her. If you don't do it, I will."

"Jo, you can't."

"She loves you more than anything in this world. You owe it to her."

"I know, I know."

I reached for his hand. It was selfish of me to encourage him to tell his mother in advance because that would give her more time to talk him out of this stupid decision he thought would make him a better man. He was already the best man I knew. I couldn't let him go. If Nick left, I'd be crushed.

"Jo, you can either support me in this decision, or we can fight about it for the next month, wasting precious time. No matter what, I'm not changing my mind."

I stood up and crossed my arms over my chest looking out to the lake. Why were the waves so calm when all I could see ahead in my life was a storm full of hurricanes, thunders, tornadoes and cloudy days? Why was he doing this to me? Why was he doing this to us?

"I need to go."

I turned on my heel and started running. This morning when we went out for our run had felt so perfect, and now Nick was ruining it.

"Joelle," he called after me, but I didn't stop. He said that I couldn't talk him out of this decision. Well, I wouldn't allow him to talk me out of mine, and so I headed for the bakery.

Marge was packing a five-layer cake into a box when I walked through the door.

"Hi, Jo." The smile dropped off her face as soon as she saw me. I ran to her, slamming into her body. She took me into her arms as if she were my mother. Truthfully, she was the only mother figure I'd known in my life, and I felt as close to her as I had to my own father.

"Honey, what happened? Is Nick okay? Oh, my God, Jo, is he hurt?"

"No. He's okay. I just had to come here because I need your help."

"All right. You know I'd do anything for you."

"You need to stop him. He can't leave."

As soon as the words left my mouth I felt like the coward I'd accused him of being. But it was too late now.

"Stop who and leave where?"

"Nick. He's going to join the navy. He wants to be a Navy SEAL, and then he'll go to war and die, just like his father."

"What?"

"In one month. He already made the decision and didn't bother talking to anyone about it."

"My son's going into the Navy?"

"Yes, you have to stop him. Please tell me that you will."

"Come here, Joelle. Have a seat and a glass of water."

She pulled a chair away from one of the two tables at the bakery where the customers often enjoyed a coffee and pastry in the mornings before work, and then sat across from me. Why was she so calm about this?

"Jo, I'm so glad that you care about him so much, but Nick is his own man. While I'm not happy that's he's not here himself telling me this, I'm afraid that I can't do anything about his decision."

What? I set the glass of water down and reached for a tissue to blow my nose.

"Of all the people, I thought you could help." I wiped my cheek with the back of my hand. "You're the only one who can help."

"Nick is almost an adult. I can't make these decisions for him."

"But you're his mother. You're supposed to keep him safe. Do you want him to die?

"Of course not. Sweetheart, I know it's hard to understand, but if he's anything like his father, which he is, he'll do this – and neither I nor you will be able to talk him out of it."

That was when Nick opened the front door. "You're playing tattletale? Seriously?"

"No, I'm making decisions that will help me keep you here."

"You can't keep me here, Jo."

That felt like a stab straight into my heart. Everyone was against me today. My only chance to keep him home, his mom, was slipping away from me, and I couldn't do anything to stop it. I felt like the world was closing in on me too quickly. I whipped my body around and headed for my house, bolting through the door.

"Joelle?" my father asked, but I couldn't stop to talk to him. I couldn't take another person telling me that they wouldn't do anything to stop Nick from leaving.

"I need to be alone," I said, and ran upstairs. I shut the curtains so that Nick couldn't see me through the window, making sure that I locked it as well. But instead of heading for his own bedroom, Nick came to mine. I could feel his presence. I pushed my face deeper into the pillow, burying it there. The edge of my bed dipped as Nick sat down. He remained quiet for a while before scooting next to my body, twisting it on its side so that he could spoon me.

"Jo, I'm so sorry," he whispered into my ear, his lips grazing gently against the outer cartilage. "Hurting you was the last thing I wanted, but I need you to be okay with this."

"Leave me alone." I pushed his hand away.

"I will, but not now."

That's right, in a month's time he would be gone, and I'd stay behind, on my own.

"I'm never going to be okay with you leaving."

He smoothed his hand over my shoulder, then kissed it gently. "I know it won't be easy, but when I come back—"

"If you come back."

"No, Jo. *When* I come back, I'll be a better man. My mother always told me that my father came back from the military a changed man. A better man. That's who I want to be — a better man."

I turned around on the bed to face him. "But you're already a good man, Nick. You're the best man I have ever known, and I can't imagine my life without you. Not now, and not ever."

"Jo, if I don't do this, I'll regret it for the rest of my life."

I shut my eyes, trying to stop the waterfall of tears. Maybe if he saw how much I was hurting, he'd change his mind. My irritation with him and this decision he was about to make was stabbing me right in the middle of my heart. Couldn't he see that?

"It should be the other way around. You should regret leaving me for the rest of your life."

"But I'm not leaving you. People do long distance relationships all the time. There are families with children that wait for their father or mother—"

"And how many of them don't make it home?"

"Jo, I will come back for you. I always will. You deserve the best, Jo."

"I just want you."

My tears were falling freely; I couldn't stop crying. He managed to get one of his arms underneath me and pulled me closer to him. I leaned my head on his chest and listened to his heartbeat. This could be one of the last few times I heard it. I prayed that it wasn't.

"I'm scared that you'll die."

"It's only training."

"But after—"

"We don't have to think about the after just yet. We don't have to think about it for a while, but it would make my training a lot easier if I knew that you were okay back home, waiting for me."

"What else am I going to do?"

"Well, you're going to college with Molly, so that should keep you busy."

I had applied to college intending to major in education, and while I'd never had a clear vision of what I wanted to do with the rest of my life, the way Nick had, I knew that I loved kids, and our school definitely needed more teachers. Besides, Mrs. Schipper in first grade foretold my future when she praised me.

"It will be the longest year of my life, Nick."

"Just think how good it will be to see each other when I come back next summer."

When he put it that way, next summer didn't sound as far away as I thought.

"If you don't like it, you won't try again, will you?"

"I won't, I promise. I'm going to stay here with you."

Except we both knew that there was no way Nick would not like it. He wasn't a quitter, and I knew that if there was anyone who would be a strong SEAL, it was him.

He leaned in and kissed me. I closed my eyes as more tears fell. I had a feeling that I'd be doing a lot of crying over the next year.

"I will miss you, Jo. I'll miss you more than you'll ever know." His arms squeezed around me and I savored the feeling, hoping their strength now would be enough to keep me sane for the next year or so.

"I will miss you too."

With that, I began counting down the days I had left with him. And they began flying at fast-forward pace.

CHAPTER 9

"You look beautiful, Joelle."

My father's eyes glistened as he looked me over. Today was our prom date, and a week from now, Nick was scheduled to leave.

"Thank you."

"Somehow I always thought Nick would be the one taking you to prom, though."

Carter was supposed to be here in five minutes. Like we'd agreed, Nick was taking Daisy. We planned on hooking the two of them up at prom, but we weren't going to tell our parents until just before Nick left. We needed as much time alone as possible before then.

"I see him every day." I shrugged.

"Honey, other people may be blind to the two of you, but I'm not."

"What do you mean?"

"How long have you two been sneaking around? I've been trying to figure it out, but it was hard to because you've always been such good friends."

"We still are good friends."

My father gave me a knowing look. "I wasn't born yesterday, and I'm getting the feeling that I'm not the only one who's been keeping secrets."

A month had passed since we outed my father and Marge. They'd been openly seeing each other since then, going out for walks and having dinners at either our house or Marge and Nick's.

"Jo, there's nothing better than showing affection to the person you care about. Just please be careful. I don't want you broken-hearted."

The only broken heart I would have was when Nick left me next week, and I was afraid if I didn't tell someone about the turmoil inside my heart, I'd die. I finally lifted my head and connected my gaze with my father's.

"I really like him, Dad. A lot. He's... he's my everything."

He sighed and took my hand, bringing me down to sit beside him at the kitchen table.

"Oh, boy. That's what I was afraid of."

"Afraid?"

"You're in love with Nick, yet he's taking Daisy; while you're going to prom with Carter. How did you two think this was a good idea?"

In love? I did love him. I think I always had, but I thought it was because he was my friend. Did I love him as my boyfriend? Was there a difference in the way you loved someone? Nick had my whole heart, and I was pretty sure that I had his.

"I think I'm beyond in love with him, Dad."

"Then why the charades?"

"At first, we didn't want to be treated differently by our friends. And we didn't want you and Marge worried about what we were up to on the rooftop because we weren't up to anything."

"You sure about that?"

"Dad, do you trust me?"

"Of course I do. I trust Nick as well. And I still think you two should be going to the prom together."

"Thank you. But don't worry. We've got it covered with Carter and Daisy."

"Are you fixing them up the way you did to me and Marge?" He laughed.

"Something like that."

"Just don't let your heart get broken, sweetheart."

The only way it would break was if Nick actually left next week.

"So, you're okay with me and Nick?"

"He's a good man, Jo." My father furrowed his brow. "I'm assuming you're okay with him leaving soon, then?"

"I don't think I have a choice. I'll concentrate on my education, I guess. College. Maybe some distance will do us good; you know, bring us closer together. I..."

When I looked into his eyes, the pride shining there was overwhelming. I was afraid I would start crying. My father wiped a tear from the corner of his eye. "Your mother would have been so proud of you, baby girl."

"Thank you."

"Be careful tonight. And if Nick breaks your heart, tell him he'll have to deal with me."

I threw my arms around his neck just as Carter pulled up to the front of the house. Dressed in a light gray suit, he looked very handsome from a distance. Having always kept my focus on Nick, I'd never noticed when the rest of my class grew up.

He greeted my father and gave me a bouquet of white roses, placing a matching corsage on my wrist. I took his offered arm and walked out. Nick was standing on his porch, getting ready to go pick up Daisy. I waved at him, but he didn't wave back, only nodded. Was he upset? He had agreed to the idea of fixing up Daisy and Carter, so why was his jaw twitching so hard?

"We'll see you at the party!" Carter called out, and that twitch in Nick's jaw hardened.

I didn't look toward Nick again because I was afraid he'd combust. It was only a five-minute drive to the old barn our class had decorated for the event. Since our town didn't have an official hall, all events, including our prom, were held near the lake.

"You know, I'm grateful that you agreed to come with me. But for the life of me, I can't figure out why Nick asked Daisy and not you." He turned on the ignition and the old engine roared. We could have walked the distance, but Carter had borrowed his father's car to pick me up.

"Why? She's very beautiful and smart."

"I know she is, but I still thought you two would be going together. Did you know there was a bet going at school about the two of you?"

"Really?"

"Yup, and I lost twenty bucks when he asked Daisy."

"Oh, sorry about that. But we're just friends. Nick's like a brother to me."

"Yeah, I guess it would be strange going to prom with your brother, but you know what would be even more weird?"

"What?"

"Not going with your best friend whom you've secretly loved for years. If he didn't ask you, why didn't you ask him? There's nothing wrong with a girl asking a guy out."

Carter was the second person tonight to mention love to me, and I frowned. My conversation with Carter before prom wasn't going as I had planned. I was supposed to be selling Daisy to him so that we could hook the two of them up, not talking about Nick and me. Maybe there was a way of turning this around?

"I know, but I'm an old-fashioned kind of girl."

Carter parked the car near the barn and turned my way. Yup, that's how long it took to drive to our prom. Add another five minutes and we could have gone to the other end of town at the base of the mountains. He reached for a water bottle behind his seat, opened the hood, unscrewed a cap, and poured it in one of the containers.

"The car runs on water?" I asked.

"No, but the radiator is leaking, and it overheats. I'll fix it over the summer."

He closed the cap and shut the hood. "Now, you say you're an old-fashioned girl, but as I recall, you asked me to prom."

Shit. I did, didn't I?

"Jo, we've been friends for a long time. Heck, I've tried to make a move on you for years without success, kissing you at our camping trip, running into you *accidentally* in gym, and it wasn't until I figured out that no one would ever be good enough for you, with the exception of Nick, that I realized you two were meant for each other. He's the one you've always had eyes for, and it won't change no matter how much you deny it. So to say that I was surprised when you mentioned prom and maybe the two of us going together is an understatement."

"Well, everyone else had a date already," I blurted out. That didn't sound right either.

"Wait. Did you ask me out of pity?" His brows rose.

"Not out of pity, but you were the only guy available."

No, no, no! Why was my mouth running away from me today?

Carter laughed instead of getting upset. "I was ready to beat Nick up when he asked Daisy. He was supposed to ask you, and I was supposed to ask Daisy. But he beat me to the punch."

"Wait... you like Daisy?"

"Yes. I mean... I like you too, but I always thought you and Nick would finally hook up. It doesn't change our friendship in any way, and I hope we'll always remain close."

Yup, I was getting dealt the friend card. I started laughing so hard that I couldn't stop. Here we were, trying to figure out how to get Carter and Daisy together, and all we should have done was leave them alone and let nature take its course.

"I'm so sorry, Carter. We thought you guys needed help. We wanted to fix you two up at prom."

"Wait – are you saying you were trying to hook me and Daisy up by going out with us to prom?"

"Yes."

"That's twisted, Jo."

"I know. We didn't want to hurt you or Daisy. I've been trying to convince Nick to tell you guys the truth for years."

"You've kept this a secret for *years*?" His eyes grew wide as he shook his head.

"Remember when we got lost at the camping trip?"

"Holy shit! I mean, I knew you liked each other, but I didn't realize it's been this long."

I looked at Carter from the side, sighing. "I can't believe it's almost over. I mean school and all. I'll miss you when I go to college, Carter. You're a good friend."

"Well, I'll be here when you come back."

That's right; Carter had decided to train as a firefighter for our little town. He was taking on the life that I wanted Nick to have chosen so that he could be close to me.

"Why are you shaking your head?"

"It's nothing. I just wish Nick was staying too." I didn't want to be upset at him, not when we only had a week left together. "Actually, would you mind helping me pull a prank on Nick? I'm so sick of crying over him for leaving. It's time to have some fun."

"Now that's the girl I remember. What do you want me to do?"

"Come on. I'll tell you about it inside."

We took our customary pictures as a couple by the barn door and then went inside to find our table. The barn was decorated with giant sunflowers, haystacks, pitchforks, wheelbarrows, and other farm tools, completing the farm theme we were going for. It wasn't that difficult to come up with decorations when every second house in town was an actual farm. White lights were strung on cords that spanned the width of the barn, spaced every few feet apart. The intimate lighting sent shivers up and down my arms.

Nick and Daisy joined us soon after we arrived. We exchanged hugs and a few polite words. Nick didn't look too happy, but at that moment, I didn't have time to baby him. He was the one with the great idea of keeping our relationship a secret, so he could suffer some more.

There were six tables of eight set up for prom. Given that our school was so small we only had one graduating class, it was a tradition to have prom with the graduates from a neighboring town. Each year a different school hosted the event, and this time, it was our turn. The seating arrangements had been mixed to avoid rivalry and each table had almost an even number of teens from each school.

When the time came for a first dance, I took Carter's hand as he led us to the middle of the dance floor. Nick's face took on a new shade. It wasn't even close to red, but more like purple.

I put my arms around Carter's neck and he lowered his hands to my waist, the way all other couples were dancing. I was wearing a halter top long blue dress that curved just over my hips before flaring at the bottom. Feeling another man's hands on my body felt odd, but Carter was a gentleman, which couldn't have been easy for him. Carter was one of those guys who spoke his mind before thinking, and I constantly had to remind him how to act around ladies. But not tonight. Tonight, his acting was perfect. Was he acting?

He leaned in to my ear, whispering, "Would it be pushing it if I kissed you?"

"If you value your life, then yes. I'm not sure how much longer Nick will be able to play this game."

"Which means that I'm doing my job. He better stand up for your honor soon, because I'd love to dance with Daisy."

"Well, what do we do, then?"

He lowered his hands from my hips and slid them down to my ass, squeezing it, forcing my body much closer to his, feeling his every manly muscle and curve.

Oh!

I touched my hand to his cheek in the most loving manner I could muster. It took seconds for Nick to be at our side with Daisy. He bumped my shoulder, anger burning in his eyes.

"What the hell are you doing, Jo?"

"Ahm, dancing?"

"Hey, the song's not over yet," Carter complained.

"Piss off, Carter! And get your fucking hands off her ass."

"Why?" he asked, dumbfounded, stopping our slow swaying motion. "I mean, it's what happens at proms, you know. You dance, you kiss, steal a little touch here and there—"

"Because that's my ass!" Nick growled and let go of Daisy, stepping between us, right into Carter's face. "And if you say another word about any other part of her body, I swear I'm going to rip your balls off."

By that time, a few of the other couples had stopped dancing as well. It felt like the entire hall quieted, and everyone was looking at the four of us. Daisy, whom I'd spoken to about our plan in the bathroom, was standing to the side, chuckling.

"Hey, the last time I checked, it was my ass!" I touched Nick's tense shoulder.

Nick looked from me to Carter in confusion as we both said, "Gotcha!"

"Wait, what's going on?" he asked.

"Nothing, you silly monkey. Now come and dance with me so that Carter can dance with Daisy."

"Wait, but what about—"

"Nick, just shut up, will you!" I finally grabbed him by his neck and pulled his mouth to mine in a lip-lock.

His shoulders lowered in relief as he found my waist and brought me to him, making everything right again. God, it felt so good to kiss him out in the open. A few of our friends cheered and clapped. Someone yelled, "Finally!" and I took my mouth away from his, continuing the dance.

Daisy was already in Carter's arms, practically glued to him, and his hands were down on her ass now.

"It was a joke?" Nick asked.

"Yes. I'm sorry, but Carter figured it all out before we even got here."

"Shit! I was about to punch him."

"My hero." I kissed him again.

"If you plan to pull another joke on me any time in the future, then I suggest no one grabs your ass but me."

Nick's voice was low and tender, like he wanted to grab me right then and there and have his way with me in the middle of the dance floor.

"Noted. But I don't think we'll have that much time to practice your ass grabbing skills. You're leaving in a week."

His body tensed for a brief moment, making me realize that his decision was weighing as hard on him as it was on me.

"Then let's make the best out of the time we have left, Joelle."

What was happening? What was that dazed look on his face all about? And those dreamy eyes... what was he planning?

"I've been meaning to say this for a long time, baby and I'm so sorry that I haven't said it sooner." He paused and I leaned my head to the side, wondering what it was that he wanted to say to me.

"I not only see you the first thing in the morning and last thing at night, but also in my dreams. You are my life, and I don't know how to live or breathe without you."

He reached into his pocket and pulled out a square box.

I stopped moving.

"Oh, my God." My hand flew to my mouth, covering it.

"Don't freak out, I'm not proposing," he assured me.

Thank goodness! I didn't think that I was ready for a proposal.

"But I want you to have this ring to remind you that you're mine and I'm yours and I'm coming back for you. It's a promise ring. Nothing will stop me, so all I ask of you is to wait for me. Please wait for me, Joelle, so that I can be everything you want for the rest of our lives."

By that time I was crying. This was much better than a proposal. Who knew Nick could speak about us with so much emotion? He removed the ring from the box, saying, "I should have told you this way before, and I'm sorry that I haven't. I love you, Joelle. I love you with all my heart, with everything that I am and everything that I ever will be."

I gasped.

We always knew it, but we never said it. Today was the first time I heard the words come out of his mouth.

"Nick, I love you too. So, so much."

He slid the ring, a small round diamond, around my finger, and then his mouth crushed against mine, putting on another display of our love for everyone.

Once we got that out of the way, all the girls wanted to see the ring. While I kept explaining that it was just a promise ring, I couldn't stop thinking that it meant so much more. Prom night was officially the best night of my life, and I had no idea that Nick had planned for it to get even better.

CHAPTER 10

By the time we got in my father's truck, which Nick had borrowed, it was one in the morning. I was tired but excited at the same time. So excited that I didn't notice when Nick drove to Pebble Beach, where we always skipped stones in the summer. He took my hand and led me down a path through the shrubs and the trees.

"Are we skipping stones?" I asked.

"Only if you'd like. I was hoping though that we could spend the night here. Together." He pointed to a tent that had been set up near the cliff.

Oh!

"But if you're not comfortable—"

"No, I'm comfortable. Totally comfortable." I squeezed his hand in assurance. "There's nothing more that I want."

I'd been wanting to spend the night with Nick for a long time and had been wondering whether we'd get a chance to be together before he left. And now I got my answer.

The moon lit the sky and the lake, reflected on the wet stones at the shore where the gentle waves lapped. It was a good thing that it was a full moon; otherwise, I wasn't sure whether we'd be able to find our way with only a single flashlight.

"I told my father I'd be back before sunrise," I warned him.

"Hmm, then we better get going."

In one swift scoop he lifted me into his arms and kissed me hard on my mouth, while carrying me toward the tent. I held the flashlight, lighting the way for Nick. Somewhere along the way, my shoes fell off my feet, but I didn't care. We climbed inside the tent, and as soon as Nick zipped the front closed, I felt nervous. He turned on a battery-powered lamp before removing his suit jacket. A mattress with blankets and pillows had been set up in the middle.

"Are you cold?"

"No, just nervous. It's my first time."

"I know, Jo. It's mine as well."

That was good. If one of us screwed up making love for the first time, neither one would know it. Could you screw up? His hand slowly grazed over my arm, killing off the unsettling nerves that were prancing around in my stomach. Once I closed my eyes and found his mouth, the evening felt more natural. Nick helped me with the zipper at the side of my dress, and I unfastened the buttons on his shirt. Soon enough, we were sitting on the mattress in our undergarments, almost as calm as though we were wearing bathing suits. At least that's what I was pretending to have on — it kept the nerves more balanced. Of course, when Nick wore his swim shorts, they didn't tent out as much as his boxer briefs were doing tonight. I felt my nipples harden at the sight and shifted my weight, slowly reaching around my back for the clasp of my bra. When it fell down to the mattress, Nick sucked in a sharp breath of air.

"Jesus, Jo. You look so beautiful."

He then proceeded to remove his underwear and my eyes grew wide. In the dim light of the lamp, I stared at his generous length, wondering how much it would hurt when he entered me. I'd felt him through his jeans, and on the warm summer days through his shorts, but I hadn't expected him to be this size when freed.

I grasped the sides of my panties and slid them down my thighs, lower legs, and off. Naked, we stared at each other, appreciating the natural beauty. Nick had been hard from the moment he set me down on the mattress, and I wondered whether that hurt him. I'd never felt as swollen between my legs as I did now. I craved to touch him and for him to touch me.

"I'll take it slow, Jo. I promise."

"I know. I trust you."

With that he lowered his mouth to my shoulder, slowly guiding my body to lie back on the firm mattress. His mouth trailed to my breasts. He'd touched them before but never kissed them, and I found the contact pleasurable. I pushed my chest higher into his mouth, hungry for more. He did this thing with his tongue around the rim that was a trigger for my hips to push into him as well. When he felt me press against his thigh, his hand weaved down my body to my center, where he touched me, slowly sliding his fingers between my folds.

I could barely breathe. The echo of my moans as he played with me filled the tent. My hips were moving back and forth along with his. I felt his girth on my stomach and positioned myself to feel more of him. I lowered my hand to feel him and curved it around his width, lining myself closer to his center.

"Not yet, baby. I need you nice and wet first. It will hurt less."

"How do you know this?"

"Guys talk."

Oh! Well, I liked that part. At least one of us knew what we were doing. I lifted my arms over my head, holding onto my hair, concentrating on what was happening to my body as he cherished it with his kisses and touches. I liked both his hands and his mouth on me, especially when he rubbed me with his fingers. A swell was building in my lower half, my body getting hotter with each lick of his tongue over my skin and the hot kisses that followed. The relentless teasing of his fingers between my legs stirred up my inner sexual needs, and I wanted him to touch me like that forever. The faster he circled his fingers, the more I writhed underneath him. I couldn't understand what was happening to my body. When I'd masturbated on my own it was always quick and fierce. But his teasing and his touches had been building up the pressure, and the sensation was so different. Him stroking me, was a hundred times better and stronger than doing it solo, and it built until it broke me apart, and I shuddered at the burst of pleasure from beneath his fingers.

"Oh, God! Nick..."

He kept on stroking and I kept on shaking, wondering whether the sensation of leaving this planet was real or my lust-infused imagination. I was floating, my mind spinning as spasms consumed my body. And then slowly the orgasm settled, and Nick gently slid his hand over my thigh, kissing me tenderly. I watched him, breathing hard, remove a condom from a side pocket, rip open the foil, and roll it down on himself.

"Ready?" he asked.

"Yes, please." I wanted so much more of this elation; while my body had returned to earth, my mind was still in the clouds. Nick positioned himself above me, lining up. I felt his tip block my entrance, and I held my breath.

"Relax, Jo. It won't help if you tense up." He lowered his mouth to mine, gently kissing me again, reducing my fear. I let my knees fall apart, and Nick moved his hips slightly forward.

"Ah!" I shut my eyes.

"You okay?" he whispered.

"Yes; try deeper."

He moved in further. A ripping pain seared through me, but once he slid in more and I adjusted, it seemed to ease. I could still feel the ache, but it was slowly being replaced by the exquisite feel of him deep inside me, stretching me for the first time. I smiled against his lips, wanting to shout, "We did it!", but I guessed that would have been immature.

Nick slid back and forth at a steady pace, slowly, watching me from above while I concentrated on how full I felt with him inside me. I used the moment to touch his body, sliding my hands along his braced arms and over his chest. His hair tickled my chest as he moved. Nick looked so handsome tonight. I sighed with happiness, drawing my finger over his left brow touching the scar from our camping trip. It was beautiful. He was beautiful and sexy and everything I'd always wanted. His breaths became heavier and his thrusts more frequent. My body jolted up each time he pushed inside me, and while the pain was still there in the background, it was so worth it. Connecting like this brought us closer. This moment of having him inside of me for the first time, marking me as his, would forever be sealed in my heart.

He let go of another grunt, his hips thrusting forward one last time. His arms shook and beads of sweat dripped off his chest onto mine before he breathed again. He withdrew slowly, ensuring I was comfortable, but even after he did, I still felt like he was inside me, and I smiled. Nick removed a moistened towel from a Ziploc bag in the backpack already stashed in the tent.

"What's that for?"

"Open your legs, Jo. You bled a little."

And he was ready for that?

He touched my knee, guiding it to the side, and proceeded to wash me.

"How are you feeling?" he asked.

"Good. Wonderful, actually."

"Yeah?"

I nodded. "It was amazing Nick. I mean, I have nothing to compare it to, but it was everything I could have hoped for. What about you?"

"I just wish we could have gone longer."

"Well, we have our whole life to practice, right?"

"Yeah, but now I'm beginning to doubt whether going away was a good idea. I could get used to being between your legs all the time."

I laughed somewhat greedily, happy that Nick was having doubts about going away. Still, he was my Nick, and I would do everything to show him how much I loved him, and that included supporting his decision.

"I can't imagine what it will be like to live without you. I mean, I've known you my entire life, but I'll be here when you come back. I'll wait for you for as long as I have to."

He covered us both with a blanket, and I snuggled into his body.

"I love you, Joelle. I will love you for the rest of my life."

"I love you too." I paused, watching the few hairs on his chest move with the breeze of my breath in the dim light. "Nick?"

"Yes?"

"I want to officially tell our parents about us. Can we?"

"Yes, I think we should."

Good. I didn't want to be crying over him and for my father to be worried. And I wanted to be able to talk about him with his mom while he was away. We could keep each other's spirits lifted that way.

"Do you think we should get going? I don't want to fall asleep and miss my curfew."

"Yes, but the night's not over yet, baby."

"Really?"

"Yeah, I heard the best view of the night sky is around four in the morning. Which means that we have about half an hour to make it to your rooftop."

"Mine?"

"Yes, yours."

I'd been waiting forever to watch the stars from my rooftop, but since Nick had always beat me at stone skipping, we'd always watched the night sky from his. Okay, so I knew that the contest wasn't fair because of his stronger arm and better aim, but I'd agreed to it, and I wasn't someone to quit when my back was against a wall.

After what seemed like only minutes of rest, snuggling against him, he helped me with my dress, every so often stealing a kiss. I was so in love with this man that I felt like I was flying on cloud nine. Now that we were officially a couple, I wanted to spend as much time with him as I could. We only had a week before he left, and I was already missing him.

When we got home, the lights were still on. We walked through the door hand in hand. In the kitchen, my father was sitting at a table with Marge, having a tea, relaxed as ever. When they saw us holding hands, they both smiled.

"Finally," Marge exhaled. "We were beginning to worry you two would never come out."

"You guys knew?" Nick asked.

"For over a year now." My father took a sip of his tea.

"And you didn't stop us?"

"Why stop something good and something that was meant to be?" He reached for Marge's hand across the table.

"So…"

"Don't let us interrupt you. Go on with your evening."

"We were just going to go up to the roof."

"All right. We'll see you guys in the morning, then." My father stood up, took Marge under her arm, and they left. We watched through the window as they walked outside, turned right to Nick's house, and went inside.

"Did they just leave the house to us?" I asked, pointing my finger toward the door.

"I think so."

"I didn't exactly expect that."

Stunned, we went upstairs to the rooftop, where a blanket had already been laid out. We both changed into our pajamas before going up. Nick covered us with a second spare blanket, and I lay down beside him, his right arm underneath me, my head partially on his shoulder and chest, and looked up at the sky. We stayed like that in silence, for the first time ever, watching the stars on the east of the night sky.

"I told you the view is better from my roof." I yawned.

He squeezed the side of my arm in agreement. "Anywhere with you will always be better for me." He paused. "I'm sorry that I'm doing this to us, especially now, but I can't even tell you how much it means for me to know that I have your support."

"Always, Nick. Always."

We didn't say another word until the sun started coming up.

"Come on, Jo. Let's get you to your bed."

I followed his steps down the ladder, onto the balcony, and inside my room.

"Stay with me?" I asked.

"I wouldn't have it any other way. Come on, we don't have much time."

He was right. We only had a week left to ourselves. Nick crawled into my bed and spooned me from behind, holding me in his arms. I didn't remember falling asleep; all I could think about was being so close to him, listening to his soft exhalations. This wasn't just my night; it was ours.

When I opened my eyes, Nick was sitting on the bed beside me, dressed in jeans and a light sweatshirt.

"Good morning." I smiled dreamily.

"Good morning."

"I wanted to leave when you were asleep, but I couldn't."

"I think I would have found your ass and dragged it back here if you had. Wait... leave where?"

Had he been planning to go back to his room before I woke? But he must have, because he was dressed already.

"What time is it?" I asked, lifting my body halfway up, supporting myself on my elbows.

"Just after two. Jo... there's something you should know."

I sat up and looked at the duffel bag on the floor beside my desk.

"What's going on? Why are you dressed? It was a late night. You should be sleeping in." I swept my hands through my eyes, wiping away the last of my sleepiness, and looked at him again. I could physically feel my eyes growing wider in slow motion. "Did you cut your hair?"

"Yes, I had to before I left for the Navy. I didn't think that it would be so hard to say goodbye. I wanted to remember you laughing, not crying."

"Nick?"

"Jo, we don't have a week. I'm leaving for the navy today."

"No, no, no." Hoping that I was still dreaming, I blinked several times, but it didn't work. I was still in my bed, and Nick was dressed, telling me that this was it.

I shook my head, feeling my throat tighten. He wiped the tears off my cheeks as I struggled to keep myself upright.

"Please don't cry, Jo." He took me into his arms, gently whispering in my ear, "You're the strongest woman I know, and you can overcome anything. I will be back sooner than you think."

"Nick, please..."

"It would be harder counting down the days. I'm... I'm sorry."

"You're *sorry*? Nick—"

"I didn't want you crying. You mean too much to me to be in so much pain. Please don't cry. I will love you no matter where I am. And I'll write to you. I'll do so whenever I can, the old-fashioned way with pen and paper. Waiting for the letters will feel more special than email."

"I love you too. I just… I thought we had more time."

"We'll have a lifetime together, I promise."

I pulled in a longer sniffle. There was no way I could control the river of tears streaming down my cheeks. After the best night of my life, I had to face my worst day.

"We should go downstairs. Your father will drive me to the station." He looked at his watch. "We don't have much time."

I still couldn't believe that this was happening to me. The man I'd loved my entire life, whom I'd spent almost every waking hour with, was about to vanish from my life for an entire year. I quickly pulled on a sweatshirt and shorts. He swung the duffel bag over his shoulder and took my hand.

We walked downstairs without saying a word. I wiped my nose with my sleeve every few moments. My father and Marge were already waiting in the kitchen, their faces almost as somber as mine, yet I couldn't imagine anyone else bearing the torment and sadness that was tearing my heart apart.

He took me into his arms one last time, whispering, "I'll be back before you know it."

"Promise?"

"Yes, baby. There's nothing more that I want from life. You and me, together, in this little town."

We followed our parents outside. My father was already standing by his truck, looking at his watch.

"But we can have all that right now." I tried to make the argument one last time.

"I don't want to be a coward. I need to be strong for you and for me. I love you, Joelle. I promise you that will never change."

"I love you too, Nick. Come back home to me."

He nodded and kissed his mother goodbye. She gave him a box of his favorite cookies she'd made earlier. Nick turned around and got into my father's car. I could have gone with them. In fact, I should have gone with them, but I'd been struck with this news only a few minutes ago, I was so overwhelmed with emotion that I didn't even think about the possibility. Marge could have managed both our stores for the day. But then again, if I went with him, I was afraid that I'd never let him go. As soon as the truck pulled away, I turned around and slammed into Marge's body. She held on to me tightly, smoothing my hair like a loving mother.

I turned back once more to see a wave from Nick, but there was nothing left but dust. Nick was gone.

CHAPTER 11

The day Nick left was the most painful one of my life, or at least, my life until that point. I stayed in my sweat pants the entire day, and the next, and the one after that as well. The minutes and hours blended into one continuous blur of time, making me feel more lost than I had ever been — even when we had escaped the bear on our camping trip and lost our way in the forest. At least we were lost together back then.

I missed our morning runs, stolen glances, and secret kisses. There was no point to waking up or going to sleep. Numbness overtook my body as I sulked in the misery of going on without him. My first two weeks passed with me kneading more dough for the bakery than I had in my life, punching the raw bread when frustration set in and sometimes even tearing it apart, until one mid-summer day, Marge knocked on the front door.

"Jo? Do you have some time to help me at the bakery?"

My father touched my shoulder. "I can handle everything here. Go see what Marge needs."

"Yeah, sure."

I followed Marge back to her store, dragging my feet along the floor. Inside, I put on an apron and a hair net, grasped the piping bag full of cream cheese frosting for the cupcakes, and started squeezing the white goodness on their tops. It took a lot of concentration, which I didn't have right now, but the monotonous activity was satisfying, especially after I looked at the finished rows of cupcakes with their perfectly piped snow caps, all lined up like little soldiers.

"You know, I too wish he hadn't left," Marge said, after the first batch was done.

I lifted my head in confusion. She'd supported Nick's decision before he even made it, so I wondered why the change in opinion.

"I thought you said it's for his own good."

"I did, but I still wish he was here."

"How did you deal with it when your husband left? I mean, you had a child already. I don't know how you've gone through it all alone."

She pulled a second stool toward the counter and gestured for me to sit.

"I felt lost. I was just about your age when Kyle left. I didn't want him to go, but I also didn't want him to lose his dream. When he came back, he was a changed man. He had matured and there was finally a peace within him that was strong and real. He knew exactly what he wanted from life, and having seen everything that he had made him cherish his days with his family that much more. I think being apart made Kyle stronger. It takes a special kind of man to join the SEALS."

She was right. I knew that Nick was special. He was the bravest and strongest man I'd ever known.

"But your husband died. Aren't you afraid for Nick?"

"Of course I am. It's a risk, but risk is everywhere. He could have stayed here and been a wonderful teacher, police officer, or even a baker, but I wouldn't want him to regret the choice and be someone else. Or he could have joined Carter at the firehouse, and that's dangerous as well. My point, Jo, is that you can't change what God has planned for you. The most difficult battles you face in your life are the ones you don't expect. They make you stronger."

"Is it bad for me to hope that he'll fail? Or that he'll change his mind and quit?"

"You too?" She gave me an understanding smile. "You'll get through this, honey. I know you will. It will get easier with time, and I'm here for you, and so is your father."

I looked at the three batches of fresh cupcakes I'd decorated. "It does help when you're busy, I guess. Marge, do you mind if I come here in the mornings and decorate these for you this summer? I don't feel like running anyways, when Nick's not here, and piping these feels right."

"No, I don't mind at all. Actually, I'd really appreciate that. Do you have time to do a few cakes as well?"

I had all the time that I needed before I went to college in September — a choice I was more confused about now than before, but I couldn't quite figure out why.

"I'd love to."

As I spread the buttercream over the cakes, I wondered how many Nick had decorated in his lifetime. It must have been in the thousands. And while I'd done a few more since the time he helped me bake for Marge, the professional way in which Nick moved his wrist and spun the turn table was definitely a skill I'd need to practice for thousands of hours if I wanted to decorate as fast.

Two hours had passed before I was done. I looked over my work, pleased, and set the cakes underneath the display glass just as the front door opened.

Daisy and Carter walked through the door, hand in hand, and sat down at the table for two.

"Are you guys checking up on me?" I asked.

"Can't two friends come over for a visit without being harassed?" Carter's over-the-top look of innocence reminded me why I loved my friends so much.

"We're worried about you. We haven't seen you around, Jo. I hope you're not planning on hiding out until Nick comes back," Daisy said.

I sort of was, but I wasn't about to tell her that. "I'm just trying to keep busy."

"Great! That's the exact answer I was waiting for."

Wait, what?

"Come out next weekend with us. There's a dance being held at the old barn. The fire department is raising funds to update their equipment. It'll be fun."

"Thanks, guys. But I don't want to be a third wheel."

"You won't be. Molly's going, and so is most of our class."

"I'm afraid I wouldn't be any fun."

"I'm pretty sure that we can wipe that frown off your sad face for a couple of hours. Come on, we're leaving for college in a month and a half. There won't be another opportunity to party together for a while." Daisy pouted.

I shifted my weight from one foot to the other, wondering what Nick would have done. If we were together, I was sure that we would have gone, but on my own?

"I don't know."

"If you're not having a good time in the first hour, I'll personally drive you home," Carter offered.

"I'm taking that offer very seriously."

"Does that mean a yes?" Daisy asked, warily looking at me, waiting to pounce with a hug.

I nodded.

"Yay!" She shot off her chair and threw her arms around me, squeezing hard. "It wouldn't be the same without you. I promise we're going to have the best time ever."

For the first time since Nick left, I felt a tiny lift in my mood. Maybe they were right. A night out dancing was definitely one way to relax.

"This will be good for you, Jo," Marge whispered from behind me.

"Thanks."

I packed up the batch of cookies Daisy and Carter had ordered earlier and took another order from Carter while Daisy was busy checking out some of the cakes I'd just decorated.

"This is for the firefighter's fundraiser, but Daisy can't know about it. When will you bake it?"

"Carter, it's an order for one cupcake. I'm pretty sure I can handle it."

He looked back toward Daisy who was busy checking out one of the cakes, and then lowered his voice even more. "Can I trust you?"

"Of course you can."

"Then you need to come with me to the city tomorrow."

"Why?"

He covered his lips with his finger. "I'll let you know tomorrow, but you can't say anything to anyone."

My mind grew more curious and I got exciting tingles all over, wondering about Carter's secrecy.

"I promise I won't. I'll be ready at nine?"

"Perfect."

"What are you two whispering about?" Daisy asked.

"Carter says your favorite flavor is chocolate. I told him vanilla, but he's not listening."

"I L.O.V.E vanilla. Not *everything* vanilla" – she winked – "but cupcakes, definitely."

"See, I told you so," I grinned, before realizing what Daisy had meant, and then felt my cheeks heat. Up to this point, I hadn't even thought whether Nick liked everything vanilla either, simply because we'd just become intimate before he left. I made a note to ask him in one of my letters.

"I'll see you two at the dance, then."

Daisy hugged me again. "See you soon."

Once they left, I gave the single cupcake order to Marge. "What do you think it means?"

She covered her mouth as if she knew something that I didn't. "Well, if it were my guess, I'd say that Carter's planning to propose."

"Really?" I almost squealed. "Oh, my God! You're right. He's going to put the ring in the cupcake, isn't he?"

"Well, I don't think right in the cupcake, but possibly on top of it. Jo, you have to find out, though, because if I know ahead of time, I can make it that much more special."

"I'm going to town with him tomorrow. He said he needs help with something and I shouldn't say anything to anyone. Wait, I just broke a promise."

"Honey, your secret is safe with me."

I looked at my watch and realized that I'd been at the bakery longer than planned, and there was still another load of breads to bake before the afternoon.

"Do you need anything else?"

"No, thank you. I'll see you tomorrow around two?"

"Sounds perfect." I stopped before heading out the door. "Have you heard anything from Nick?"

"No. Not yet. But I'm sure we will soon."

"Okay."

I went back home to help my father, but the batch I'd planned to help him with was already in the oven.

"I'm sorry I started without you, honey. It's all done now."

"I didn't expect to be there so long."

"Oh, don't worry. I don't mind at all."

"So, what's next?"

"Nothing. Why don't you take some time for yourself?"

Myself?

He then reached into his apron pocket and waved an envelope that was addressed to me.

"I think someone's been waiting a long time for this."

It took less than a second to register Nick's handwriting. My heart jumped up as I rushed across the room to get my first letter. "Thank you so much."

I skipped every second step upstairs and locked myself in my room to read it in private. My fingers trembled and hands sweat as I pulled the scissors through the envelope, ripping it open. It had been hard to wait for an envelope, but it was so much more romantic than an email. I knew I'd keep it beside me and reread it often. Maybe even sleep with it under my pillow.

My Dearest Joelle,

I hope this letter finds you well. Before you start reading, please wipe the tears away. It hurts too much knowing that you'll cry each time I write. I don't want you crying.

I chuckled. Him asking me not to cry was like trying to stop Niagara Falls from flowing. Still, I pulled my sleeve over my cheeks and eyes, drying them, so that I could at least read the letter.

To say that I miss you would be blasphemy. Not a second passes that you're not on my mind. You fill my days and nights, motivate me to pull through the torturous minutes and hours of training, and remind me of what I need to do. You give me strength I didn't know I had.

I have to be honest, I don't know how often I can write to you, but I will every time I can. I wish I could say that I was counting the days to my return, but everything here blends into one continuous string of time and it's hard to tell the days from the nights. Sleep is a luxury I don't always have. I don't know how long it's been since I've been gone until I look at the calendar. That only makes me crave you even more. When I lie down in my bunk, I look out the window and see the night sky, yours and mine, and I wonder whether you're on your rooftop. Hoping to connect with you on some level, I pretend that you are watching the same stars I am.

The rigorous physical activities are hard. They push you to your breaking point until your mind starts playing with you and hallucinations begin to be a part of your life, but I'm soaking it all in. I don't want to turn around in eleven months and think that they've been a waste. I can already feel that I'm changing. Little things don't matter. Only you do, our future and safety. I am now more determined than ever to make this world a better place for us to live in, I promise.

The most painful and difficult part by far is being away from you. I miss your sweet lips and your body. I miss everything about you, but knowing that I'll come out stronger for the both of us is worth it.

Please say hello to our friends, your dad, and give my mom a kiss. I'll try to write soon. I love you, Joelle.
Forever yours,
Nick

I used my other sleeve to wipe my eyes again. It would take some time before I could read a letter from Nick without crying. I quickly got a pen and paper and sat by my desk, trying to think of what I wanted to say to him. The words came all on their own.

Dear Nick,

I won't lie, it's not the same here without you. When you left, I felt like I lost my best friend. My days are long and nights even longer. I try to keep busy at the bakery, both yours and mine. Still, I feel lost more often than I care to think. I'm not sure what to do with myself. Carter and Daisy stopped by today to invite me to a barn dance next weekend. The firehouse is raising money for new equipment. As much as I don't feel like being there, to me, it's another few hours without you that I hope will pass more quickly.
I thought about going to the butcher so that he'd let me chop up some meat when I get frustrated, but he said that knives and a lost mind don't mix. So instead I beat the dough in the morning as if it were a punching bag. I hope I can find my mind again soon, because right now, all that I'm capable of doing is living through the memories of the

two of us. I'm not sure how I'll be able to study with you so far away.

Even if I'd rather you stayed home, I want you to know that I'm proud of you, Nick. I go to the rooftop and think about you every night the weather allows and I watch the stars – the same ones you do.

Wish you were here. I miss you with everything that I am.
Yours always,
Joelle

I kissed the letter, sealed it, and addressed it to the APO address on the envelope I'd received from Nick. I must have jogged to the post office and back at record speed. By the time I returned home, my father was closing up the store.

"That was fast," he said.

I couldn't stop smiling.

"You know, today was the first day that I thought I could live through this year without Nick."

"That's good, honey. And once you're back at school full time, the year will pass even faster."

I took a cloth, soaked it in running water, and began wiping down the counters.

"Dad, how did you know what you wanted to do?" I pushed my arm in a circular motion.

"I didn't. I took over my father's business, which had been there for a couple of generations."

"So you didn't have a choice?"

"I didn't think about it that way. I had an opportunity, and I took it."

"Oh."

"Why are you asking, sweetheart?"

"I'm not sure about college."

"Where's this coming from? Don't you still want to be a teacher?"

"I don't know. I think I made the decision to go because Daisy did the same, and I... I'm just not sure it's my thing. Actually, I'm not quite sure what my thing is. Would you be upset if I didn't go yet? I don't want to waste a year on something I'm not sure about. I'd rather do what I enjoy."

He got a mysterious smirk on his face as if he knew something that I didn't.

"I'd be upset if you had no plan at all. I'm assuming there's something else you're interested in?"

"That's the problem. I'm not sure. I mean, I know I'm not going to be a doctor or a lawyer, but I do want to do something I love."

"What do you love?"

I wasn't sure about that either. I loved my father, and Nick of course, but as far as hobbies, well, I was pretty sure that stone skipping or running wasn't a career choice. Then the main kitchen oven rang with the afternoon batch of buns and breads.

"I love the smell of bread first thing in the morning. I love the way I feel when I bite into Marge's cupcakes. And even better, I love watching people bite into them as well – the way their eyes light up when they see a cake that resembles a purse, a shoe, or a ball. Marge creates art, and it's just so beautiful."

"Well, I don't want to push this on you, or anything, but have you ever thought of being a baker?"

A baker?

"Like you?"

"Me, or Marge, or both. You have the experience. And it may be a bit selfish of me, but I could retire earlier." He winked.

"A baker..." I whispered, suddenly feeling elation fill my heart.

"I think you just got your answer. If you'd like, I can make a few phone calls. There's a wonderful pastry school in Pinedale. And with the world of the Internet, you can practice off YouTube. I'm sure Marge would love to teach you as well if you'd like."

I hadn't felt nearly this excited about becoming a teacher. My heart was drumming in my chest as ideas and possibilities filled my mind. It was all happening so fast. I could already see my own store, an online ordering system, boxes upon boxes being loaded into a truck to make the deliveries.

"I think I'd really like that."

And with one little suggestion, my father managed to bring meaning to my life once again.

CHAPTER 12

Molly, Daisy, and I decided to have a girls' night out by the lake. When we arrived at Pebble Beach, I couldn't help the memories flooding back to me of our prom night, when Nick and I made love for the first time a few feet away from here. We set up a campfire and our camping chairs. I set the batch of muffins, cookies, and cupcakes I'd made earlier in the day on a table made from a few planks that had been piled by the forest. Molly had brought a healthy plate of fruits and veggies with dip, and Daisy had opted for the junk food: chips and caramel popcorn. With the amount of food the three of us could carry, you'd think we were throwing a party for at least a dozen.

The sun was about an hour from setting. I stretched my legs out, removed my shoes, and warmed my feet by the fire. Evenings in Hope Bay tended to be cool even in summer time.

"So, roomie, are you packing yet for college?" Daisy asked.

"Actually, I've been meaning to talk to you about that."

"I don't like the way this is sounding."

"I don't see myself as a teacher. I think I was born a baker, though I hadn't really figured that out until now."

"Wait, are you backing out?"

"I really struggled with the decision, Daisy, but the only thing that makes me happy is baking."

"You mean baking and Nick, don't you? I can already picture you two on that counter top, with flour sprinkled all over the kitchen and a few chocolate chips here and there." She removed her daisy printed hat and put it to the side.

"Eww, Daisy. Never!" I couldn't stop laughing, yet Daisy was serious.

"Why not?"

"Because for one, we knead the bread there and two, it's the kitchen and it's not sanitary."

"Sanitary, my ass. A few drips of sweat never killed anyone."

"I swear I'm going to think twice when I'm over at your house for dinner."

"I'd disinfect the table before we eat."

"Table? Daisy! Where else do you have sex?"

"Everywhere." She sighed dreamily.

"You keep that up and Carter will knock you up before you finish college." Molly removed her shoes as well and dug into the batch of cookies I'd brought. I had a feeling that the fruits and veggies would be quite lonely tonight.

"So you're really quitting on me?"

"I promise you can practice your teaching techniques on me." I crossed my finger over my heart. "And Marge is taking me to San Antonio Texas tomorrow to bake a special-order cake. Get this – we're flying out on a private jet, and she said she'll let me do the whole thing."

"Wow! Soon you'll leave this tiny town and be a famous baker."

"Nah. I'm a Hope Bay girl at heart. This town is my home."

"Well, it won't be the same without you at school, but I'm glad someone will be here in town, making sure we have fresh bread each morning while I sweat teaching little rugrats."

"You're going to be a great teacher," Molly said. "Kids love you. They always have, because you're fun."

"Aww, thanks. What about you, Molly?"

"Oh, I still want to be a nurse. It means I'll need to go away for a few years, but I'll be back. There's no way I'd leave this town permanently."

Her comment sobered me as I wondered about my and Nick's futures.

"I'm sorry. I didn't mean it that way. I know you miss Nick, but what he committed to takes a lot of courage."

"I know. I just wish time would pass by quicker."

"You know what I would miss the most if Carter left?" Daisy asked in a dreamy voice.

"What?"

"The sex. Carter's just so amazing, and so, so giving. He does this thing with his—"

"Whoa, girlfriend. That's TMI." Molly perked up.

"Oh, you'd know what I meant if you were under him. I swear, he's had some special training in the sex department."

Interested in the conversation a bit more due to my lack of experience, I set the bag of chips I'd been devouring aside, waiting for Daisy to continue.

"So, you guys do it often?"

"Three times a week at least. Sometimes four, or maybe five. Who keeps track of these things? What's important is that when we're horny, it's on. I just don't know how I lived without it before. That's why I said I would miss it. Actually, I think I'd go crazy. How do you do it, Jo? How can you stand being away from the man you love? How can you not want him all the time?"

"Well, I do want him and I do miss him, but I don't have as much experience to compare to. We only did it once, the night before he left."

"Prom night?"

"Yup. Right there on that hill." I pointed. "He set up a tent and had everything ready."

"That's so sweet," Molly said dreamily.

"Wait, did he pop your cherry that night?" Daisy licked the cupcake icing clean off her fingers.

"He popped mine, and I popped his."

"Awww, that's so sweet," said Molly again. She was a romantic at heart, and she was waiting until she got married to have sex.

"Ladies, you don't know what you're missing. It hurt like a bitch after I lost it to Carter, but the next time was so much better. And then every time after that, it was just mind-blowing. He likes it on top, on the bottom... actually, he likes all the positions and surprises me every time we're together."

"Wow, that's... amazing?" I asked.

"Yeah, it is." Her smile was goofy and nostalgic. "We can't get enough of each other."

"Well, you two were definitely meant to be together," I said. "Like me and Nick."

"You're going to go nuts when he comes back."

"You think so?"

"Yeah, once you get a taste of the forbidden fruit, you want the whole orchard. You should think about a place where you guys can do it because you'll want to use those few weeks you have him back to your full advantage."

"Well, you'll have to tell me some more, then. I want to make sure that I'm ready and that he's pleased."

She leaned in closer. "Then you gotta blow him. That's an easy one. Carter also likes it when we're on his bed on the side. Our legs are crossed like scissors, and I reach down to cup his balls, and that puts him totally over the edge."

I almost spat out the chips I'd been chewing. This was way too much information, even for me.

"I'm afraid I'll lose my virginity just listening to you, Daisy," Molly laughed, before her concentration flew to the lake. "You know what we should do?"

She stood up and removed her shirt.

"Oh, oh! I have a feeling Molly's high on fresh air again."

She giggled. "Come on! We haven't skinny dipped in ages." Molly begged.

"I'm game!" Daisy joined her, unbuttoning her jean shorts.

"Well, I'm not going to sit here and watch you, am I?" I laughed, and took my shorts off as well. Once we were closer to the shore we each removed our undergarments without looking at each other, and slowly stepped into the lake.

"It's colder than usual," I said, as I swam out. The sun was just beginning to set, and its orange reflection rippled in the water. I loved my town, and the scenery was yet another reason why I knew staying here to be a baker was the right decision. Living anywhere else wasn't even an option.

"There's a shift in the weather. Enjoy this, because they're saying we're going to get a storm by the end of the week."

"Those folks are never right about predicting the weather. One job you can always screw up and never be fired from," I laughed.

"I hope so, otherwise the firefighters' fundraiser will be ruined. Carter's been working so hard to make sure everyone in town attends."

"It's so nice to see you two happy."

Daisy dove underwater and resurfaced, spitting some of it out in a fountain, the way kids did. She was going to be a hoot when she taught at school.

"We're madly in love. I can't wait to share my life with him."

"You're that sure?" Molly asked.

"Yup. If he'd propose tomorrow, I'd say yes without even hesitating. Heck, if he asked me to elope, I'd say 'let's go!'"

"Is it bad that I'm jealous of you two?" Molly swam up to us. "I mean, sometimes I doubt my choice to hold off until I'm married, and I don't even have a boyfriend."

Molly was a beautiful girl. The problem was that most of the guys in town felt intimidated by her beauty. I had hoped that Andrew would finally make a move, but even he was afraid to ruin the perfection that was Molly. And it didn't help that she had extremely strict parents. They were awesome parents and raised her well, but going out and socializing other than on designated nights was not making Molly's life any easier.

"Jealous? No, honey. Your man will come. Saving yourself for the right guy takes more confidence and self-discipline than any of us have. You don't give up that v-card until you find the right man. One day, he will steal your heart and treat you like the wonderful lady that you are. But first we'll have to make sure that he's deserving of you. He'll definitely need to pass the Jo and Daisy interview."

"I didn't know there was an interview." She laughed.

Neither did I, but knowing Daisy, she was very serious about it.

"Of course there's an interview. We're not going to give you up to just any dweeb that decides he wants to get laid."

"I love you guys. I don't know what I would do without you." Molly hugged us both. I loved my girls. They meant everything to me, and I'd miss them when they both left for college.

I dove under the water once more and when I surfaced, someone whistled from the shore. The three of us turned away from the setting sun.

Oh, no!

Carter and Andrew were standing at the shore, waving our undergarments in the air.

"Carter Jacob Clark, you put those down and leave, or...!" Daisy threatened.

"Or what, baby?"

"Or I will come out and get them myself."

She wouldn't, would she? Yeah, she would. Daisy never joked when she made threats. I made sure that my upper body was still covered underwater as I swam closer to her.

"Daisy, what are you doing?"

"If he doesn't set those down and leave, he'll get a piece of his own medicine."

I laughed. "You have no idea how much I love you."

"Ditto. Are you coming with?"

"Are you kidding me? If Nick ever found out that Carter saw me naked, he'd kill him. This one's all yours."

Daisy lifted her head higher and slowly dog-paddled through the water toward the shore while, along with Molly, I watched the game of chess between her and Carter. Slowly, the water level lowered on Daisy's body, exposing her breasts.

"What are you doing?" Carter yelled.

"I'm coming for my bra and panties," she called out.

"Are you crazy? Get back in the water, now!" Carter was spitting mad and I couldn't stop laughing at the way his girlfriend called him out.

"You asked for this. Well, now you got it."

"Turn around, Andrew," we heard him order.

"And miss the show?" Andrew chuckled.

"You'll miss much more when you're dead."

Molly and I couldn't stop laughing, and I was sure that we each even peed a little. Well, at least I did. Andrew finally turned around just before the water dropped below Daisy's hips as she sauntered toward Carter, who handed over the undergarments.

"I swear if you ever do that again, I will... I'll lock you up and not let you out until you understand that you can't expose yourself to other men."

"You lock me up, baby, and one day you'll wake up tied to your bed with no one to help you." She stood up on her toes and kissed him.

Thank goodness sound carried well over water. I wouldn't have missed their cute argument for the world.

"Now leave, because I'm sure my girls are freezing in that water."

"I don't get it. Why skinny dip?" he asked.

"It's the same reason why you guys fart in the fire. Go figure that one out."

"I love you, you crazy woman."

"I know. I love you too."

"I'll let you go for tonight. But tomorrow, you're mine!"

"Grrr!" Daisy made a wild animal sound and hooked her fingers into a claw shape, scraping the air.

He slapped Daisy on her ass before disappearing into the woods with Andrew.

"And don't you dare peek from there! I'll know if you do," Daisy yelled toward them. Once she was certain the beach was clear, she turned our way. "Okay, ladies! It's safe to come out now."

I paddled with Molly toward the shore. "Thanks, Daisy. I don't know what we would have done without you."

"You would have turned into wrinkly old prunes," she laughed.

We got dressed and added more wood to the fire. Soon the flames rose high enough to keep a constant warmth floating around us. As I sat there, following the orange sparks up into the night sky, I wondered how many more gatherings like this one we would have before the summer's end. Little did I know, this would be the last one for the three of us.

Dear Nick,

It may seem odd, but I want to talk about sex. It's on my mind all the time, and I think it's because Daisy can't stop talking about all the sex she's having with Carter. Daisy's beginning to remind me of a female rabbit in spring. She and Carter are going at it like two monkeys, and I feel like I'm missing out on all the good stuff with you. I mean, we had sex, but I don't really know what you like, and I want to know. I don't know what I like, either, but I want to learn about it with you. If I told you the things Daisy does with Carter, you wouldn't believe me.

And she said that she kept the best parts to herself. Daisy doesn't know it, but Carter's going to propose to her. Please keep this between us, although by the time you get this letter, they'll already be engaged. I'm going to town tomorrow to help him pick out the ring. It's exciting. I wish you were here.

I hope you don't think it's weird of me to write about the sex stuff. Probably better than me telling you about the cakes I've been decorating with your mom. I'm getting better at them too. In fact, I can't wait to go to your mom's bakery each morning so that I can try something new. Which brings me to another discussion I wish we could have had on one of our rooftops. I'm not going to college. I can't see myself there and the only place I'm truly comfortable is the bakery. Are you disappointed? I've been watching a lot of YouTube videos about baking, and your mom has been a great asset as well. I can't wait for you to taste my blueberry muffins. They're to die for. Last weekend, I flew with your mom to San Antonio to create and decorate a special cake, and under her supervision I did it all! I baked, assembled, and decorated my very first special order for an exclusive client. Can you believe it? Little me? And the best part was that they loved it. I must say that it was beautiful. I'm attaching a photograph with the letter.

Miss you more than I did yesterday.

Love always,

Joelle

CHAPTER 13

My Dearest Joelle,

I would never be disappointed in you, and honestly, I never saw you as a teacher anyway, so I can't wait to try your blubbery muffins, and much more. I'll support you in whatever you choose, my love. Always.

So, you've been decorating cakes? Well, I can't say that I'm surprised. I want to see every single one. The one you sent me is a masterpiece. Please take more pictures. I want to see every single one of your creations.

I can't tell you what I'm feeling when I read your letters. I wish I was there on that rooftop with you, talking about our future, which of course includes the sex part. What do I like? I don't know, but I'm pretty sure that anything involving your body would be more and better than I get through my dreams at night. Yes, I dream about you every night. I wake up hard, thinking about our night together. Do me a favor? Tonight, after you shower, put on your sexiest underwear and a t-shirt, climb in your bed, and touch yourself. I want you to feel what I felt when I touched you. I want you thinking about me and how my hand is on my cock when I think about you. Now I'm getting hard while writing this letter and I wish I had time for a quick shower myself so I could jerk off to the beautiful image I have in my mind of your naked body. You are my everything, Joelle. Counting down the days.

Yours always,

Nick

P.S. I hope you're keeping these letters hidden.

The day of the fundraiser I paced up and down the bakery, biting my fingernails. Last week, Carter had taken me on a secret trip to the city where I helped him pick out an engagement ring. Marge was just as excited as I was. She would be the one decorating the cupcake and setting the ring into the cream on top. I still couldn't believe they were going to get married. But from what Carter told me, they both didn't want to wait long.

"Hey, when you know it's right, what's the point of stalling?" he said, once we had the diamond ring in a bag. It was a perfect cushion cut that I knew Daisy would love. Nothing big, but just right.

Daisy and Molly were both starting college next week, so today was bittersweet. It would be our last outing together before everyone left town for school.

I tapped my foot on the porch, whose wooden planks echoed from my cowboy boots. Carter was picking me up in ten minutes. I had the cupcake ready in a box, and he was going to hide it in his trunk before we got Daisy. My yellow strapless dress fluttered in the wind, and I pulled the denim jacket close around me. Although it was still summer, the winds had shifted, and this evening the air felt cooler than earlier in the day. Marge came outside, smoothing her hands over her bare arms.

"Feels more like fall. Look at those colors." She pointed to the setting sun. The bright oranges and pinks were like from a painting.

"It does. They're saying we have a chance of thunderstorms later on."

"You be careful, sweetheart. There could be an unexpected tornado coming with this storm."

Although we'd never had a tornado in town, there were a few warnings every once in a while.

"I will. Are you guys closing yet?"

"Soon, honey. We'll definitely drop by later in the evening." Marge and my father would be joining us after they closed the stores and finished prepping for the next day.

"Marge, do you think I'd be a good pastry baker?"

"Well, your skills are almost as good as Nick's, and the cake you baked this week was a true work of art. Don't tell my son, but I don't think he would have been able to pull off that last minute change."

I still couldn't believe how much had happened that week. A private jet, a ginormous ballroom party, and a cake that was the center of it all, which I'd baked all on my own. If time flew by for me at this rate, I'd be back in Nick's arms sooner than I thought.

"That's impossible. Nick is amazing."

"So are you. You have a talent for art. Remember when you guys made a portrait of our houses from different shades of rock?"

"Yeah, but we were only kids."

"Doesn't matter. They were beautiful. You have a talent that comes from the heart, and that cannot be learned or taught by anyone. Remember, I've seen your work firsthand and would have no objections if you wanted to bake or decorate for me permanently. So yes, I do think you'll make an amazing pastry chef."

"Thank you. My father said something similar."

"If you ask me, I'd say you were born to bake, honey."

"Really?" I hadn't realized up until now just how much her approval meant to me, and I smiled. Part of me felt like I'd always be here, in this little town, so now I wasn't sure why I'd ever thought I could move away to go to college. Deep inside, I'd known that I'd remain tied to Hope Bay, where I was born, grew up, and fell in love.

"Yes. Really."

Carter's truck pulled up to the house along with another strong gust of wind.

"Be safe!" Marge waved. Far in the distance, a good dozen miles or so beyond the town limits, the clouds were a dark green color, bordering on black, puffing gray mist through the few breaks of their perfect structure.

"Looks like it's going to be a wild night." Carter opened my door and I slipped in. We opened the cupcake box lid and Carter placed the ring we picked out for Daisy right in the middle.

"She's going to love it." I sighed, secretly wondering what my engagement to Nick would one day look like.

"You think she'll say yes?" Carter's voice vibrated with nerves.

"I hope so, otherwise it's a waste of a perfectly good cupcake."

"Hey, that's what you're worried about? A cupcake?" He turned on the ignition and backed the car out of the driveway.

"Carter, I'm not worried about anything – which means that yes, I think she'll say yes."

"What if she doesn't?"

"Well, then you'll have an extra ring to wear."

"Shit!"

"Carter, I'm kidding. Now concentrate on the road. The wind is getting stronger."

On the way to the barn, we picked up Daisy, Molly, and Andrew. Everyone was watching the bank of clouds outside approaching our town. It was almost surreal. I remembered seeing a movie, *Independence Day*, and the puff of cloud that pushed through the atmosphere when the ship approached — that's what the storm ahead looked like: an invasion.

"Heard anything from Nick?" Molly asked, as Carter parked on the designated grass by the barn.

"He says the training is hard and he misses me."

"Don't worry. A year will pass so fast you won't even know it."

"Yeah, but what about afterwards? He could be deployed for even longer."

"I wouldn't think that much in advance. Life has a funny way of making difficult choices for you. I mean, look at my parents. They divorced when I was just a baby, only to find each other again when I went to high school. You've known Nick your entire life, and he'll be back. You two will grow stronger and appreciate each other that much more. In the meantime, have some fun. Get to know the *you* that you didn't know existed. And more importantly, dance like there's no tomorrow." Molly smiled, pulling on the handle to open the door.

"Thanks, Molly." I hugged my friend before we headed inside.

Music blasted through the barn; a local band was set up on the stage. Around us, red, orange, and yellow decorations filled the hall. Fresh flowers were propped in vases on each table, and white lights were strung around the perimeter and along the high beams above. Everyone was laughing, cheering, and dancing. The local firefighters had parked their fire truck halfway through the main barn door and, wearing their uniforms, were serving food from the hot containers their wives and other volunteers had prepared. At the end of the table, near the pies, cookies, and desserts, I noticed Marge's fire engine cake that she'd donated, and smiled.

Soon enough, while rain poured outside, the party was in full swing, and no one cared that the wind was picking up and giant drops had started to hammer against the rooftop.

I was seated at a table with both Daisy and Molly. Carter was standing by the fire truck, talking to his father, Captain Clark, and then to Daisy's father. They shook hands and patted each other's backs in a way that men have perfected through evolution.

Molly and Daisy had taken on the mission to make me forget about Nick and cracked jokes one after another. It worked. I'd been laughing so hard that my stomach muscles were beginning to hurt, and I was sure I'd get a few permanent wrinkles.

"Good evening, ladies." I heard an unfamiliar voice behind me and turned. A tall, handsome man stood with his head held high, a petite raven-haired girl under his arm. They both wore a pair of cowboy boots, hats, bandanas around their necks, and khaki pants complete with leather chaps and shiny belt buckles. And it wasn't fake leather, either; I could smell its velvety aroma waft around us. Whoever had invited them to our fundraiser might have exaggerated our country clothing theme, but I loved it. The couple had class and carried their own atmosphere of *I can blend in anywhere* with them.

"Well, you're not from around here, are you?" Daisy scanned the fit new arrival from the bottom up as if he were the main course, completely ignoring the arm candy at his side. Carter would have to put that engagement ring on her finger before she ran away with this hunk. "Going to a Country Convention?"

"Daisy, don't be rude. Hi, I'm Joelle. This is Daisy and Molly," I said, introducing my friends.

"It's a pleasure to meet you." He kept his back straight and bowed his head respectfully. "Fortunately we missed the invitation to the Convention, so tonight we're privileged to spend time with you beautiful ladies. My name is Bennett Claremont, and this is Juliet Small."

Swoon. Mr. Claremont definitely had a way with words.

"We're acquaintances of Maxwell Clark," he added in a proud and commanding tone.

Carter's older brother? I didn't know that Max knew anyone out of town, let alone someone with a personality that easily filled the barn. And may I add handsome? Yes, he was definitely easy on the eyes; hence the stunning date standing beside him, who looked familiar, and I wondered whether we'd met before. He carried himself with poise, like a businessman. No one in our town had manicured hands or an expensive watch. Yet despite the obvious wealth, I found the couple approachable.

"Maxwell mentioned a fundraiser and, well, what's better than a good cause?"

This was the first time I'd heard anyone refer to Carter's brother, a firefighter like his father, by his full name.

"Thank you for joining us, and welcome to Hope Bay," I said.

"It's a pleasure to meet you." Juliet extended her hand to each of us, her gray eyes captivating me. I had a feeling she was someone I could easily be friends with.

"Are you guys staying long? Because if you are, we can show you around town," Molly offered.

"Thank you, but no. I'm just catching up with Maxwell. We went to college together."

The band began a new song.

"Bennett, I love this song." Juliet looked up adoringly at Bennett, and I got shivers over my arms. I'd always looked at Nick the same way.

"Well, it would be a shame to let a good song pass, wouldn't it? Ladies" – he bowed his head again – "Enjoy your evening."

Their walk to the center of the dance floor appeared synchronized. He twirled Juliet before showing off a polished, near-perfect two-step. Not in a bad way. Heck, if I could dance that well, I would.

"Look at those moves." I felt my mouth drop open. I was sure that at this point everyone's attention was on the new couple mastering the dance. Juliet was light on her feet, and Bennett couldn't peel his gaze away from her.

I sighed, wishing Nick were here. This year away from him would be the longest of my life.

"That right there is top-dollar dance school." Daisy nodded, approving of their moves. Or perhaps she was just checking out Bennett's tight behind. Those chaps were so fitted I wondered how he was able to move like that.

"Come on, let's join them!" Molly pushed away from the table.

"You don't have to ask me twice to get another whiff of that expensively delicious perfume Juliet was wearing." Daisy hopped off her chair.

Thunder sounded outside, and I jumped, along with a few others in the room. I saw a bright flash of lightning between the barn walls, and when the ladies at the table beside ours turned toward the door, I knew that I wasn't the only one beginning to get concerned about the storm. This place was old, and I was afraid that a stronger wind would one day blow down the building. The barn was one of three in town that had been standing unoccupied for decades; another of them stood a field length behind our bakery.

I danced with the girls at first, then with Carter and Andrew and a few others before we formed a circle and, along with Bennett and Juliet, trotted to the center and back as if we'd practiced the steps for hours. At one point, the music quieted and Carter stepped in the middle of us all, with a plate and a cupcake on top. The ring was so nicely set in Marge's frosting that you could only see its center in the middle — that is, if you knew it was there.

"What is he doing?" Daisy bumped my arm.

"I don't know." I bit my lip, hoping that my friend would stop looking right in my eyes. If she didn't, I'd spill Carter's secret before he got down on one knee.

He reached out for Daisy, who pranced to the middle. The music stopped, and everyone's attention fell on the couple. I saw Daisy notice the diamond center of the buttercream daisy flower that Marge had crafted. She covered her mouth with her hand just as Carter knelt on one knee.

"Daisy Anne Fraser, I've never met anyone like you. You're the breath that fills my lungs and the pulse in my veins that keeps me alive. Will you do me the honor and be my wife? Will you marry me?"

Everyone was quiet. Tears streaked down Daisy's face, and I wiped the wet corners of my eyes.

"Yes. I'll marry you!"

The cheers were so loud that they overpowered the rain and thunder outside. Daisy took rounds of congratulations, including mine. She wore the diamond on her finger with pride, showing it off to everyone at the hall. Carter gave me a thumbs-up from across the room by the stage, and instead of returning the gesture, I ran toward him and jumped into his arms, hugging him.

"I'm so happy for you two."

"Thanks, Jo. I couldn't have pulled this off without you."

Something roared in the distance and shivers covered my arms. The sound of an oncoming train filled the barn, somewhat confusing me. It got louder and louder, and by the time I realized we were in danger, full chaos ensued.

"A tornado," someone screamed. The lights flickered on and off a few times before the power went out. One of the firefighters turned on the fire truck's headlights.

Everyone was rushing around in confusion, not knowing what to do. Although there was chaos, I didn't hear as much screaming as I thought. The sound of the approaching wind, howling like a freight train, got louder. Carter swung his leg forward, breaking the plywood covering the bottom of the stage side. "Climb in!"

I got down on all fours and crawled toward the back. I searched for the darkest corner and straddled one of the thicker posts holding up the stage, praying that I wouldn't get sucked out. I heard Carter call everyone in.

"Daisy!"

One by one, others climbed underneath the stage. As I huddled, I strained my eyes to find someone I recognized. If it weren't for the few streams of light coming through the boards from the fire truck's headlights, I wouldn't have been able to see my hand in front of my face.

"Jo?"

"Molly? Oh, my God! I can't believe this is happening. Have you seen Daisy?"

"Daisy!" Carter was screaming at the top of his lungs. "We need everyone under the stage, now!"

Holding onto the beam, I desperately searched through my purse for my phone, hoping both Daisy and Carter would soon climb underneath.

"Dad?" I could barely hear him through the static.

"Joelle? Where are you? The weather is really bad."

"There's a tornado heading our way. I'm under the stage."

Something snapped outside, and I was sure it was part of the rooftop. Was Carter still out there? Where was Daisy? The space under the stage seemed pretty full by now and I hoped they were both here.

"Honey, I'm coming!"

"No! You take cover, Dad. Dad?"

The connection broke apart, and then I couldn't hear anything. The sound was unlike any I'd ever experienced. It was like all the sounds in the world had combined into one. Wind howled and tore through the barn. At one point,

I thought I'd gone deaf, as the tornado ripped apart everything in its way. It was just me and the post I'd been holding onto, and I imagined the stage above me ripped off along with everything else. The faint light through the boards from the fire truck vanished, and I silently prayed to not die until I saw Nick once more.

And then it was all quiet.

I'm alive.

Someone was crying further away, and I thanked God I wasn't the only one to survive.

"You okay?" I asked Molly.

"Yeah, I think so."

The stage was still above us.

"Is it over?" someone else asked. The space slowly emptied as we made our way out from underneath the stage. That's when I saw Carter, frantically looking around the room.

"Daisy!" he called out, and I ran to him.

"Where's the last place you saw her?"

"By the fire truck."

We both turned at the same time toward the barn door.

"Where's the fire truck?" I asked.

We ran outside to a world I barely recognized. I turned around in a circle to assess the damage. If it weren't for the few parked cars that remained untouched by the tornado in the parking lot and the now magically clear skies and the moonlight, we wouldn't have been able to see anything. The wind had activated automatic alarms on a few cars, and the sirens echoed, bouncing off the mountains. Trees to the left of the barn had been torn out of the ground, and some of those still standing had been snapped in half, like matchsticks. When I looked back to the barn, the front half of it was gone. Boards from the roof as well as from its sides had been ripped off, which meant that the tornado had cut through the structure, missing the far end by the stage where we'd been hiding, but judging by the look of the mud and debris all around us, not by much. The fire truck was on its side, a hundred feet away from the barn, and so we headed in that direction.

I searched through the debris, despite Captain Clark's instructions to stay back. I shoved the stray branches to the side when I saw a foot with a daisy sandal sticking out from underneath the rubble.

"This way!" I screamed, and climbed up the mound of trees, boards, and twisted metal the tornado had deposited. Daisy was pinned under a tree trunk. Her eyes were closed, and her dress stained with mud, ripped to shreds but still covering her body.

"Daisy! Daisy!"

She opened her eyes.

"Somebody help! She's alive," I screamed.

"I'm here, honey." I took her hand, careful not to add any more pressure to the tree that had trapped her.

"What happened?" she asked.

"I think you were sucked out of the barn by the tornado, but you're okay now."

"I don't think so, Jo. I think this is it for me. I can feel it."

"Come on. Don't talk like that. You're the strong one. This is just a hiccup. You just got engaged, baby, and Carter's been searching all over for you."

"Daisy!" I heard him not far away.

"Take care of my man, Jo. Promise me you'll take care of him."

"Daisy, don't talk like that. You're going to be fine, and you'll take care of him yourself until you're old and gray."

"It hurts so much," she moaned. Her pain seared through me, and I saw blood pooling underneath the tree.

"Don't move, Daisy. Just hold on. They're coming."

"Promise you'll take care of him, Jo."

"I promise, Daisy. I promise. Now you promise me to hold on for as long as you can."

She sighed and her eyes closed. Peace swept over her face, and my heart constricted. She didn't open her eyes again.

One of the firefighters was first at my side, with Carter right behind him.

"Hurry! She's losing blood." I squeezed my friend's frail hand, on which she wore her engagement ring, but she didn't squeeze back. "You hold on, Daisy Anne. Hold on."

"Joelle, move aside."

I wiped the tears from my face with the back of my hand and stepped away. Carter and Captain Clark threw branches blocking the main trunk to the side. Four more men joined them, and together they lifted the heavy tree; I could see their pulses straining through their bulging neck muscles. God only knows where they found the strength, but they were able to get it off her.

Daisy was covered in blood. Her eyes were closed, and though it was dark, I could see that her skin was white, almost translucent. Bennett and Juliet were helping Mrs. Gladstone, who had apparently hurt her leg, walk toward an ambulance.

"Joelle!" I heard Marge's voice first, then my father's, as they called for me.

"I'm here!" I ran to them both.

"Thank God you're all right." My father wouldn't let go.

"Daisy, she's... Dad, she's really bad. I..."

"Honey, she's in good hands now." Marge pointed to the team of paramedics carrying her to an ambulance. Carter was beside them, holding her hand. One of the paramedics was above Daisy doing chest compressions, and another one had attached an air bag and was squeezing the bag, forcing air into her lungs. The third was putting pressure on her belly where the blood I'd seen earlier was gushing. A piece of a branch was sticking out of her abdomen, and I brought my hand to my mouth in shock.

"We're going to pray for her, baby. We'll pray as hard as we can."

I was supposed to remember this night as a happy one, when two of my best friends got engaged and we celebrated the beginning of their lives. Instead, I would remember it as one of the worst ones of my life. Five people lost their lives that night, including my best friend Daisy.

Dear Nick,

I wish I was writing to you with better news. A tornado hit our town. We were at a dance to raise money for the firehouse. It was almost a direct hit to the old barn. Nick, Daisy died... It's still so hard to believe. She didn't make it underneath the stage where we were hiding and was sucked out of the.

Carter's a mess. He proposed to her the same night and moments later, Daisy was gone. I tried to call him over and over but he's been avoiding me. I can't even imagine his devastation. I'm not sure if I could live through the loss he's feeling. I mean, losing someone you love so much... I miss you and wish you were here. I lost my best friend and I need my boyfriend now more than ever.

This letter sucks because there's nothing good I have to say, but I do want to keep you updated. My house and my father's bakery were torn down as well. The tornado hit our side of the street but thankfully spared yours. We're both staying with your mom now and I live in your room. It smells like you. I hug your pillow every night. So much has changed in the little time that you've been gone and there are another ten months I have to get through without seeing you. I don't know what Dad's plans are about the bakery, but the whole town's a mess. Cleanup will take months but should be done by the time you come back.

At least I'll see you, right? I mean, Carter won't ever have Daisy again. I feel like you're so far away. I need

*you, Nick. I need you so, so much. I'm feeling very sad and
I wish I could hug you.
Yours always,
Joelle*

CHAPTER 14

My Dearest Joelle,

I'm sorry. I'm so sorry that I can't be there for you, for my family, and for our friends. Knowing how much pain you and everyone else in town are going through is tearing me apart. The days and nights are still blending into one, and while it feels like the training is easier, I think I'm just getting used to it quicker. I can slowly see the light at the end of the tunnel and can't wait to tell you all about it.

Want some good news? I'll be home for most of the summer. I feel much stronger than I was and that I can accomplish anything I put my mind to. So can you, Joelle. You can be anything you set your mind on. How is the baking going? Any new recipes?

Miss you with every fiber of my being.
Love always,
Nick

I placed a bouquet of flowers in a vase by Daisy's headstone and said a quiet prayer for my friend. Pulling my winter coat together, I walked between the graves, marking a new path with my feet. The wind whistled quietly, adding an extra layer of frost to my skin, and the compressed snow squeaked under my soles. This winter was running well into early spring, and I longed to see green grass and gardens full of daffodils and tulips. When I left the graveyard, I caught a movement in the corner of my eye.

Carter?

I changed my direction and headed toward the man sitting on a bench outside the front gates and, as I'd suspected, it was Carter. It had been seven months since Daisy died last August, and despite my numerous attempts to see Carter, I'd failed. I sat down on the bench beside him.

"Have you gone in yet?"

He shook his head, sighing, "No. It's still too hard."

From what friends had told me, Carter hadn't been at Daisy's grave since her death. He mourned his loss from outside the cemetery and kept his grief to himself. Carter wouldn't open the door when I knocked or answer any of my calls. If it weren't for Captain Clark, who assured me that Carter was dealing with Daisy's death in his own way, I would have taken that front door off its hinges. Months had passed with no word from Carter, and today was the first time since the funeral that I'd been given a chance to talk to him.

"It will never get easy, Carter. But if you'd like, I can go inside with you."

"Thanks, but not yet."

"How is the firehouse?" I asked. "I heard you finished your training."

"Yeah."

"Are you going to apply?"

"Probably, but not yet."

"Well, I'm sure they could use your help this cold spring. There've been a lot of power outages."

"Daisy was pregnant."

"What?"

"She was pregnant. We were going to have a baby."

"Carter, I'm so sorry." I removed my mitten and reached for his cold hand, covering it with mine. "I didn't know."

"I'd have been a father in a month. Can you believe that? Me, a father?"

"Of course I can. You're a wonderful man."

"What kind of a man lets his girl die?"

"This wasn't your fault."

"I should have been with her. Holding her hand. I'd never have let the tornado snatch her."

"Sometimes things happen that we can't understand, but you can't blame yourself."

"It's not easy."

"I know, but you'll get through this, Carter. You have to."

"What's the point?" He turned his head toward me. His light brown eyes appeared so dark I wondered whether they'd changed color. And then he looked down again. That connection I'd been wanting to make with him was gone.

"I'm here for you, Carter. If you ever want to talk, or do something to get out of here and clear your mind, I'm game."

"Thank you. I just haven't been ready." He lifted his head once more and met my gaze. The sadness in his eyes tore at my heart so hard that my chest ached. I turned my body toward him and he leaned in, resting his head on my shoulder. His body slowly slid down until his head was on my lap. He lifted his legs up to the bench, and sighed.

"Have you talked to anyone else about it?" I asked.

He shook his head but kept it on my legs. I drew my fingers through his hair, combing it gently, pressing the tips of my fingers to his scalp. He closed his eyes. I wasn't sure how long we sat like that, but I wouldn't move for as long as Carter needed me. When he finally pulled away and sat up, a fraction of that pain I'd seen earlier in his eyes was gone.

"I'm sorry, Jo. I don't like being a fucking wuss." He pulled his fingers through his hair. It had grown longer since the last time I'd seen him, and while I would have normally suggested a haircut, the style suited him. It reminded me of Nick's before he'd cut it. Besides, it would have been rude, especially at this difficult time.

"You're not. You're human and you're hurting. You need someone to talk to, Carter. I'd like to be that person if that's okay with you. I mean, I loved Daisy too. She was my best friend."

"I know. It just feels like I not only lost a part of my life, but also part of me disappeared."

"Can I come over for tea sometime?"

"Sure, but I moved out of my parents' place."

"You did? Why didn't you tell me?"

"I haven't really told anyone. And I know you've been busy at the bakery."

Oh! Since our house had been demolished by the tornado, I'd decided not to bother with pastry school. It just didn't make sense, since I lived with two of the best bakers in the world. That, and I didn't have the money to pay for it and didn't want to ask Dad. I objected when he offered to pay for my school when he was looking for a way to rebuild our house. He had enough to worry about with our new living arrangements. I loved working with Marge and was sure her knowledge and experience were better than those of any teacher at any pastry school.

"I bought the house Mr. Grafton used to live in, with the garage and all."

"The haunted house?" I gasped and covered my mouth with my hand dramatically. His mouth curved up a little. Mission accomplished! I curled my lower lip to the inside of my mouth and his grin widened. My heart pounded with delight.

"It's just an old house."

"It's the garage that sold you, isn't it?"

"Yeah." He gave me a bashful grin, reminding me of the boy I'd known my entire life who had been forced to grow up sooner than most. It also reminded me of how cute that boy had always been.

"My parents helped out, and I'll pay them back. I've been fiddling with a few old cars, fixing them up. My father's broken truck is next."

"I'd love to see it, if that's all right with you."

"Yeah, sure." He shrugged.

I looked at my watch. I didn't want to leave, but I had a retirement cake to finish.

"I have to go, Carter. But I'll see you around?"

"Yeah, sure, Jo." I tried to stand up but he grasped my wrist and whispered. "Thank you."

"You're welcome."

He let go of my hand and looked forward into the distance, lost. Just before I turned around I saw that young, capricious face disappear, replaced by a grieving one.

The next day I was swamped with receiving orders. It looked like everyone in town wanted a cake for the weekend. First I was busy planning them out, then fulfilling earlier orders, baking cookies and mixing tiramisu mascarpone filling for the Ladies Club at town hall, who'd ordered five tiramisu cakes. I didn't even want to know what they were planning to do with them all. Since both Dad and Marge were sharing baking space now, the crammed scheduled hours meant little time for negotiation, so I couldn't put something off for later. And all the while I'd been thinking about visiting my friend to see if I could get that spark of him back again.

It took me two weeks to find the time and work up the nerve to go see Carter. It was finally looking like spring outside. With a blast of warm southern air, the surprising snowfall two and a half weeks ago had melted away and the grass took on its bright green shade within twenty-four hours. Daffodils bloomed, tulips opened, and the smell of new beginnings lingered in the air. I knocked on the front door, but no one answered. The drapes were drawn and I couldn't see anything through the window. I knocked again, lightly tapping my foot on the porch.

Something clattered to the side of the house. I followed the noise until I reached the garage. A pair of legs, which I assumed belonged to Carter, were sticking out from underneath a car. By their twisting motion, it looked like he was trying to turn something.

I cleared my throat, and he stopped. After a pause, Carter rolled out from underneath the hood, the arm loops of his overalls and the entire top half draped over the bottom. His torso was smudged with grease and dripping with sweat. While I wanted to laugh, there was something about the image of him like that, half naked... sweaty... dirty... that forced my mouth to open. He pulled his arm over his brow, smearing grease over his forehead and bringing me out of my confused daze.

"Jo?"

I took a step back and leaned over, blocking the sun from his face so that he could see me.

"Hi." I waved with a full hand splayed out as if I was about to count out on my fingers. "I brought muffins. And cupcakes. Would you like to try my cupcakes?" I asked, reaching out with the box.

"Hrmph." he cleared his throat, trying not to laugh. "Your cupcakes?"

"Yes, my cupcakes. You know how good my cupcakes are, don't you?"

What the hell was wrong with me?

"Jo, right now I'm looking at your long pale legs, and when you say it that way, you make it sound like you're talking about..." I saw his cheeks turn red as his gaze ventured higher to my chest.

I crossed my arms over my breasts. "Carter! Stop looking at my boobs."

"Sorry, can't help it."

He finally got up and walked toward me in his half-naked glory.

"You better put something on or you're going to catch a cold."

Carter reached for the box I was holding, opened it, and swept his finger through the cream frosting before licking it all off in slow motion. My jaw snapped when my mouth fell open as I followed the tip of his tongue leaving a clean trail behind. My arms peppered with goosebumps.

"I'm sorry, I didn't mean to make you uncomfortable."

"I'm not. I'm perfectly fine," I lied. There was no way I would admit to him that he was causing an uproar inside my body. I mean, who in their right mind walks around half-naked when spring has barely started? "Your father's car?" I pointed to the Buick he was fixing, the same one we'd driven to prom in.

"Yeah. If I can get it going again, I get to keep it."

"Is that hard to do? You know, fix it."

"Don't know yet. I'm taking it apart first to see what's wrong."

"Oh, okay."

"Would you like to come in for tea or something?"

"It looks like you're busy. I don't want to interrupt."

"I've always got time for you." He winked. It was genuine and even a little bit happy, which was a good thing because making sure that Carter was happy and moving on from his loss was my goal. "I'm gonna grab a quick shower, if you want to wait for me."

"Okay."

"Wanna sit inside or outside?"

"I'll wait outside. The weather is nice, and apparently my legs need some sun."

He scanned me from the bottom up and back down again, stirring a weird feeling in my stomach once more, and said, "There's a patio set in the back. I won't be long."

I wanted to tell him to take his time, because in all honesty, I had to pull myself together while he was showering, but Carter was gone before I got another word out, and I exhaled in relief.

CHAPTER 15

As soon as Carter disappeared through the side door, I pushed the gate open and strolled to the back yard. Tall trees ringed the perimeter, followed by a forest. Mr. Grafton's yard turned out to be the size of a quarter of a soccer field. He was one of the other people who had died the night the tornado hit the barn. Evidence of old garden work was stacked to the right, propped against the falling fence: shovels, buckets, rakes, watering cans, and a weeder. The rusty edges of the tools flaked off here and there. Over-bloomed tulips and daffodils swayed to the gentle breeze, their last petals falling to the ground. There was enough space here for a future pool – make that three pools – and a garden. I wondered what Carter planned to do with the place.

I cleared a dusty chair and took a seat, extending my legs in the sun, and gently lifted my dress so that my thighs could catch some rays as well. Carter was right. My skin wasn't usually this light, but the long winter and staying indoors while trying to keep up with the bakery's orders and practicing my new pastry skills had taken a toll on my tan. If I didn't get some sun before Nick returned at the end of June, he wouldn't recognize me.

Ten minutes later, the back door squeaked open as Carter stepped through with a jug of lemonade, two glasses, plates, and a wet rag underneath his arm. I immediately lowered my feet and straightened my dress. He was dressed in a pair of sweat pants and a white t-shirt. Carter must have made use of the nice weather earlier in the week because his skin already looked sun-kissed.

"Made lemonade last night and had some left over. Is that okay?"

"It'll go well with the cupcakes." I smiled. "Thank you."

He pulled out another chair, set the tray with the lemonade aside, and wiped the glass table before taking a seat in the wicker chair across from me. Carter sipped on his drink while I did on mine. My gaze darted up every few seconds to see whether he was done, only to be caught in the act. He smiled politely, and I finally broke our awkward silence.

"I never realized this place was so big."

"I know. Me neither. Old man Grafton had all this land and didn't know what to do with it. I have my work cut out for me."

"What are your plans?" I opened the lid of the cupcake box and set one on a plate for each of us.

"I don't know. I have to get the garage organized first, clean this place up a bit, and then maybe once I get the business going, I'll install a pool. This backyard definitely needs a pool."

"You've got furniture in there?" I asked, looking back.

"I do, but it's old. Most of it is still Mr. Grafton's. It came with the place. I have no idea what to do with the old drapes, decorations, and girly things like that. I'll probably throw them out. The fabric and walls are stained with cigarette smoke. Daisy would have known what to do."

The mention of our best friend was heart-wrenching. I reached for his hand, squeezing it gently. "It's okay, Carter. It will get better. Maybe I can help out with the more girly things sometime."

"Really?"

"Sure, just tell me what you need. I can't promise when exactly I'll be able to do it, because with just the one bakery operating, it's been busy, but maybe I can just drop by whenever I have time?"

"Sure, that works. And if you ever have a car that needs fixing, you know where to find me."

"Thanks. I do."

There was that silence again. It was weird. I'd never been in a situation with Carter where I didn't know what to say or what to do, but maybe that was because I'd never technically been alone with him, or at least, not since we'd almost gotten lost in the woods on our high school camping trip and he'd kissed me. The memory sent some heat to my cheeks.

"What are you thinking?" he asked. "Your cheeks are bright red."

"I don't know why, but I'm remembering our camping trip."

"Yeah, that was a blast, wasn't it? Until we had to send out a search party for you and Nick."

"Actually, I was thinking about how I've never really gotten to spend time with just you. You know, as friends and all." Why was my voice shaking? If Carter heard it, he didn't say anything. "Not since we went to gather wood in the forest."

"Oh. Yeah, I'm sorry about the kiss. I shouldn't have done that without your permission."

"It's okay. We were kids. And I didn't make it easy on anyone, given how confused I was about my own friendship with Nick."

"So you were thinking about that kiss?"

"Sort of."

"You're a good kisser, Jo."

I laughed before taking a sip of my lemonade. Was there an appropriate response to such a compliment? "And you're a smooth talker, as always."

"Hey, it's a talent I'm not willing to part with."

"So, what happened to the firefighter dream?" I asked. "I really thought you'd be good at it."

"It's still a dream, but I need some time. I want my mind clear when I work. You're dealing with people's lives, and that's something I don't take lightly. So I want to wait until I know I'm ready. And I'm nowhere near ready yet. That's why the mechanic side business for now." He reached forward and wiped what I assumed was frosting from the corner of my mouth. I stilled and watched him suck it off his thumb.

What were we talking about? *Oh, firefighting!*

I licked my lips, staring abnormally at his, wondering whether he still kissed the same way he had that day. Guilt swept through my mind, and I shook the thought away.

"Well, when you're ready, I'm sure you'd be a great asset to the firehouse."

"That's what Captain Clark says. I just don't want to disappoint anyone."

"Carter, he's your father. There's no way you could ever disappoint him."

But my words of encouragement didn't seem to be getting through.

"You're strong and dependable. I know that once you commit, you won't back out, and you'll make everyone in that firehouse proud."

He finally grinned. "Thanks. Nick is one lucky man to have you. If I were him, I'd never let you out of my sight."

I bit my lip, unsure what to say, because secretly I'd always wished that Nick hadn't left.

"My life means nothing without him. I'm sorry. With Daisy gone, it must be difficult hearing things like that."

"I won't say it's not, because it is, but you're both my friends, and I'm very happy for you guys."

"Have you thought about finding someone else to share your life with? I mean, I don't know if it's too soon or if there's a standard time frame to move on, but you'll move on one day, won't you? You're a handsome man, and I'm sure there are girls in this town and a couple of towns over as well who'd be lucky to have you."

Was there a protocol one was expected to follow when they lost their loved one?

"Thanks. I'm happy on my own for now because I can't picture anyone else other than Daisy at my side. And I don't want to replace her. I want to hold on to her for as long as possible. I can't believe I'm even talking to you about her. I mean, I haven't talked to anyone about her since that day."

"It's helpful for me too, Carter. I loved her like a sister, and I know that she loved you like a soul mate. It may not get easier to live with her loss, but at least we're able to live, right?"

He took in a deep breath and then let all the air out of his lungs. "Yeah, she definitely was my... everything."

I finished my cupcake and lemonade. "A bunch of daisies would look really nice around the base of that tree." I pointed to the weeping willow in the back.

"I think Daisy would have liked that too."

"Can I plant them for you next time I'm here?"

"You'd do that?"

"Sure. Why not? I think I may plant some in front of Marge's house as well. It'll keep Daisy's memory alive."

"I was afraid after you saw this dump, you'd never want to come over again."

"That's nonsense. It'll give me something to do before summer and keep my mind occupied before Nick comes home."

A gust of wind brought the smell of manure, and Carter wrinkled his nose. "Sorry about the smell, but Betsy has bad gas."

The cow who'd been born on my and Nick's birthdays still roamed the fields by Mr. Grafton's – now Carter's – house. Mrs. Gladstone lived past the second row of trees.

"She comes over to the side yard sometimes. I think old man Grafton used to feed her."

We heard another moo.

"You think she'd like a cupcake?" he asked.

"I don't know. You can try."

Carter got up and went over by the fence. He reached his hand out to the cow's muzzle and she gently removed the cupcake from his palm.

"I think she likes your cupcakes, Jo. I may have found a new friend."

If Carter was thinking of becoming friends with cows, then the situation was worse than I thought. But I guess anything to keep his mind occupied was better than nothing at this point.

Carter came back and stretched his legs out. His shirt lifted a fraction, enough for me to get another glimpse of his toned abs. While it felt wrong to be drawn to his strong physique, like I was cheating on Nick, my curiosity won out.

"So, what's going on with the bakery? Must be hard on you with your house gone."

"We're staying with Marge. I think Dad wants to make it permanent but doesn't know how. If you ask me, they should just stay in the house, convert it to a normal home, and build a huge bakery beside it, instead of re-building our house."

"That's a great idea. You should tell your dad."

"You think?"

"Sure. And are you going to work at the new bakery?"

"I'd like to, but I have other plans. If my father can still manage it all for a while, I was thinking of starting up an online business where people could place their orders on the Internet, and we'd ship the cakes and cupcakes right to their front door."

He sat up straight, his eyes going wide. "Jo, you should do it."

"You think?"

"That's the best idea I've heard in years. Wait, this means I could order your cupcakes without coming over."

"Carter, if you ever do that, I will personally deliver them and smash them on your front step. You live ten minutes away, and I miss seeing you. I miss everybody. Promise me that you'll come over whenever you need cupcakes."

His gaze flew straight to my chest again, and I frowned at him. "Real cupcakes, Carter. Not my boobs."

"Sorry not sorry. I can't help myself. But seriously, you should look into the delivery idea."

I couldn't help but gloat on the inside. I didn't realize that it would feel this good to talk to Carter about my life – about Nick and Daisy and my plans as a baker.

"You know, people could get addicted to your cupcakes once they try them." He took another swipe of fresh frosting with his finger and stuck it in his mouth. I was beginning to learn that Carter favored the toppings over the cupcakes.

He then shot off his chair. "Oh, my God, Jo! You should send mini-samples to bigger businesses with your site information. DELIVERED FRESH." He made a gesture with his hand as if he were writing a sign. "People will go nuts for them."

I felt my eyes grow wide and stood up in my excitement, throwing my arms around his neck. "That's a great idea! Thank you."

When I realized that I was standing against him, chest to chest and heart to heart, and he was holding me by my hips, I slowly let go, slid down his hard body, and straightened my dress.

"I'm sorry. That was inappropriate."

"What are you talking about? We're friends, right? Besides, I've known you from way before you had boobs, Jo."

That wasn't helping, because now he was actually staring at them.

"Stop that." I pointed my finger at him. "I should get going anyways. I'm sure those buns aren't going to bake themselves."

I turned around and headed for the gate. Feeling his stare on my behind, I stopped and turned once more. "And stop staring at my butt."

"Hey, you said buns – and I'm a guy. It's impossible not to stare."

Carter walked me out the back yard, as any gentleman in Hope Bay would have. I waved before heading out.

"Jo?" he called behind me.

I swiveled on my heel, expecting another sleek comeback.

"Thank you for coming over. I mean that."

"You're welcome. And I'd like to see your face at the bakery a little more often as well."

"It's not because I don't want to. I gotta watch my carbs if I'm going to stay strong and lean for the firehouse." He lifted his white shirt, showing off his six-pack again. Wow, I definitely didn't remember Carter having perfect abs. Thank goodness he lowered it; otherwise, I would have stood there until someone smacked me over my head. "But I'll definitely drop in for some of your cupcakes." He winked, wiggling his brows, and I couldn't help but chuckle.

Today had been a good day, and when I saw a falling star on my rooftop that night, I secretly wished for more good days like this one.

Dear Nick,

We're slowly moving on from the horrific nightmare. I visit Daisy's grave every few days. Carter lingers around the cemetery most days. He's lost, and I don't blame him. He runs by the bakery sometimes, then stays at his new garage, fixing cars. I think he finally broke through, though, because now he'll wave to me when he sees me. I guess that's good. We had a nice chat at his house the other day and he even fed Betsy a cupcake. Oh, yeah, Carter bought Mr. Grafton's house. I can feel that he's slowly coming around. I hope I never lose somebody I love, but of course, that's just wishful thinking because no one lives forever, right?

Dad and Marge have agreed that it is best if we don't rebuild our house and instead focus on building a new bakery — one that's large enough for both of them, and me. Once it's done over the summer, I hope to get the business going online as well. I have so many ideas! Carter said I should send out samples when we're ready.

I'm holding onto our memories together like they're gold. I never thought that a year could go by so slowly, yet so fast. I dream about you every night and yes, more often than I feel appropriate to admit, I do touch myself thinking about you. When I pretend that it's your hands on me, it's much quicker and fiercer. I bite my covers in fear that I'll scream. Should I even be writing this? I can't wait to touch you and to kiss you and I can't wait for you to touch me again as well. I feel like my cheeks are being set on fire just thinking about our reunion.

Last night I saw a falling star on the rooftop and made a wish. I know it will come true, because I know that soon I'll be in your arms. Counting down the days.
Yours always,
Joelle

CHAPTER 16

My Dearest Joelle,

One more month and you'll be in my arms. Thirty more days and I'll kiss you until my mouth is sore and touch you until I have all the curves of your beautiful body memorized.

The training is routine now. I have another physical screening test next week for a special project. If I pass, I'll have more time with you this summer. If I fail, I'm coming home permanently. It shouldn't be an issue, since I passed the first one nine months ago. Sometimes, when I lie here at night, I wonder whether it's worth it. Then the alarm sounds, the boys jump out of their beds, and we all do what must be done to protect our freedom. The adrenaline keeps me awake most nights. I fall in and out of sleep and can't wait for a full night when I have you in my arms. Maybe I'll finally sleep in peace. I can't wait to tell you all about the new friends I've made here. They're awesome guys.

*I'm glad to hear that Carter's doing better. You're an
amazing friend and he's one lucky guy to have you in his
corner. It sounds like a lot has changed at home. Have I
really only been gone a year?*
Love you with all my heart,
Nick

The bell on the front door dinged just as I reached to
stack the boxes on the top shelf. This had to be one of the
worst chores ever, and given that the shelf was so high, it
was usually Dad's job. But this morning he was busy
outside, preparing to begin the construction on the new
bakery next door. And since Marge was in the back mixing
fresh batter, that left me to tend to the customers and stock
the shelves. Once the new building was complete, we could
renovate Marge's house to be a normal home we all lived
in, with a family and a dining room. The store next door
would be kept separate.

"I'll be right with you," I called, concentrating on lining
the square shapes evenly so that the stack would not tip
over, as all the while my knees wobbled on the small ladder.

Whoa!

I felt myself sway from one side to the other as I tried
to push the last box on the very top. The ladder flew from
underneath me and I tensed my body, ready to hit the floor,
but a set of strong arms caught me. I looked up and met
Carter's brown eyes as he held me close to his body.

"What are you doing here?" I breathed heavily, a little
shocked and relieved that I wasn't on the floor.

"Apparently catching you."

"No, I mean here. At the bakery."

"You invited me to come over more often, didn't you?"

"Yes, but—"

"And your father offered me a job with the construction." He slowly set me down on the floor and I straightened my shirt.

"Thanks for catching me. I might have broken an arm or a leg." I wiped the drop of sweat off my forehead. The rush of almost crashing to the floor had turned on my perspiration as if I had a sprinkler under my armpits and on my head.

"Anytime. I promise there won't be any broken bones while on my watch."

"So, you'll be here..."

"Every day until it's done."

"That's awesome! It means you'll be a fresh mouth to taste my new cupcakes."

Carter looked like he was holding in a laugh, his lips straining at the corners.

"What did I say?"

He shook his head, mumbling underneath his breath, "I have a feeling that you and your beautiful cupcakes are going to drive me nuts."

"Hey." I punched him in his arm. "Are we still talking about my cupcakes, or something else you shouldn't be thinking about?"

"I wouldn't dare talk about something else." He winked. "But I can't promise that my mind isn't elsewhere."

"Here." I passed him another stack of boxes and pointed. "You're taller. They go there."

"Yes, ma'am." He climbed up the ladder and easily shelved the remaining boxes. "Hey, listen. So last week I saw that the soil around the weeping willow was moved around."

"Yeah, I planted the daisies. You weren't home, so I just went to the back."

"What about the shrubs?"

"I might have cleaned up a bit too."

His brows rose.

"And added two rose brushes, peonies, a few gerberas, and some lilies."

Carter opened his eyes wider each time a flower name escaped my mouth.

"Okay, I don't know what half of those are, but thank you. I now officially owe you."

"It was my pleasure. If you like, I can add some to the front of the house as well."

"Only if it's not too much to ask, and if you'll let me pay you."

"Nope."

"Come on. At least for the bulbs and whatever else you used to plant them. You're trying to get a business going as well, so I'm sure you'll need all the funds you can get."

"Okay, how about... we'll see."

"So long as *we'll see* means I can pay you back." He winked. "Anything special on the menu today?"

"Morning glory muffins."

"Never heard of those."

"They're like carrot muffins but with pineapples and nuts."

"Okay, I'll have one of those and a coffee, then. And if you could keep track of which ones I'm trying, that'd be great. I want to be surprised every morning I come here?"

"Every morning?"

"Yes, until the job is done, at least."

Right.

"Cool. I'll make sure you get the fresh ones. Wait, what am I talking about? They're always fresh."

Was I feeling nervous again? This was just Carter, my friend who wanted to try my muffins... our muffins.

Geez, Jo. Get a grip on yourself.

"See you around." He waved.

"Yeah, see you around."

Over the next month, Carter came in each morning, ordered his coffee, and grabbed a new muffin I'd prepared. After we'd gone through them all twice, he switched to tasting cupcakes. I'd never seen anyone devour our baked goods the way Carter did, but he'd done that ever since he first stepped into Marge's bakery. These days he still moaned the same way he had as a kid, and his eyes rolled back in their sockets. Except now I enjoyed watching him do it more than I remembered doing when he was younger.

After the construction day was over, we'd drive his father's old car that he'd finally fixed back to his house in the late afternoon, where he'd work in the garage while I spent an hour getting dirty in the front garden.

It looked almost perfect now, and when I took a few steps back, I couldn't believe how much it had changed on the outside. The next step would be to take care of the old furniture inside. Half of it was good enough to keep, and the other half needed either a major revamp or to be trashed and burned so that no one's eyes would ever hurt looking at it, the way mine did. I had yet to find a way to break that news to Carter.

When I took another step back, I tripped over the curb and fell butt first into a bucket full of water.

"Ahh!" I screamed, but it was already too late. I was sitting in the bucket, half-submerged, laughing, when Carter ran from the garage around the corner.

"What happened?" he asked.

"I... I fell." It was difficult to get the words out between my bursts of laughter. "And I can't get up."

That's when Carter lost it as well. He fell to his knees, hands on the grass, laughing with me, physically rolling over. Actually, he was laughing at me.

"Some help would be nice," I managed, but still kept laughing. He finally reached for my hand and pulled me out of the container, bringing me close to his body and not letting go.

"You okay there, Betty Crocker?"

His hands were on my hips, holding onto the wet fabric. I in turn held onto his arms because I didn't want to go back down into that bucket, and the way my legs were shaking underneath me, there was a good possibility of that happening.

"Yeah, I think so. I'm all wet now."

Carter held me so close, that the moisture from my jeans transferred to his. "Come on, I have a pair of old sweat pants you should fit into."

"Thanks. I got you all wet as well." Especially the front of his garage jeans, which now appeared more fitted than before. I followed him inside. The place was looking much better each time I came here. New drapes hung in the windows, and Carter had bought a throw for the scruffy couch. The bright light coming from the back patio door made the home appear larger than it was. I followed him to his bedroom, and then waited at the threshold as he fumbled through the clothes in his chest of drawers.

"This is the smallest pair I have." He handed me the sweats and a t-shirt as well.

"Thanks."

"I'll go to the bathroom. You can change here."

"Okay."

As soon as he left, I pulled down my pants and panties, and then removed my shirt and quickly jumped into his clothes, which were quite loose. I rolled up the bottoms of the sweat pants as well as the band around my waist, folding it outward. When I was done, I went back out to the hallway. The bathroom door was open, and in the reflection I saw Carter in his boxer briefs. He flexed his arms in the mirror, then stood sideways and examined his toned abs, like most guys probably did every morning. Yup, they were definitely tight. But so were his ass, his legs, and the rest of him. There was not even an ounce of fat on this guy, despite all the muffins and cupcakes I fed him each day.

"Don't worry, Carter. You look good."

He turned toward me, showing off his physique, flexing like a professional body builder.

"You think?"

My gaze inadvertently traveled lower to his crotch. Yeah, he definitely looked good.

"Trust me, when you're ready, the girls will be clawing at one another just to get close to you."

"What about you?"

"What about me?"

"Would you want me?"

Well, that was a loaded question. Carter had a knack for surprising me with questions I didn't know how to answer. I had a boyfriend. But if I said no, I'd offend him.

"Ahm, yeah. I would."

His mouth curved in satisfaction.

"Nick will hardly recognize you," I said.

"I don't think I'll recognize him either. I bet he's all buffed up for you. How long do you have left now?"

"Two more weeks. I think he's busy with his final tests."

"Probably. Hey, we should throw him a welcome back party. Isn't Molly coming home from school as well?"

"I think so. Doesn't it feel like we're the only two left from our class in town?"

"I think we are. Okay, so I'll get the word out for a little gathering. Will you do the same? My house?"

"I'll bring cupcakes." I perked up.

"You better."

His brows wiggled again. Whenever he did that, I wondered whether he was truly thinking about my cupcakes... or my boobs.

* * *

"Carter, you gotta try this, " I said, carrying the tray full of fresh cupcakes toward him. The construction crew was putting up the framing today. The sun was wringing the last beads of sweat from the men. I'd finally got a tan on my legs as well; working in Carter's garden had definitely helped.

"New recipe?"

"Sort of. Marge loves black forest cake, but there isn't a black forest cupcake at the bakery, so I just made one up."

He took a bite, cutting halfway through the cupcake, moaning as if he'd just eaten the most delicious food ever.

"Jo, you know how much I love your cupcakes." He winked. "But this one's the best one yet."

I'd also been using Carter as my test dummy, making him eat anything new that I baked. "Oh, my God, the cherries inside are perfect. How did you make this frosting?"

I saw my father watching us out of the corner of his eye and shaking his head.

"Wait, are you playing with me again?"

He'd done it before when I misjudged the amount of nutmeg for my pumpkin spice recipe. Carter hadn't wanted to be rude and had gulped down the most disgusting muffins I ever made.

"No, I'm serious. I wouldn't dare play with your cupcakes."

I smacked him in his arm. "Carter! You're so annoying sometimes."

"Just sometimes? Man, I must be slipping."

"You have some…" I pointed to the corner of my mouth to indicate the cream he had left on his, but that only confused him. I reached toward him and wiped it off with my thumb, and then licked it off. I mean, it'd be a waste of cream if I didn't. And it wasn't like he hadn't done that to me before. Carter froze, and I wondered why. His mouth opened slowly as he pointed to something behind me.

When I turned, it felt like everything went into slow motion, and at first I thought I was dreaming. In fact, when I laid my eyes on Nick, I barely recognized him. A black duffle bag was draped over his wide shoulders. His crew cut had grown out to a more pleasant length. I scanned the rest of his rough yet lean body in awe. Even his face was chiseled. Everywhere I looked, Nick was full of pure muscle. There were muscles upon muscles, layers of lean tissue in places I didn't know could have been beefed up — ever. The gray t-shirt he wore barely fit him, the limits of its seams tested around every curve.

Holy shit!

"Surprise!"

I dropped the remaining cupcakes I was holding into Carter's hands, which were thankfully ready to catch anything I threw at him, and jumped into Nick's arms. He spun me around in a circle, pressing his hot lips to mine, holding me as easily as a feather. The pure strength emanating from him was so intense that I had to pull away, let him set me down, and look him over again, because I still couldn't believe that this was my Nick. My soul felt like it had just been given a new life.

"You're home, you're really home. Dad, Marge, Nick is back!" I just couldn't stop screaming and crying and laughing all at the same time. "What are you doing here?

You're not supposed to be back until next week. We had a party planned out and everything."

"We'll talk about that later. I got a chance to leave early and thought I'd surprise you."

"You did!"

Oh, my God, did he ever!

"Welcome back, Nick." My father broke away from the construction work, shook Nick's hand, and then hugged him, patting him on the back in that feral way only men knew. Carter was next, greeting his best friend. They exchanged a few quiet words I couldn't hear, and I wondered what it was about. Marge wiped her hands on her apron and ran out to embrace her son. All the while, I couldn't stop staring at this new man who'd come back into my life. There was so much commotion around Nick's surprising arrival that I felt a little dizzy. As if sensing it, Nick was at my side in a second.

"Are you okay?"

"Yeah, just a little overwhelmed. We weren't expecting you until next week, and now here you are. There's so much I want to tell you." My heart was misbehaving in my chest and my mind was still spinning.

"And there's so much that I want to tell you as well. Looks like we'll have to get through a family reunion first before I can have you alone."

Alone. I couldn't wait to be alone with him. Part of me felt like I'd have to get to know this new man all over again, and I was excited to do so, but when I watched him talk to his mom, Carter, and my dad, I knew that my Nick was back. In a different body perhaps, but back.

"I'll see you tomorrow, Jo." Carter waved at me and I waved back. "Don't worry about a new cupcake in the morning. I'm pretty sure you'll have a busy night." He winked, and my cheeks heated. I wished he wouldn't say things like that in front of my father and Marge.

I prayed that Nick and I would have a busy night, but given that we were about to spend our first night in the same house as our parents, I wasn't sure how we'd make it work.

Since the construction stopped for the day, we went inside and I helped Marge set the table for dinner. We had spaghetti. I watched Nick eat one plate, and then get seconds and thirds. I wasn't sure where he was fitting all the food, but apparently the new body needed more fuel than the old one.

When evening came, I realized that I'd been using Nick's room. When I got up from the table and went upstairs to move my things to the guest room, I startled when Nick walked in.

"What are you doing?"

"Giving you your room back."

"No, that's okay. You stay here, and I'll take the guest bedroom." He then lowered his voice. "Although ideally I'd stay here with you."

"Nick—"

"I know. I know. I won't be disrespectful to your father or my mother. But I do insist on you keeping this room. I'll take the guest bedroom."

"Okay."

"Wanna head up to the rooftop?"

"Yours or mine?" I joked, knowing full well that my house and rooftop were long gone.

"How about ours?" he asked.

I smiled, biting my lip. He always knew the perfect thing to say.

We climbed up the ladder from his balcony. It felt like years since we'd been there together, but as soon as I lay back, with Nick's arm underneath my head, everything came back to me. Everything was normal again.

CHAPTER 17

"It's hard to believe we've been looking at the same sky at night but were so far away," he said, sighing. "It feels so good to be home, to have you in my arms."

"Aren't you tired? Do you want to rest?" I asked.

"No, baby. I have so much adrenaline pumping, I won't be able to fall asleep for a while."

"How are you feeling, emotionally? I mean, you've been gone and secluded, and now you're back."

"I couldn't be happier to be back, but I'm also proud of what I accomplished."

"I'm proud of you too, Nick. You set out a goal and never gave up."

"And you – I mean, from the looks of the new cakes, cupcakes, and pastries, it looks like you've had your hands full."

"As soon as the new bakery's running, I'm going to open the online store. We'll start shipping to nearby cities. I've planned a marketing campaign. I'll be able to have a delivery system with a larger radius than I originally thought, which will also reduce our shipping costs. And I followed through and sent samples the way Carter suggested. I already have two large orders for cupcake wedding cakes this fall, and the website design is almost complete."

"Look at you, my businesswoman. You have no idea how smart and sexy you sound."

I chuckled, "You're just saying that because you love me."

"I do love you. And I missed you."

He curled his arm underneath my head, lifting me higher and bringing my lips to his. The strength of him, holding me, still surprised me. It was all new and exciting. I opened my mouth wider, welcoming the swift strokes of his tongue, feeling my breasts swell at the intensity of our kiss. It felt like I was getting to know him all over again, kissing and touching him for the very first time. The outline of his leg muscles was pressing against my softer thighs. I was getting lost in his body, my hands exploring all the new contours of a fit man, and liking it. Soon enough, I was on top of him, pulling my fingers through his shorter hair, circling my hips over his erection, feeling the heat between us ready to burst.

When Nick pulled away, we were both heaving. "You take my breath away," he whispered. "I've been thinking about this day every minute while away. You kept me sane.

You're the one who helped me push through the physical and mental pain. I couldn't have done it without knowing that you were waiting here for me."

I looked up, exposing my neck as he sent simmering hot kisses along my skin. "I've been waiting for you too, Nick. It's been so long."

His hand swept over my curves, down to my hips, then lower to my dress, which he slowly scrunched up until my behind was exposed. I pressed my pelvis harder against him, wanting to feel all of him on me. He kept kissing me, his lips making a journey all over: my cheeks, neck, and back up to my ear, while grasping my ass with his full palms, squeezing it gently.

"Best buns I've held in my entire life."

I laughed, my ass tightening in his grip. Counting the number of buns that he'd held at the bakery, that was definitely a compliment.

"The only human buns you've held?" I asked.

"The only human ones I've ever held and ever want to hold. I want to make love to you, Jo, but I'm not sure this rooftop is strong enough to hold the force I want to take you with."

"I want you too, Nick."

A growl rumbled from his chest as he whispered against my cheek, "We'll have to settle for something easier for now."

He slowly rolled me off him so that we were both on our sides, facing each other. His hand slid underneath the elastic of my panties, fully palming my ass, and then his fingers drew lower and to the back. I arched my back and tilted my ass higher, panting at every touch and stroke of his scorching fingers, wanting him to reach further. He fondled me from behind before switching to the front, cupping my sex through my panties. His fingers swiftly moved the lace aside and weaved between my folds, sliding through the moisture, dragging it back up to my clit, then rubbing, stimulating me. I wanted to moan louder, yet knew that I couldn't because our parents would hear us, so I bit my lip, holding onto the sound for now while letting out only a soft whimper.

Nothing else mattered, only the feeling that Nick was drawing out from within me. The touch was igniting my body, and I felt beads of sweat form on my forehead as the inferno of emotions roared with each breath I exhaled.

All I wanted to do was feel. I wanted to feel him on me, under me, and inside me — everywhere. The most incredible rush was consuming me from the inside out and outside in. How had I lived so long without this, without him?

The orgasm came shockingly fast. I grasped Nick's arms, holding on and biting into his shirt as he swirled his fingers a few more times, drawing the remainder of my euphoria out.

"Jo? Nick? Are you guys up there?" his mom called out. "We're locking up for the night."

I quickly came back to earth, realizing what had just happened and that Marge was only a few feet away. She only had to take one step up on the ladder to have us in view.

"Yes, we are. We'll be down in a sec," Nick answered.

"Oh, my God, what if she saw us?" My whisper was only loud enough for Nick to hear.

"Don't worry. She didn't."

"What if she did? You think they're checking up on us?"

"Probably."

"Argh! I wish we could go away somewhere."

"And if we did, what would we do?" he teased.

"We'd make love until the sun came up." I kissed him.

"Then I'll make sure that happens sooner than later."

"How?"

"Let's go down for now. We'll figure out the rest later."

I adjusted my dress and made my way down to the balcony and then to the bathroom, where I changed into my pajamas. I said goodnight to Dad and Marge, then Nick, before retreating to my room. The ceiling seemed infinite, and my eyes wouldn't close. I could still feel the rush of the orgasm Nick had blessed me with in my veins. He touched me with so much need and determination. And I liked it; in fact, I wanted more. My gaze flew to the closed door, then back to the ceiling. I wasn't sure how long I stared, but one thing was certain: falling asleep would be impossible.

I turned and twisted. The sheets wrapped uncomfortably around my body, and I yanked them away. Despite the light breeze I could feel through the open window, the room felt hot and stuffy. Maybe the full moon was the source of my madness – you know, like the way it acted as a beacon for werewolves, and it was messing up my hormones. I removed my sleeping shorts and my top, relief washing over me as I splayed my naked body on top of the cooler covers. Still it wasn't enough. The wall separating me from Nick felt thousands of miles thick. He was so close, yet so far away.

I must have suffered through at least two hours of this torture when I heard the handle on my door twist. I tugged the covers over my body, holding my breath.

Please let it be him!

"Jo? Are you asleep?" I heard Nick's voice and exhaled in relief.

"No."

He quietly tiptoed toward my bed. As he sat down, my body was lifted upward, allowing me to see him in the faint moonlight. He looked like he'd just come out of my dream.

"Why are you pulling the covers so high up?" He tapped my nose.

"Because I'm naked underneath."

"What?"

"I was hot, okay? And I couldn't fall asleep."

"I couldn't fall asleep either. I want to see you."

What did he mean by that? I was there, right in front of him.

"Naked, Joelle. I want to see you naked again."

"Oh."

I'd only seen him naked once, and with all the changes his body had gone through, I wondered whether *everything* had changed. I slowly loosened my grip on the sheets. There was no way I'd be brave enough to pull the covers off myself, and I knew that Nick knew that, because no sooner had I let my arms fall to my sides than he slowly lowered the covers off my body, his gaze following the trail of heat the pads of his fingers left behind as he traced them over my skin in a downward path.

Once the covers were down, Nick sucked in a quick breath and adjusted his crotch. I was glad it was dark and he couldn't see the new shade of red on my cheeks. His face was glowing in the moonlight filtering through the window.

"You're so beautiful."

His hand slid over my stomach and then higher to my breast. He gently pinched my pebbled nipple between his fingers, and I felt my mouth open and eyes close. It felt so good. Too good. He rolled it, tightening the pressure, and I felt a trickle of moisture between my legs. If I thought that I'd been tortured when he wasn't here, then I was wrong. What he was doing to my body now was the sweetest and most delicious torment. I heard him shift on the bed and opened my eyes just as he surprised me with a soft kiss.

"Don't move," he whispered.

"What if someone comes in?" I asked.

"I checked before coming here. They're both sleeping. Don't move, Jo, and don't make any noise."

Nick removed his t-shirt and shorts. I wished I could see all of him, but the lamp on the nightstand was shading his crotch.

"Touch me, Nick."

"I'm going to do way more than touch you, baby." He was above me in seconds, kissing his way down my body, starting with a tender stroke of his tongue around the rim of my nipples, gently pulling them out, and then dragging his lips between my breasts down to my navel.

YOURS AND MINE

I was panting, completely turned on by his touch and agonizing kisses that were taking their sweet time adoring my body. My hips bucked higher and higher with anticipation of his lips reaching their destination. All the while Nick had both his hands filled with my breasts, squeezing and manipulating them.

As he touched the upper part of my pubic area, I stiffened. His hands finally let go of my engorged breasts and lowered to my hips. He inhaled deeply, and I squirmed. It took all the patience I had not to reach down and touch his hard cock I was feeling against my legs.

And then it happened. His lips took a hold of my clit and I lost it at the first lick, shaking underneath him, tensing my ass. Yet I wanted more, and couldn't stop shaking. As soon as the first orgasm left my body, obliterating me, Nick slid a finger inside me. It felt thick and welcome inside my body. I gripped my muscles around him, thrusting my hips forward, wanting to feel more of this delicious stretch.

"Do you like that, Jo?"

"Yes," I panted.

"I'm going to add another finger."

I wasn't sure why he was telling me this, but it only turned me on that much more. I waited for the perfect strain on the inside as he filled me.

"It's been a year since we made love. I need to get you ready, so it doesn't hurt."

He pulled his tongue between my folds while pumping his fingers in and out. It felt so good. Too good. I didn't want him to stop. With the way he sucked on my clit, massaging my inner walls, pressing into that perfect spot I didn't know existed until now, I was certain that whatever seductive university he'd attended, he'd graduated from with a major in orgasms. It only took seconds to feel another swell building in my body.

"Nick—"

"Shh." He pulled away from my flesh, and passed me a pillow. "Bite this. Don't scream."

I nodded and he resumed his tantalizing foreplay. Was that even foreplay? I wasn't sure because it was happening so quickly, but whatever it was, I wanted more of it. The sound of his slurps and my deep breathing intensified. As soon as he closed the suction around me and flicked the tip of his hard tongue once, I lost it. Tears of joy rolled down my cheeks, the pillow muffling my scream, and my body trembled underneath him, completely taken by this new blissful release.

He kept licking and I kept throwing my hips higher to push myself deeper into his mouth. When he finally stopped, it took a moment for me to figure out where I was. Everything in my head was spinning. I was afraid that I'd wake up and this would be one heck of a wet dream. But it wasn't, because Nick was already sliding up my heated body, lining himself up at my entrance.

Oh, my God! This is actually going to happen!

"Jo, I don't have a condom. I came straight here from the bus, and—"

"I'm supposed to get my period in two days, so we won't get pregnant and you're the only one I've ever been with and my gynecologist gave me a clear pass two months—"

"Me too. You're my only one. So, are you okay with this?"

"I've been waiting for this for almost a year. Please, Nick. I need you."

He lowered his mouth to mine, sealing my plea inside me, while slowly sliding in, pushing his cock forward inch my inch until we were connected.

My knees fell apart and I stilled. Nick pulled away, watching what I assumed was my perplexed face from above.

"You okay?"

I nodded. "It feels so good, Nick."

My lids felt heavy and my head lolled to the side as he thrust inside me in a rhythmic motion. I loved the way my body responded to his, the way he rocked me, controlled me, filled me, and tantalized me. I lifted my legs at one point and wrapped them around his waist, pulling him deeper inside me, and that's when he stilled with a groan, biting his lip and fisting the bed sheets.

"Those legs of yours were always trouble." He lowered his body onto the bed. I scooted closer to the wall and he wrapped me into him. He felt hot and sweaty and so right I didn't want to peel away. He leaned into my ear, whispering, "I'm spending the night here."

"What if someone comes in?" I asked.

"No one will. I'll sneak out before dawn. Besides, we're adults." He kissed my forehead and then turned me on my side, spooning me from behind. My ass wiggled on its own, and I felt him grow hard again.

"And the likelihood of me being inside you before the sun comes up, is... it's a guarantee."

I pushed my ass against him and felt him slide inside me. His hands wrapped around my body from behind, one cupping a breast and the other reaching to my sex, jolting me awake. If he wasn't inside me, then he was spilling down my inner thigh from within me. I didn't count how many times we made love that night, but I did remember that I barely slept and that he snuck out before the first glimmer of light.

CHAPTER 18

I stood by the counter, kneading the dough for the few sweet breads that had been ordered for the weekend. Nick had been home for five days now. Each morning, he went out for a run, and then showered, had breakfast, and went out to help my father with the construction. That of course was right after he snuck out of my room before dawn. I'd been with him every night since his return. For the past three nights, we hadn't made love because I got my period and I wasn't that comfortable with the thought of having him inside me when I bled. Not yet, at least, because knowing that I couldn't get enough of him would finally push me through my inhibitions.

We spent the evenings by the lake, skipping stones. Most of our time alone was taken up by kissing, touching, fingering, stroking, and fondling. I didn't want to pull apart. Life seemed perfect for now. He was back home, in my life like a normal boyfriend. But the nagging question in the back of my mind that I yet had to ask him wouldn't leave me alone. I was afraid to ask because I was afraid of the answer I'd get. Call it an instinct or a gut feeling, but I was sure that Nick wanted to tell me something now that he'd returned, and I knew I wouldn't like it. But I didn't want to waste the little time we had together worrying. Two months was barely enough to make up for the past year.

Tips of warm fingertips snuck underneath my apron and drew along the exposed skin over my stomach, right underneath my navel before they reached into the band of my sweats. I could still barely believe that when he touched me, he was actually here.

"Nick, someone's going to come in."

"I don't care. I want to touch you."

"What if it's your mom?"

"Then she'll see what we're up to, and she'll leave."

"Nick!" I finally managed to push him away with my behind and turned around. The moment I did that I was captured between him and the counter, my ass cutting into the marble behind me.

"Tell me you don't want me."

"I... I want you."

He lowered his lips closer to my ear, trailing them along the cartilage, making the hairs stand on my neck, arms and... well, all over my body.

"Then let me fuck you, Joelle."

I sucked in a quick breath. His eyes were on fire, setting me ablaze all over again. Nick had never spoken this way to me. And it was hot. Actually, I was beginning to sweat from just thinking about the way he could do... *that*.

"Not here," I whispered. The shadow of defeat covering his face broke my heart as he slowly backed away. "But..."

Lust filled his eyes again in one blink.

"Maybe this evening," I whispered. "My period's over."

He was at my ear again. "There's no pillow in the world you can bite hard enough to stop the scream that will come out of your mouth when I fuck you."

Oh, my!

Someone cleared his throat at the threshold and my body fell cold.

"Nick, you have some flour, here" – my father pointed to Nick's ears – "and here," he said, indicating Nick's shoulders. His finger kept on waiving over the different parts of Nick's body as he kept repeating the two words.

"Actually, it's everywhere." Then he looked at me, the culprit with flour-covered hands. I felt like a kid who'd stolen candy from the corner store.

And if things couldn't get any worse, Marge walked through the swinging kitchen door. She assessed the situation with her keen eyes and sighed.

"I think we should talk." She pointed to the chairs.

"Mom, I'm a man," Nick defended.

"Then listen to me like a man would."

I took the stool to my left and passed it to Nick. I reached for the other one and sat beside him.

"We know you're in love. I mean, we've been in love too when we were your age, but we're worried."

"What about?" I asked. When I looked to the side, Nick was as confused as I was.

"You've been locked up in the house. It's just work and sleep for the both of you. I mean, you guys look tired as hell, and I don't think that spending minutes together through the day when Nick isn't helping with the construction is doing you guys any good. When are you going out? When are you going to have any fun? You're missing out on so much. Skipping stones by the lake isn't exactly socializing."

Oh! I guessed they didn't know about all the fun we were having at night when they were asleep in their own bed.

"We want you to spend time with other people too. You're still so young," Marge added.

"You were both young when you fell in love. And if I recall, Dad, Mom was right about my age when she had me."

"So were you, Mom," Nick said to his mother.

"Are you guys planning a family?" my father jumped in.

"No, we're not. We're just trying to make a point. We like spending time together. Love it, in fact." Nick was trying to do his famous sweet-talk and was looking for an angle. I was afraid that if he didn't come up with something good soon, I'd blabber that we were spending some good quality time together at night. We were doing what all other couples were doing. Having amazing sex! Okay, so maybe I'd skip the amazing part.

Our parent's faces remained stone-cold. Geez, it was like they were insisting on us being reckless outside the house.

And then Nick opened his mouth again. "However I think you're right in this case. We should go out and catch up with everyone else. For reals this time."

For reals? Was he for reals? Who was he?

"I haven't seen Carter's house yet. Let's visit him. And maybe we can stop by Molly's to say hello, and check up on Mr. Andrew the firefighter."

Our parents' eyes lit up.

"Okay, sounds good. This is the last batch I have," I said, playing along, and that's when I saw that secretive spark in the corner of Nick's eye. Carter had left earlier in the day, so I knew we wouldn't walk home with him. We'd be alone. That was it! Nick wanted alone time for the two of us, so that I could scream when he...

I felt my cheeks heat from the thought and turned around to finish kneading the dough and twisting it into a braid.

"Good. Also, if you make me a grandmother too soon, I will kill you."

I whipped my body around. *What?*

Marge wiggled her stern finger at Nick, turned around, and walked to the front of the store. My father pointed two of his fingers toward his eyes, then back at us in the infamous *I'm watching you* gesture.

Marge knew? Or maybe she didn't. What did she mean by that? How much did my father know?

"Relax, Jo." Nick's eyes sparkled with devilish lust. "No one knows about me eating you out at night."

Jesus, that alone made me want to drop my panties and lift my skirt. Could I? I waved a bit of air over my face, trying to cool off.

I swiveled on my foot to face him. "'For reals'? Who says 'for reals'?"

"I'll explain later."

What was there to explain?

"You better hurry with that dough if you want me to fuck you from behind," he whispered in my ear, winked, and left. I stood speechless for a moment, still shocked by what had happened in the last five minutes, wondering where Nick got that dirty mouth from. He had come back a new man, and I liked it. In the span of five days, my boring life had turned from ordinary and predictable to rousingly exciting – thrilling, in fact – and hot. Definitely hot.

Nick resumed his work with my father outside. At the pace they were putting up that drywall, the new bakery would be standing tall in a week. The new counters, mixers, freezers, and shelves my father had bought with the insurance money we received from the tornado were arriving in four days. Then the construction on this house would start and we'd finally have an official dining room and a family room with a fireplace.

I kneaded until my fingers hurt. Once done, I ran upstairs, showered, changed, stocked up the front, checked my emails to see if I'd heard from the web developer, and then waited for Nick outside on the porch. I didn't think he'd get ready that quick, but as soon as he did, he took my hand, we waved to our parents, and left. My father let us take the truck.

The day was hot, and sweat began sticking the shirt to my back and the seat to my shirt. While Carter's house was only ten minutes' walking distance, we didn't want to waste precious time on our feet. Preferably, I'd be on my back, or maybe my hands and knees?

"Okay, where are we going?"

"To Carter's," he teased.

"Come on. You forget that I know you better than anyone."

"You do, don't you?"

"And, you just passed the street that goes to Carter's house."

"Hmm, right. I did, didn't I?"

"Nick!"

"There's a clearing in the forest on the other side of the lake; I remember my father taking me fishing there when I was young. He said it's a special place because no one knows about it, and it's where all the fish hang out."

"I thought you didn't know how to fish."

"I don't. It was the only time my father tried to teach me, but each slippery sucker got away."

"Then why would we be going fishing?" I asked, somewhat confused.

"We're not, babe. We're going to a spot no one knows about. A spot where you can scream all you want." My thighs tightened. The expectation began to build inside of me as soon as he said the word 'scream.' I still had a difficult time believing that this handsome man was mine.

Nick pulled into the clearing. For a moment, as he was driving along an unpaved road in the woods, I'd been afraid that we'd get lost. I stepped out on the grass and walked toward the shore. Behind us, the forest sealed off the entrance. He was right: unless someone knew about this spot, no one would ever find it.

The breeze was calm, creating a few ripples on the otherwise glass-like lake. I felt his arms snake around from behind me, skim over my hips, and splay flat out over my stomach before reaching for my breasts. Nick wasn't wasting any time.

"Lift your dress, baby."

I did as he asked, sticking my ass outward and bending over. I braced my arms on the boulder formation in front of me, wondering what he'd do next. Nick unbuckled his jeans and reached inside to free himself. The motion was so hot that I felt a drip inside my panties. I watched him take himself into his hand and stroke his already-hard dick. My hands itched to touch him, yet watching him like this was so much better. I licked my lips, flipped over on the rock so that my back rested against it, lifted my skirt up, spread my legs wide for him to see, and reached into my panties. He stilled for a moment, as if unsure of my intent. I just wanted to touch myself. I wanted him to see what he was doing to me. The corner of his mouth lifted, and Nick continued the strokes over his length. My pussy was throbbing, wanting to feel him inside me, but this... us exposing ourselves to each other, was beyond erotic. Up until now, I'd only seen him at night. He took a step closer. I concentrated on the pulsing vein that ran along his length. Nick could barely wrap his hand around himself; I knew that I couldn't. My thumb never managed to touch the tips of my fingers when I pumped him.

I shimmied out of my panties, turned back around, and lifted my ass on full display for him, my hand now between my pussy and the rock, rubbing quicker.

"You're driving me crazy, Jo."

"I'm expecting a good fuck, Nicholas."

"Nicholas? Well, then how can I say no to that? But first..."

Without a warning he was down on his knees, licking my wet slit from behind, pulling his tongue all the way from my opening up to my ass.

Holy shit!

I felt my ass cheeks tighten as his tongue thrust inside me. I removed my hand from myself because my knees felt soft and I had to hold onto the rock. He slid in two fingers, his thumb circling just over my clit as he kissed me and licked me from behind, and I lost it.

"Ah! Holy lord of... Nicholas!" I screamed, but he wouldn't stop. He wouldn't pull away until the last drop of my orgasm was in his mouth. Spent, I lay flat on the rock and finally felt fresh air sweep over my swollen folds when Nick stood up. As I looked back, he reached into the pocket of his jeans and pulled out a foil packet. Nick rolled down the condom and part of me wished we could still do without it, but I wasn't ready for cute little babies any time soon.

"It'll be rough, Joelle. But let me know if I'm hurting you."

I was so turned on by this point that nothing Nick could do would ever hurt me. I wanted it all. I wanted to feel him as hard as possible. No sooner had the thought entered my mind than he slammed into me, his pelvis slapping against my ass and his balls onto my sensitive pussy. I could have come right then again, but I wanted this to last as long as possible.

"You okay?" he asked.

"Perfect. I want... more of that."

He grinned behind me, without moving again. His hand eased up the middle of my back, higher, to between my shoulder blades until he reached my hair. His fingers weaved along my scalp. Nick collected my hair into one bunch, as if he were making a ponytail, twisted it, and pulled my head back.

"You better hold onto that rock, Jo."

I squeezed my fingers around the stone, ready for the onslaught I was about to receive. The raw nature of this moment was making me squirm. Nick pulled out and thrusted forward again, this time not pausing before his next drive forward. My whole body flew up from his forceful onslaught. Each time he came close and his balls slapped against my pussy, a jolt of electricity buzzed through me, sending a spark of blissful current through my body. The remaining energy kept collecting between my legs, and I slowly lowered my hand till it lay between the rock and me. Nick pulled a little on my hair, bringing my attention to him. "No touching yourself, Jo. This time you're going to come just from my fucking."

Yup, I could definitely do that. With the announcement, his diligent stabs became rougher, and my pussy grazed the hard surface underneath. I shifted my hips slightly, finding a perfect round bulge of the rock that gave just enough friction when Nick pushed my body forward.

"Oh! Nick... harder."

This must have been what Daisy was talking about. He felt so good inside me, I could never get enough. The force of his shoves was awakening a woman inside of me that needed much more sexually than I'd realized. I could hear his exertion behind me. At one point, he let go of my hair and held both my hips, pulling me onto him as he impaled me from behind. I couldn't take it much longer. The swelling between my legs felt like the size of a balloon. On the next thrust, that last rub against the rock punctured the pressure, and I screamed.

"Oh, God!"

My echo came back to me just as Nick stilled behind me and let out a loud groan. Betsy mooed in the distance, drawing our attention to the field at the side of the lake, where she was being mounted by a bull. We both laughed. When I looked back, Nick's forehead was dripping with sweat. I wasn't sure when he'd removed his shirt, but his body glistened in the late afternoon sun as beads of moisture rolled down his chest and abs, and I couldn't stop looking, wondering how long it would take me to get used to his new buffed body.

"I'm pretty sure someone heard me." I splayed my body over the rock. Nick was still inside me, and he lowered to kiss me.

"Doubtless."

"Nick, my throat actually hurts from screaming so much. Betsy must have heard me."

"Betsy's a cow."

"Yeah, but that farm is by Carter's house."

"Does it matter?"

No, I guessed it didn't. He ignored my worry, moving on to kissing my lips. "Besides, your throat is just beautiful. That was amazing, Jo."

It was. It definitely was.

He pulled out slowly and I felt completely spent.

"Shit," he cursed.

"What's wrong?"

"The condom burst."

"What?"

"It broke when I was inside you. Jo—"

"It's okay. I don't ovulate for another five days or so."

"You sure?"

"Yeah, I'm sure."

"Good. I wouldn't want our baby born when I'm away."

Our baby. Wow, that sounded so wrong and so right. There was no one else in the world whose baby I'd want to carry, other than Nick's, but he was right. The timing was completely off. Nick had to go back to the navy, and I wanted to start the online bakery business as soon as he left. I lowered my dress and smoothed my hands over it when my gaze found the lake.

"Unzip me, please." I turned around.

He didn't ask why, but pulled the zipper on my back down and I stepped out of my dress.

"You're the sexiest woman I ever met." His eyes glowed with hunger, and I bet that if I let him, he'd take me again. But with the sun so hot today and me still sweaty, all I could think about was that cool lake.

"Feel like taking a dip?" I asked.

Amused by the idea, he lowered his pants to the ground and removed his running shoes. I reached to the back and unclasped my bra. He sucked in a sharp breath and I proceeded to lower my panties. His cock twitched and started getting hard again.

"You better get in that water before I catch you."

I ran to the shore. The water felt cold at first, but as I dove in, the temperature of my skin dropped and adjusted. It was perfect. Nick swam up behind me.

"Carter tells me you planted some flowers at his house."

"I did. I thought it would help him to deal with Daisy's passing. He didn't talk to anyone for months."

"He seems better now."

Nick took me in his arms and I wrapped my legs around his torso and my arms around his neck. The trapezius muscles extended from his shoulder blades all the way up his neck. They made him look so strong. I smoothed my fingers over the area. Every time I touched Nick, it felt like I was touching him for the first time.

"He is, but sometimes I think he's putting on a show for everyone."

"Why?"

"I don't know. It's a gut feeling, you know. I mean, when you were gone, I got him. I knew what it felt like when you didn't have your loved one, but he lost Daisy permanently. It was hard."

"Well, I'm glad he's got a good friend in you."

"He's been good to me too. He always reassured me that you'd be back. He made time fly by quicker."

"Speaking of time..."

I heard a slight vibration in his voice, and I didn't like it.

"I returned home ahead of schedule because they need me back a bit earlier as well."

"How much earlier? I thought you said in your letter that we'd have the whole summer."

"That was before I agreed to take on a special mission. I have to go back at the end of July."

"But that gives us only four weeks."

A feeling of impending anger was blossoming in my chest, but Nick was not done with the bad news just yet. I shook my head, my intuition slowly kicking in.

"For how long, Nick?"

"Twenty-four months."

"Two years! You'll be gone for two years?"

"My training went better than I thought. They have a special program for people like me that's integrated with work and missions. I'll be deployed on a special project."

"What do you mean, people like you?"

"Someone who can study others, switch character, and adapt."

I remembered how smoothly Nick had swayed our parents' attention earlier in the day.

"I caught a sergeant's eye, and he handpicked me for this, along with a couple of other guys. I shouldn't even be telling you this because it's top secret, but I don't know how else to explain it, and there's no fucking way that I'll lie to you, Jo."

"Two years?" I felt the swell in my eyes increase. The more I thought about it, the more I wanted to cry.

"I'll finish the remaining training required for the mission in the first three months, which means I'll be deployed the rest of time."

"Is it dangerous?"

"I don't know, but when I complete it, I'll have six months off. From then on, the missions won't be longer than six months at a time."

"I don't know if I can survive with just writing letters."

"That's another thing I want to talk to you about. I don't know where I'll be stationed until we get there."

"But you can write me and tell me where you are, right?"

He shook his head and I jumped off his body.

"Nick! No contact at all? Seriously?" My sobs stopped as fast as they had begun because this was hurting too much. I could feel the anger overwhelm my body. I couldn't believe this was happening again, and that it would be much worse this time.

"I can't say no to this, Jo. It's for the betterment of our future. I won't have to be deployed every few months for long periods of time. I may even be able to work from home, and maybe travel for a few weeks only. I don't want to be away from you and from my family for long periods of time,

Jo. I want to be here with you and our future children. I don't want to miss birthdays and graduations. This way I'll still get to do something that matters and still have those who matter the most in my life."

I selfishly wondered whether I did truly matter the most. Didn't he realize that he could have been a firefighter or even a damn baker, and be close to me? I felt like he was abandoning me — us.

I was walking away from him. I never thought I would, but I was so angry now. Our intimate relationship was just beginning to grow. I was starting to get to know this new man that had come back into my life, whom I loved more than my own life, and he would leave me again.

"Jo, wait up."

He caught up to me and turned me around. Shivers covered my body, but it wasn't from cold. I had a bad feeling about this. My stomach was swirling with so much emotion, I couldn't understand it all. My intuition told me not to let him go, but I knew that I couldn't stop him from doing something he loved and believed in because I wouldn't want him to stop me from achieving my dreams either. I tried before and it didn't work.

"Baby, I love you. Two years will fly by, and before you know it, I'll be back and we'll be ready to start our lives, maybe think about having a family of our own. I'll look for a house near our parents, so that we're close to our family, and our kids will be able to run to their grandparents' without us worrying. In fact, I already have something in mind."

"You do?"

"Yes, I was planning to show you in a couple of days."

He was making our future sound so perfect; why was I having such a difficult time with his decision? Because what he was saying was way in the future. It meant that he had to complete a secret mission first, and I'd have no contact with him.

I leaned my head against his chest and he wrapped me into his body. We were standing knee deep in the water, and my tears mixed with the drops flowing down my hair.

"I just love you so much, Nick. It's the danger of your mission that I'm worried about."

"Would it help if I told you that I'm good at what I do?"

"I have no doubt about that."

"There's nothing that will keep me from coming back to you, Jo. Nothing."

"Do you promise?" I looked up into his green eyes. They said the same thing that he was saying – that he'd be back.

"I promise." He lowered his mouth to mine, sealing my lips with a passionate kiss. "Let's get out of the water before you get sick."

We drove back home in silence. Despite our hot sex, today was the first day since Nick's return that I felt sad.

CHAPTER 19

The construction of the bakery was finally over, and this afternoon we were celebrating with a grand opening. The summer was in full swing, and my father had set up a tent at the front of the building for additional shade from the scorching sun. I'd spent the night before and all morning baking five hundred regular-sized cupcakes in five different flavors and another five hundred mini ones. The kids were stuffing their faces, drinking lemonade, jumping on a trampoline, and playing tag. A fun house at the side of the bakery, which included a bouncing castle, a dunk tank, and a face painting station, resounded with roars of laughter. The town's mayor had closed off the road on one side, which gave everyone additional parking spots.

I wiped the sweat off my forehead, took another sip from my water bottle, and stacked another layer of cupcakes on the multi-platform tray. When I twisted to the right, I felt a twinge in my left leg muscle, and remembered how that leg had been over Nick's shoulder last night. This morning I got up two hours earlier than usual to ensure that the decorations were prepped for the opening. Maybe I wouldn't have been so tired just from the baking, but given that Nick had come to my room at one in the morning, we hadn't gotten as much sleep as we were supposed to.

A woman's voice called out my name, jolting my head up. When I saw Molly, I almost dropped the platter I was setting up and rushed toward my friend.

"Oh, my God! It's so good to see you!" I hugged her. "I missed you. You look good."

"Thanks! I've been working out at the campus gym before classes."

"Well, I can definitely see the results. Holy shit, Molly! Now, please tell me that there's a new man in your life."

"Nope, still haven't found the right one."

I leaned in closer. "So you're still a virgin?"

"Yes, and proud of it."

I saw Carter look up from the side and wondered whether he'd heard us. If he had, he didn't say anything, but he did come over to say hello. "Nice to see you, Molly. Those buns of yours are looking good." He leaned back to get a better look at her behind, and I rolled my eyes.

"What buns?" she asked.

"He means your ass."

Her cheeks covered with a rosy shade.

"Don't worry. He calls my boobs cupcakes."

Nick looked up from the porch where he was talking to the construction crew who would start the house renovation on Monday. I was afraid he'd heard me.

"Once Andrew gets here, we'll have the whole gang back," Carter said. "Well, almost whole."

"Carter," I touched his arm. "I'm sure Daisy's looking over us from heaven. She's with us in spirit now and always will be."

"You're right. I'm sure she is. So, which cupcake haven't I tried yet?" he asked.

"Ahm, I think you're the only one who's tried them all. You know you're my number one tester, don't you?"

"Hell, yeah!"

"Yo, Carter! Stop hitting on my girl!" Nick jogged up to us.

Carter only laughed in response. "I will for now, but once you're gone, all bets are off, buddy."

While I knew that Carter was teasing, Nick didn't seem to like that answer.

"You better cool it, Carter." Andrew patted his back from behind. "I hear Nick's got new killer skills, and I'm afraid he'd love to try them out on anyone who gets too close to his girl."

"Hello, Mr. Firefighter." I hugged Andrew.

"Hey, if I knew you'd greet me as Mr. Firefighter, I wouldn't have waited so long to start my training." Carter winked. He'd finally decided it was time to redo his six-month course to become a firefighter. Better late than never. The firehouse was still short a couple of guys to have a complete shift turnover without anyone working overtime, but when Carter was done, they'd all finally have regular working hours.

"What did I just say about hitting on my girl?" Nick asked.

"Don't worry. He flirts with everyone, including the cattle at Mrs. Gladstone's ranch." I stepped up on my toes and planted a kiss of reassurance on his lips.

"Hey, that cow likes me, and you know it." Carter's normally humorous tone changed to serious whenever he mentioned Mrs. Gladstone's cows, especially Betsy.

"The easier question is, which cow doesn't like you?" Andrew chuckled before running off to greet one of the firefighters.

"Come on, Molly. Let me show you the best cupcakes before Nick over there rips off my balls." Carter took her under his arm and picked up one of my favorite cupcakes: black forest.

As soon as they left, Nick was at my side. "Why does he call your boobs cupcakes?"

"I don't know. Why don't you ask him?"

"He shouldn't be thinking about your boobs at all."

"I don't think he's thinking. He's just being Carter."

"I don't like it."

"Are you jealous of your best friend?"

"I'm jealous of any man who hits on you."

"No one's hitting on me, and you're being weird."

"Just protecting what's mine."

"Well, then protect away." I kissed him again. "Have you told your mom that you have to leave in three weeks?"

"This morning. She cried."

"Are you surprised?"

"No. But I was hoping that someone would be happy for me."

"Nick, I am happy for you. What you're doing for this country is very honorable. I just wish it wasn't that dangerous, and for so long. I mean, I won't even know if you're alive."

"Of course you'll know. The military would inform you if..." He stopped.

My hand flew to my mouth. "Don't even say it, Nicholas."

"I'm sorry. I promise I'll be safe. They only send out the best of the best, and I guess I'm the best."

"That, you certainly are."

"Hey, I have a surprise for you."

"You do?"

"Yes, and I'd like to give it to you right now."

I pulled him off to the side. "Does it have anything to do with you and me getting naked?"

"No, but I'd like to think we'll get naked anyway." He winked.

I saw my father step out of the bakery and wave to us, and I waved back. "Do you think they know that you sneak to my room in the middle of the night?"

"I don't think so. There's no way your father would allow it. In his eyes, you're still that little girl who liked piggyback rides."

"I guess you're right. It was hard on him, you know, raising a daughter on his own. Thank God your mom was here."

"Excuse me, can I have everyone's attention, please?" My father clanked a fork against a vase full of field flowers, and the crowd quieted and turned his way. "Thank you for joining us today. We've come a long way since last summer, and the destruction the tornado brought to our town will be felt for a long time. We've lost members of our community whom we will always remember, and we gathered together with strength and perseverance to overcome the new challenge in our lives. I have lived in this town my entire life, and I've always known that I could depend on the good folks who live here as well. I'd like to take this moment to thank you all for your continuous support of our bakeries, which have been merged, and to tell you how grateful and privileged our family is to bake for you every day. That's why it's so important to me to make this announcement in front of everyone gathered here." He then turned toward Marge and reached for her hand. She had a somewhat confused look on her face. I got a funny feeling in my stomach, and I squeezed Nick's hand, whispering, "Oh, my God."

"What's going on?" he asked.

"Just watch."

A few people gasped, the way I had, as my father's intention dawned on them.

My father cleared his throat, and he knelt on one knee in front of Marge. She gasped and covered her mouth. The tears were streaming before he even reached inside his pocket. "We might not have started our journey together, the way our kids did, but I've loved you for so many years, my sweet, that it only makes sense for me to promise to love you for the remainder of the years I have left. I would be the happiest man on earth if you would do me the honor and agreed to be my wife. Marge Tuscan, will you marry me?"

"Well, isn't that interesting," Nick said to himself.

"What is?"

"Nothing. I'll tell you later."

Marge nodded feverishly, saying yes, and he slid the ring on her finger. Everyone cheered, and champagne bottles began popping up into the air. I wasn't sure how and when my father had organized this, but it was one of the sweetest proposals I had ever seen. I wiped the tears off my cheeks and turned to Nick.

"They're getting married!"

"Come on, let's go congratulate them."

Hand in hand, we rushed over to our parents, hugging them.

"I'm so happy for you two." I squeezed my father.

"So we have your blessing?" he asked.

"Are you kidding?" I looked to Nick. "Of course you do."

"Good, because we'd like to make this official in two weeks."

"What?"

"Nothing big, just you two and a few of our closest friends."

"But only if you'll agree to be my maid of honor, Joelle," Marge added.

"Yes! Oh, my God, of course, yes! This is so exciting. We have a wedding to plan. Nick, did you hear that?"

"What do you say, best man?" my father asked.

"Really? Me?"

"I wouldn't want anyone else."

"Yes, definitely. I'm not too sure what my duties are as best man, but I'll do my best."

"Well, one of them will be to walk me down the aisle." Marge's voice was shaking.

Nick squared his shoulders and held his head high. I thought I saw his eyes glisten, but he held the tears back.

"Just name the time and the place, Mom. Congratulations." He reached for my father's hand and gave him a firm shake. "Walter, can I speak with you privately for a moment?"

I wondered whether Nick wanted to have a man-to-man talk with my father before giving away his mother. Which may have sounded funny, but Nick had always been very protective of Marge.

As they stepped to the side, Marge took me under her arm, and we walked inside the bakery to get more cupcakes.

"You're okay with this, Jo? Me and your father getting married?"

"I couldn't be happier."

"I know you haven't had a mother in your life, and I'm sure that's always been a big hole that could never be filled, but—"

I stopped her, "Marge, I never felt that hole because of you. You were the closest to a mother figure I've ever had, and I do think of you as my mother. I always have. I hope you're okay with that."

Her eyes welled up. "And I think of you as my daughter, honey. I want you to know that no matter what obstacles life throws at you, that you can always come to me."

"I know, and I will."

"Are you and Nick happy? I mean, he's not staying as long as he was supposed to."

"I'd rather we had longer too, but we're very happy. Actually, I'm over the moon. It won't be easy seeing him leave, though. How do you do it? How can you be so calm about it?"

"You're forgetting that my husband used to be in the navy. This is nothing new to me, but you... you're so young."

"I know. I guess it just takes time getting used to."

"You'll get the hang of it. And I'm sure once this mission is done, Nick's schedule will be more manageable, and he won't need to leave for so long. At least that's what he says."

"I hope so. You think we can get the wedding ready in two weeks?"

"Well, we'd like it to be just us and a few close friends, nothing bigger than a picnic, maybe."

"Whatever you need, I'm here for you."

"Thank you, Joelle."

Nick rushed back to us, a little flushed, and took my hand. "Come on, let's get out of here for a while."

I waved to Marge and followed Nick's lead. "Okay. Where are we going?"

"That's the surprise."

He gave me a quick kiss, took my hand and led me to the back of the house. "Can you jump the fence?" he asked.

"It will be hard with this dress on. But I can try."

Nick gave me a boost up, and with a quick flip I was on the other side. I was secretly afraid that my dress would get stuck on the fence and I'd end up hanging upside down with my butt shining up. Thankfully, I didn't. When I saw him fly over it himself, I did a double take at his shoes to see if he got the additional thrust from hidden rockets or propellers, like Astro, the boy from the comics.

I followed him through the back field that led to the old Camden barn. It had been for sale for years, and I wasn't even sure who the owner was anymore, but the field around it was at least fifty acres of land or so, and the only other visible establishment from here was our bakery and our house.

Nick pushed the main barn door, opening a sliver of space to squeeze through. Inside, the now setting sun streamed between the wooden boards from the outside, creating ribbons of light that carried dust and particles. At the far end, old hay was stacked about fifteen feet high, and the smell of dried grass filled the air. Overhead, on the exposed upper level, some old tools and pitchforks were propped against the wall. The only way up was a ladder.

I sneezed.

"Bless you."

"Thank you. So, where's the surprise?" I asked.

"You're standing in it."

I looked around, wondering whether I was missing something.

"I'm going to turn this into a house," Nick said. "Our house."

"Are you kidding me?"

"Jo, I'm not the kidding type when it comes to you and me."

"I'm not sure if I want to live in a barn." My nose wrinkled and I sneezed again. "Especially one filled with hay."

"This" – he stretched his arms out wide – "is not just a barn. I mean, it would still look like a barn on the outside, but on the inside, it will be all wood. New wood. Clean exposed beams, open concept, stone fireplace, high ceilings, a chandelier made of deer antlers, dining table carved out of wood, and sheepskin rugs everywhere. Up there," he said, pointing to where the ladder led to the half second floor, "will be our bedrooms and the nursery. It will be beautiful. Imagine that ladder's a swirling wooden staircase. I'd paint the roof red, and build a greenhouse in the back and a garden at the front where you could plant your flowers. Can you see it? Because I can."

The way he described it, I could see it. Except for the sheepskin rugs. I preferred something more minimalistic.

"Oh, and I forgot to add that there will be a jukebox right there." He pointed to an empty space. "So that I can dance with my wife to any one of her favorite songs."

"Wife?"

And then he did the unthinkable and knelt down in front of me, reached into his pocket, and pulled out a square box.

"Nicholas..." I gasped.

"Joelle Kagen, I cannot live my life without you. You are my best friend, my only love, and my soulmate. I think it's time to replace that promise ring with something more permanent. If you will wait for me while I'm gone and have me when I return, I would be honored if you would agree to be my wife."

He took the oval-cut stone between his thumb and forefinger and slowly slid it on my ring finger, patiently waiting on his knees until I cried out, "Yes!"

I was in his arms, being spun around in the air until everything around us blended and his lips were once again on mine, kissing me so passionately, I thought I'd seen his soul.

"I love you, Nick. I love you so much."

"So, wanna christen our future house?"

"Thought you'd never ask," I laughed.

He spun me around in the air again, and then his hands didn't leave my body again until I was spent.

CHAPTER 20

I stood at front of the aisle, opposite my father, as Nick walked Marge toward us. Watching him come forward was surreal, and I wondered whether I'd have all these emotions running through me when we got married ourselves. Probably. The town church was packed. Despite not having announced the official wedding and the lack of any invitations, everyone seemed to be present. To celebrate their nuptials, Marge and my father had organized a picnic by the lake for anyone who wanted to join them, and given that nobody wanted to miss this latest happening, I was pretty sure that everyone in town had shown up.

Marge wore a long white dress that shimmered with light pink when she moved. It fit snuggly against her body, a sexier outfit than I was used to seeing her in; way different from the flower-printed aprons she wore every day. Her hair was swept to the side, pinned back with a silver rose. Matching flower stud earrings with a small gemstone in the middle sparkled as she walked down the aisle. She looked breathtaking, and I saw my father wipe his cheek. When they arrived, I hugged her and kissed her before Nick passed her hand to my father and took the best man's spot at his side.

Goosebumps swept over my body as I took in the ceremony. While our parents spoke their vows, I kept my gaze connected with Nick's and twisted my own engagement ring, wondering how long it would be before it was the two of us pledging our love to each other in front of family and friends. At one point he winked at me, and I felt my heart palpitate. I blew a cool breath up to my face just as the priest pronounced our parents married and they kissed.

The church roared in applause and there were a few whistles from the firefighters. My heart was beating faster and faster, my breaths became shallow with excitement, and the noises around me grew more distant as my vision blurred. The next thing I knew, I was staring up into Nick's eyes, watching his mouth move in slow motion. The world slowly faded back into focus, and a hum of whispers buzzed in my ears: *Is she okay? What happened? Get her some water.*

"We lost you there for a moment, Jo." He let out a breath of relief.

"How are you feeling, honey?" Marge brushed my hair out of my eyes.

"What happened?" I looked around, but all I could see were feet. Lots of feet. Loud whispers echoed through the room as I realized that we were in church.

"Oh, my God! I ruined your wedding."

"You didn't ruin anything. We're married, and that's what counts." My father passed me a bottle of water and I took a sip, slowly feeling it swoosh through my veins.

"You fainted, honey." Marge was crouching beside me.

"Carter broke your fall. You're lucky he was sitting on this side of the aisle." Nick was looking above my head. I felt something soft move underneath me. As I shifted, so did the cushioned backing, and then something poked into my ass. I turned around to see Carter's face. I was lying on top of him.

"I'm sorry. Did I hurt you?" I asked.

"You, hurt me?" He chuckled. "Good one, cupcake."

"Thank you." I rolled off him. Carter hurried to stand up and got out of the way.

"Doctor Burke is coming to look at you." Nick helped me sit up.

"I don't think that's necessary. I don't want to stop the celebration."

"We'll still party, but we want to make sure you're all right."

"I think I just got overwhelmed. And the heat, too. It's pretty humid out today."

"Have you eaten anything, Jo?"

Eaten? I remembered rushing this morning. I'd finished the last batch of cupcakes, added fresh pansies to the wedding cake, and then showered and did my hair. By the time I put on my dress, we were leaving.

"I think I skipped breakfast."

Nick reached inside his pocket and pulled out a granola bar, tore the paper, and passed it to me. "Next time, I'm checking if you ate," he warned.

"Yes, sir." I winked and took a bite of the bar. It was one of the most delicious things I had ever tasted. "Dad, Marge, I'm so sorry."

My father helped me to a chair. Nick wouldn't leave my side. He never let go of my other arm and made sure I finished the granola bar to the last crumb.

"Nothing to be sorry about. It wouldn't be a wedding without a little bit of mischief. How are you feeling?" my father asked.

"Better. I think we can get this party started."

"Good, because I'm starving." I saw Carter pat his stomach. If he was trying to cover up that he was worried, it wasn't working. I had seen him peeking from behind Nick when I was still down on the floor.

Doctor Burke pushed through the crowd. He'd gone to his car to grab his black doctor bag, and now he set it down beside me. He wrapped the Velcro band around my arm to take my blood pressure and grabbed my wrist to take my pulse, took my temperature, and asked me whether anything was hurting from the fall.

"No, I'm pretty sure Carter cushioned me," I said.

"Well, your pulse is still a little low." He passed me a box of orange juice. "Drink this before you do anything else and check back with me at my office next week."

"Yes, of course."

Once I got cleared to enjoy the wedding, Nick secured me under the arm to his side, never letting go, and we made our way to where the festivities were being held by the lake.

There was no pageant of cars honking because like everything else in this town, the lake was a stone's throw from the church. Despite the heat, everyone walked to celebrate the new union.

Tents had been set up over tables laden with home-cooked food the families had prepared. It was a full-out potluck galore, barbecue style, because who didn't like hot dogs and burgers? Carter proudly stood by the grill, flipping the meats, calling out to kids to get their hot dogs.

"Are you sure you're feeling okay?" Nick asked. "You still look a little pale."

"Yes, I'm much better now. I think it was the stress of the day, and not having breakfast."

"Do you want anything else to eat?"

"What I really want is for you to stop worrying so much."

"That will never happen. Fruits. You didn't eat any fruit today."

"Nick, really. I'm okay."

"You say that now and then you'll faint later." He looked up to see my father waving at him. "Looks like I gotta help move a table. I'll grab you some water on the way back."

He kissed me and hurried over to my father. I watched him jog. It looked almost like slow motion and was so sexy that I felt my breasts swell and nipples ache at the sight. I adjusted the top of my dress, wondering whether the fit on the girls was a bit too tight, when I heard a voice from behind me.

"Making sure your cupcakes don't spill?" Carter asked.

I rolled my eyes and ignored his comment. "Just the man I was looking for. I'm sorry about what happened at the church."

"You fell, and I caught you."

"No, I mean, when I was on top of you and made you... uncomfortable."

"Oh, that."

Was Carter actually blushing? Well, that was a first. "I'm sorry, Carter."

"I know you didn't mean it. And *I* didn't mean to get hard, either. It would have happened with any girl."

"Well, that makes me feel special." I let out an over-dramatic sigh.

"Would you rather I only got hard for you?" he asked.

"Eww, don't even say that."

"You asked for it."

"Well, I'm sorry I asked. But seriously, thank you, Carter. You're always there when I need you."

"Don't tell Nick or he'll cuff me."

"I have a feeling that would be an easy punishment, coming from Nick."

"Yeah, you're right. He'd make me dig my own grave."

"Don't say that. You guys are best friends — almost like brothers."

"Yeah, we are." His mouth curved in that sexy way to one side. I was pretty sure that I'd gotten used to it over the years, but it didn't stop the sensation of dancing endorphins in my stomach. Hey, I was human, and not blind to the attraction that was Carter Clark.

Carter took a seat beside me and watched Nick set another table up. Or maybe it was just me watching? I was pretty sure that Carter was just staring out into the distance.

"Penny for your thoughts?" I asked.

"You'd be bankrupt," he laughed. Carter wasn't usually someone who overthought life. He mostly acted on instinct, like Nick did; but today, something about him was different. "Next thing you know, it will be the two of you walking down that aisle." He gently nudged me in my side.

"Oh, I'm sure it will be some time before that happens."

"If I were Nick, I'd knock you up before someone else stole you."

"Like who?" I laughed.

"I don't know. Me?"

"Carter, you're like a brother to me."

"Ouch." He motioned with his fist into his heart.

"And I know you'd never do that to your best friend. Besides, what would Molly do? She's had a crush on you ever since I can remember."

He shook his head as if I'd just spoken the impossible. "Nah-ah. Molly is absolutely unattainable."

"What are you talking about? Why?"

"You're gonna think that I'm a jerk, but she deserves better than me. Because you know, she's... pure."

Pure?

"Don't you think she'd be better off with someone like you who respects her, rather than a guy who just wants to pop her cherry?" I asked.

"I haven't thought of it that way."

"Well, you should."

"She has school to finish. But fuck yeah, she's gorgeous."

"And I bet you one hundred bucks that she'll come back home in three years, still untouched. You know, this shouldn't be a tough sell."

He laughed, then looked Molly's way. "It's not a tough sell, Jo."

I leaned in closer to him and looked around, making sure that no one else could hear me. "You're a pussy."

His mouth opened wide. "Joelle Kagen, just when I thought there was nothing you could say that would shock me..."

"Please. I think you're just afraid of rejection. I think you like her so much that you're afraid you'll blow it if you approach her with your usual manly flirting."

"Oh, yeah? Watch and learn, Jo."

He raised his chin higher and walked to where Molly was standing by the drink station, pouring punch into plastic cups for the kids. I watched them eagerly, wishing I could hear what they were saying. By now, Nick came back and sat by my side.

"What are you looking at?" he asked.

"Carter's making a move on Molly."

"Well, isn't that interesting?"

"Why?"

"Because Carter sucks at making moves. His mouth gets away from him and he says the most inappropriate things."

"Oh, come on. Have some faith."

"Look, he's about to strike out." He pointed.

The frown on Molly's face wasn't easing. Whatever Carter had said to her must have been bad.

"Oh, no. I think you're right." I covered my mouth.

Molly took the pitcher of water she was holding in her hand and poured it right over Carter's head. My heart broke for him. He was trying so hard and was a very nice guy. I wondered what he'd said to Molly to get her that upset.

"I feel bad for him."

"Carter knows how to get back up on his feet. Don't worry. He'll get it right one day."

"Yeah, but that was just sad." I lowered my voice as he approached us at the table. His shirt was soaking, and so were his pants. He reached for the hem and pulled his shirt over his head, slapping the wet fabric on the table and sitting across from us. Carter was officially shirtless at my parent's wedding.

"Well, that went just as I planned," he mumbled.

"Only you could fuck up a good thing, brother."

"Easy for you to say. You guys always knew you were meant to be, and didn't even have to try."

"Ha!" Nick laughed. "We didn't always know, but we were friends first. Friends who cared about each other."

"I do care about Molly." He turned around to have another look at where Molly was filling up the cups. "I care about her long legs, that low-cut dress, and the pretty pink underwear she's wearing."

"Now how do you know they're pink?" I asked.

"Guys are meant to know this stuff. It's intuition."

"So what's going to happen now? What did you say to her to make her that angry?"

"I might have mentioned something about someone waiting to be deflowered by the right guy."

"Oh, Carter!" I lowered my head to the table.

"I thought it was bad after it slipped out, but I got nervous, okay? I just can't find a way to talk to her without screwing it up."

"I think you're just trying too hard. If there's anything I know, it's that Molly likes you. You'll get it one day, and when she realizes that you're the only one for her, she'll make you as happy as Jo makes me." Nick leaned in and kissed me on my shoulder.

"You know, I'm really going to miss you when you're gone. I could use you as my wingman."

"Hey, I could be your wingwoman," I said.

"Yeah, but it doesn't really matter, does it? She's going back to school in a month."

"Which will give you some time to work on those gentleman skills. You can practice on me. Right, Nick?"

Nick paused for a moment before he connected his gaze with Carter's. "Yeah, he can practice, as long as he doesn't touch you."

"Of course not. Carter's a friend."

"I was your friend once."

I was flattered that Nick was so possessive and jealous, but he had no reason to be.

"Okay, given that I'm leaving soon, I think I owe you. Watch and learn." Nick stood up and walked toward the table where Molly was standing.

"Looks like I'm not going to be the only one without a shirt soon," Carter gloated, and moved around the table to sit beside me for a better view.

"Nick's a gentleman. I'm sure he can handle himself," I said with pride.

The two of them were having a conversation now. Molly was smiling and even laughing a little, and then she blushed before peeking our way; at Carter, more specifically. She curled a lock of hair around her finger and bit her lip, nodding, before the two of them came our way.

"No way," Carter whispered.

"Told you," I gloated.

"I'm sorry about the water. If you'd like, I have an extra shirt in my car."

I nudged Carter with my elbow because he was sitting awestruck, with his mouth open.

"Uh, yeah, thanks. I'd like that."

He got up and followed Molly to the parking area. I was almost as awestruck as Carter.

"What did you say to her?"

"I told her the truth. That he liked her, got nervous around her, and ended up saying the wrong things."

"And that worked?"

"I took a chance. She could have said that it was too bad, but I think she likes him as well."

"That's good." I got up from behind the table. Feeling a little lightheaded, I hugged Nick, using his body as support. I didn't want him worried that I wasn't eating enough. "You make me so proud."

"Thanks, Jo. You make me proud as well. I'm glad Carter will have you when I'm gone. Someone needs to keep him in line, so he doesn't get into trouble when Molly's away at school."

"I'll try to put in a good word for him as well. She'd keep him in line."

"All the single ladies, please come forward. It's time to catch the bouquet!" Mrs. Gladstone yelled at the top of her lungs. She was used to calling out to her cows, and I chuckled when she used the same tone of voice when she called out "all the single ladies," like they were her cows.

"Are you going?"

"I guess since we're technically not married, I'm still single." I kissed him on the cheek and hurried toward the group of girls.

Marge winked at me before turning around. The moment she did, I felt like a swarm of bees was buzzing around me, squeezing me into the center. Except they were girls, all single girls. From the corner of my eye I saw Molly standing at the side. I waved to her to come over, but she shook her head.

It was all over before I got a chance to lift my hands in the air. The bouquet was coming straight for me. I felt a push on my right, then on my left, also from the back, and as I concentrated so I wouldn't fall or get stepped on, the flowers hit my head and were snatched by Katie, a girl from our school, one year younger than me.

Marge mouthed, "I'm sorry" toward me and blew me a kiss. I went back to Nick, pouting. I never realized just how much I'd wanted to catch those flowers.

"What's the matter?" Nick took me into his arms.

"I didn't catch the bouquet."

"You don't believe in the superstition, do you? We make our own destiny, Jo. You and I, well, there's no doubt in my mind that one day this will be us." He pointed to our parents.

"I love you, Nicholas."

"I love you too, Joelle."

That last week Nick was home, my mood shifted from bad to worse. I stopped jogging, stayed in bed longer than usual, and dreaded the final goodbye. As much as I wanted our time together to last longer, it only seemed to speed up, and then Nick was gone.

CHAPTER 21

"Jo!" I heard Carter call me from outside, and I opened my eyes.

"Yo, Jo!" he called out again, in a loud whisper.

What in the world is he doing?

I put on a pair of sweats and a shirt and went out to meet him. My father and Marge were already at the bakery, and given that I'd been feeling under the weather, I had stayed in bed longer than usual. Still, this was way too early for Carter to be calling me outside my window.

I opened the front door and met him on the front porch. "Do you know what time it is?"

"Seven?"

"Quarter to."

"I thought you bakers wake up early."

"And I thought you were studying for the firehouse."

"I'm off today, and I'm knee-deep in trouble."

"What happened?"

He pointed to his left, where a familiar cow was standing by the roadside, chewing on the chrysanthemums I had planted by the driveway. It had been two weeks since Nick left, and I couldn't get myself to smile, no matter how much my parents, Carter, and Molly tried, but something told me that today would be the day I broke through.

"Betsy escaped. She came to my house this morning, and now she won't stop following me."

"Carter, what does this have to do with me? Couldn't you have brought her back to Mrs. Gladstone's and tied her up, instead of walking her here?"

"I would have, if she didn't moo at me each time I approached."

"That's what cows do. They moo." I chuckled at Carter's perplexed face. He was acting like a complete city boy, as if he'd never seen a cow before.

"Yeah, but this one's different. Watch."

He took a wary step toward Betsy, who of course never stopped watching him from the side, and stopped when she bobbed her head up and down.

"See, she's going to attack."

"Awww, Carter, she loves you."

"What?"

"Don't you remember? It's what she used to do to Nick when we passed by the farm. She wants you to pet her. I guess now that he's gone, she's found a new buddy."

"She loves me?"

"Step closer, and she'll kneel and let you rub her head."

I watched him pace toward the cow as if he were approaching a tank that was aiming right at him. The scene was getting funnier by the moment, and while I wanted to warn him about what would happen if you approached Betsy from the left side, I didn't. Everything inside me was twisting into knots filled with laughter as I composed myself on the outside. As Carter reached out toward Betsy's head, she did what she'd always done to Nick — licked him from the jaw right up the center of his face, over his nose and to the top of his head, setting his hair standing.

I burst out laughing.

"What the hell, Betsy?"

"I told you she loves you."

"You knew this would happen, didn't you?"

"Sort of. You need to be on her right to pet her, otherwise she'll lick you."

"Lick? I feel like I just took a shower. Stay, Betsy. I'm grabbing a cupcake and taking you back home."

"If you don't pet her, she'll break out again," I said.

"How did Nick deal with her?"

"He stopped by the farm each time we jogged."

"To pet her?"

"Yes."

"And that made her happy?"

"I guess. It worked. She hasn't escaped since we were fourteen."

"Jo, will you come with me to bring her back?"

"Are you afraid of a cow, Carter?"

"Me, afraid? Hell, yeah."

"Let me brush my teeth at least. And move her over by the tree, so she doesn't chew up all my flowers."

I turned on my heel, changed into leggings and a tank top, and quickly brushed my teeth. I grabbed a single cupcake on the way out.

"Is that your breakfast?" Carter asked.

"No, this is for Betsy."

"Aren't you having breakfast?"

"No appetite."

I jogged down the three steps and took Betsy's rope, which was attached to the leather strap around her neck. "Come on, Betsy. Let's teach Carter how to deal with women."

She mooed as if understanding me, took the cupcake out of my hand, and followed. We walked down the road with Betsy behind us. I let go of the short rope. Given that Carter was her new best friend, he could also be her guide.

"I haven't seen you around in two weeks, Jo."

"Oh, you know. I've been around."

"Crying over Nick?"

"I'm pretty sure that I'm out of tears."

"I'm worried about you."

"I'll be fine. I've done a year before; I can do two now."

"You know I don't live far away if you need to talk, don't you?"

"I do. Thank you. I may take you up on that. What's going on with you and Molly? Are the rumors that I heard true?"

"Yes. We went out on a date."

"That's great news. Carter, I'm so proud of you."

"Yeah, but it didn't end that well."

"Why not?"

"She didn't like bull riding."

"You took her bull riding? What were you thinking?"

"I was hoping if she got used to the riding motion, she might warm up to the idea of riding something else, if you know what I mean."

Oh, I knew what he meant. What I couldn't understand was how someone like Carter could be so brainless.

"You can't think with your" – I looked down at his crotch – "penis all the time. Especially when it comes to Molly."

"I promise, I don't."

"Liar."

"I was just trying to get her loose. I mean Molly's an amazing girl, but sometimes it feels like she's got the wrong thing stuck up her ass."

"Carter!"

"What?"

I shook my head. "You're taking the wrong approach with Molly. You need to share her interests, enjoy her company, and be there for her."

"I totally want to enjoy her... company. I really like her, but I get nervous around her and say and do the wrong things. She's just so different from Daisy. Maybe I shouldn't even be thinking about Molly that way. What if we really aren't compatible?"

"You can't force it. You need to let it happen naturally, and I'm sure you'll look much less like an ass if you're not trying to impress her."

"I really look like an ass?"

"Bull riding on the first date?"

"Daisy loved it."

"Daisy was a feisty spirit, but that doesn't mean that Molly isn't fun or adventurous. Molly may seem more reserved than Daisy, but she has so much to offer. Someone like you could really bring her out of her shell. She's such a smart and loving girl, and" – I raised my finger to ensure I had his full attention – "she's the one who initiated our skinny dipping that time at the lake. That should tell you something."

"Seriously? I would have never thought that."

"There's more than one aspect to her personality." I noticed how the sun shone off my engagement ring, reflecting the light, at the right angle spreading a prism of colors onto my finger. "Like facets of a jewel."

"A jewel?"

"Different cuts shine when the light turns, but it's still the same stone. Molly's light shines at a different angle, that's all. It's the same way some people think you're a jerk, but I know that you're a very kind man."

"What?"

"Well, your mouth does get away from you sometimes, but I know that it's always with good intentions, because there's much more to you than your smart mouth. You're a special kind of jewel, Carter."

"Thanks, Jo." Carter scrunched his brows as if he were in deep thought. I hated to see him doubt himself so much.

"You do like her, don't you?"

"I'm actually surprised how much I like her. I mean, like a lot, and I never thought we would mesh well together."

"Good, then give it some time; go out on few more dates; be a gentleman. I remember you telling me that you date to get to know someone better because you can't stop thinking about them day and night. Give Molly a chance. Let her open up to you, and woo her."

Betsy let out a loud moo.

"I didn't say moo, Betsy. I said woo."

"She can't understand you."

"Sure she can. Watch this. Betsy, can you moo?"

Mooooo!

"See? Anyway, if you want, I'll help you with Molly."

"Well, it will have to wait until she's back next summer because she's book shopping and packing this week."

"All right, then you should definitely ask her out to dinner before she leaves. No expectations, Carter. Just sit back, relax, and talk. And definitely no bull riding."

"So, do I have to buy flowers, open her door, and pull out her chair and all?"

"Carter, do we even live in the same town? Of course you do. Please tell me that's what you've been doing. And no jeans."

"What's wrong with jeans?"

"They don't say gentleman."

"Not the way I wear them. They show off my package. Daisy liked it."

"Not all women are the same! Besides, you don't need to be drawing any extra attention to your crotch."

"Are you drawn to my crotch?"

"Any woman with a pair of eyes always looks that way to see if anything is outlined. It's like a law. But with Molly, you need to tone it down."

We reached Betsy's gate, which was wide open. I led her through and scratched her behind her right ear, and she mooed in appreciation.

"Now, promise her you'll stop by every morning," I said.

"I promise, Betsy. After Molly leaves, you're my number one girl from now on."

"Hey!"

"I'm kidding. You're not gonna lick me like she did, are you?"

I punched him lightly in his right arm and rolled my eyes. "You know, talking to you makes time go by faster."

"Thanks. I enjoy your company as well. So, since Nick is gone, do you need someone to pet you too?" he asked.

"In your dreams, Carter."

"Hey, it was worth a shot."

"See, that's the kind of thing you shouldn't say to Molly."

"Of course, but when the cat's away, the mice will play." He wiggled his brows playfully.

"Molly's not leaving until next weekend."

"I'm just trying to get a head start. You know, we can keep each other company while our significant others are out of town."

I sighed and shook my head. At least Carter would remain in town to keep me entertained over the next two years.

"Of course we can."

Something swirled in my stomach. We closed the gate to Betsy's field and I touched my hand to my navel. And just as Betsy lifted her tail to do her number two, I bent over in half and puked. The nausea came out of nowhere – well, maybe Betsy helped a bit – but I couldn't stop it. My stomach was being emptied with a jetting force. I felt it tighten into one small blob. The vomit spilled out of my mouth and nose at the same time, tiring me out.

"That's disgusting!" I heard from the side. Carter passed me a piece of cloth and I wiped my mouth. When I stood back up, I realized that he'd taken off his shirt, and I'd stained it with my vomit. My head hummed, Carter's silhouette faded in and out of focus, and I blacked out.

When I opened my eyes, I was on the ground, staring into Carter's and Betsy's eyes.

"There you are. What was that?"

"I... I don't know."

"I'm taking you to Doctor Burke."

"I forgot about breakfast. That must be it."

"Jo, no one throws up because they miss breakfast. Were you feeling okay this morning?"

"Just tired."

"My house is around the corner. Let's grab some water and drive to the clinic."

"It's not far away."

"You're not walking."

He scooped me into his arms, and shirtless, he carried me. Maybe it was a better idea that I didn't walk, because my legs felt like they'd been amputated. Carter put on a fresh shirt at home, gave me a bottle of water, and holding me steady under his arm, walked me to his car. Barely a minute later, we arrived at the clinic.

Doctor Burke waved us in as soon as he saw us at the front door of the clinic, which was also his house.

"Good morning, Carter, Joelle. I hope nothing bad brings you in this morning."

"She threw up and fainted."

"Has this happened before?"

"No," I answered.

"Wait – you fainted at the wedding as well, didn't you?"

"Well, then yes."

"I remember that. You were supposed to check in with me."

"I'm sorry. It's been hectic."

Doctor Burke reached into a cupboard for a round container. "I'm going to need a urine sample. We'll draw some blood as well, but it will be a while before we get the results. Have you been eating well?"

"I think so. My appetite has been so-so."

"All right. Let's get you checked out."

After I peed in the cup, Doctor Burke took my blood pressure, which was on the lower side but still in the normal range, listened to my heart, and checked my motor skills. Nothing seemed to be out of the ordinary, and I waited patiently for him to return into the fluorescent-lit room. All the while, Carter waited at the front.

"I think I have the answer to your ailment."

"Great... or not so great. What's wrong with me?"

"There's nothing wrong with you. You're pregnant, Joelle. Congratulations."

What?

"Wait, that can't be."

"Have you been sexually active?"

"Well, yes, but..."

"This is just from the urine test; the blood work won't be back for about a week to confirm. You should start taking pre-natal medications, though. Here's a sample pack for you. The nausea should ease in a couple of months, but if it doesn't, or if it gets worse, call me. And make sure you don't skip breakfast anymore. Do you have any questions?"

Even if I did, I wasn't sure that I knew how to ask them at this moment. The shock factor of this news was definitely over the limit.

When we walked out of the back room, Carter stood up and pulled his fingers through his hair. "What's wrong with her?"

"Congratulations, Mr. Clark. You're going to be a father."

Carter hit the floor.

Dear Nicholas,

I know you may not get this letter for a while, but I don't know what else to do. We've tried calling the officer in charge of your deployment, but we couldn't get through. My father even went to visit the base, but he couldn't get any more information either. I need to get in touch with you. It's an emergency. Nick, I'm pregnant, and in six months we're going to have a baby. I'm excited and nervous at the same time. I'm excited for our future, and us, but nervous because I don't want to go through this without you by my side. I don't want you to miss the birth of our first child.

I'm feeling well and the baby is doing well too. Doctor Burke says that its heart is very strong. My morning sickness has passed and I'm eating well. Our parents are very excited to have their first grandchild, but they also wish you were here.

Wherever you are, I pray each night that you are safe. I talk to our baby and tell him or her stories about our childhood and how brave a father our baby has. I know that when you get this letter, you'll call or write. I know you wouldn't miss the birth, no matter where you were in the world, so I'll keep on praying for your safety, and that somehow you'll get this news soon.
Love always,
Joelle

* * *

Dear Nicholas,
Today I felt the baby kick. At first I thought it was gas, and then it kicked again. It was when I was tasting my new cupcake flavor: strawberry-banana. Well, the dough is banana, and the filling is strawberry. It's delicious. I also went to the city for my first wedding consultation. They want

a seven-tier cake, made up of cupcakes, with a Harry Potter theme. I'm attaching my first sketch of the cake to this letter. If it turns out as beautiful as I think it will, it will be amazing.

I'm beginning to show as well. Not a lot, but I can't wait for this little baby. Nick, I'm scared. Not of the pregnancy or the birth, but that you won't get the news and won't be here. I don't want to do it alone. I want you here, by my side. I want our baby to be held by its mother and father first.

Marge is worried about you as well. My father confirmed that you're at an undisclosed location and probably won't get any of my letters, but I won't stop writing. I can't stop hoping, because hope is all I have left. I love you.

Joelle

* * *

Dear Nicholas,

My pants ripped today. Split in two right over my ass when I was having dinner with Molly and Carter. Molly visited for Christmas and our two friends have become closer, but Carter is still hesitating over how to move the relationship forward. I think he'll get the hang of it soon. He won't say so, but I have a feeling he's just making excuses because he's still missing Daisy.

Every day I wonder whether you'll get my letters. Sometimes I cry at night, thinking how unfair life is, because you're away. Then I suck it up and think that it could be worse, right? I mean, you're fighting for us, for our safety and freedom. Still, I will not lose hope that you will be here in three months. That by some miracle you'll get my letters.

I promised Molly that she could be with me for the birth. It will be good for her nurse training, and I'll have someone close with me in the room. Marge volunteered as well. She's been knitting a blanket for fifteen minutes each morning. Your mom has been in good spirits, but I see the worry on her face draw new lines underneath her eyes the more time passes.

Hope to hear from you soon.

Love always,

Joelle

* * *

Dear Nicholas,

It's getting more difficult to sleep. The baby likes to stay up late at night. It pressed its foot against my belly today, and I could see the outline. It was beautiful. I took a picture for you to see when you come back. I've been taking lots of pictures of my belly. Sometimes I feel like I want to keep it inside of me forever to keep it safe from the outside world. Then I realize that's impossible, and I'm grateful that her or his father is doing a great job of keeping us safe.

Betsy's pregnant as well. She'll be due around the same time that I am. I think it happened when we saw the bull mount her when we went to the lake. It's possible that's when it happened to us as well, when the condom broke, but since we had sex every other day, it's difficult to pinpoint. Carter's been visiting her each day on his way to the fire station. I'm getting a lot of pregnancy advice and baby advice from all the customers.

The wedding I catered went very well, and the cake was a hit. All my business cards were gone by the end of the night, and I already received a half dozen new orders. I think the next few months will be busy ones as I get ready for the birth and the weddings.

Miss you with all that I am.

Yours,

Joelle

* * *

Dear Nicholas,

I want to stay strong, but it's not easy. I have one month left before the birth and haven't heard from you. I know you would have written if you could, which makes it that much more difficult. After all, it means that you don't even know about the beautiful miracle we'll soon have. I pray that I'll close my eyes and when I open them again, you'll be here. I wish you'd never left. I'm sorry to be so selfish right now, but I've never needed you as much as I do now. I'm hurting on the inside. I don't want to, because I need to stay strong for the baby, but what else can I do? Whom else can I speak to, to reach you?

I can't climb up the ladder to the rooftop any more. It's not safe. It's another piece of you that I've lost, and if what you said was true before you left, if your deployment will in fact take two years, then I'm afraid you'll miss our baby's first fifteen months. He or she will be walking by then.

We turned the guest room into a nursery. With the money I've been making with online sales, I was able to buy everything for the baby on my own. I feel proud. I know you would too. I wish you could be here. I'm praying for your safe return. I'm praying that we'll soon be together.
Forever yours,
Joelle

CHAPTER 22

"Good morning, sunshine. How is my grandchild doing?" my father asked.

"Good morning, and your grandchild kept me awake most of the night." I smoothed my hand over my stomach, where the baby was now sound asleep. At night, I felt a few pains. I'd read about Braxton-whatever contractions, and I was pretty sure that those were it.

"It's just making you used to getting up at night to feed it." Marge smiled and kissed my cheek. "You look different today, Joelle. Like you're ready for this."

"No, no. I want to hold it in."

"I'm afraid when it's time, you won't be able to hold it in. Jo, I know that Nick would have been here if he got your letters. You need to get ready to do this on your own. But we are here for you, Jo. For whatever you need." Marge squeezed my hand.

"I know. I think I've accepted that. It's just bad timing all around."

"There's never bad timing to have a miracle. And a baby is a miracle," my father said. "Don't let anything distract you from that."

"You're right. I'm sorry. I shouldn't be so selfish. We'll do what we have to do."

Although I still held out hope that Nick would suddenly return, inside I had come to terms that he would not be here for the birth, or the first year and a half of our baby's life. It wouldn't hurt the baby, would it? After all, a lot of other families were probably going through the same thing I was. And while I would have preferred for Nick to experience all the firsts our baby would accomplish, at least he would be back some day, and time should fly by much quicker with a newborn. I made a note to record all the baby's firsts and take lots of pictures for Nick. The last thing I wanted was for him to feel like he'd missed too much.

"Molly's coming home for a visit next week. It will be the perfect time for the baby to be born over the Easter weekend, when it's due."

"You know, honey, that you can't plan the birth to the day. With two weeks to your due date, it could happen any moment."

"I know. But I have a good feeling about this." Feeling a wave of anxiousness pass over me, I rubbed my belly again.

We were having an early spring this year. The grass was getting greener, and the smell of summer was in the air. It was as if the world was preparing itself for my baby.

Tulips and daffodils were blooming everywhere, even in Carter's garden, which I'd made him clean up and replant last fall. You could smell the warmth looming over our small town and this morning, with the bright sun and clear skies, couldn't have been more perfect.

The front door to the bakery opened and Carter pranced in, the same way he did each morning on the way to work. The fire department finally had enough men to cover all shifts.

"Good morning, Hope Bay. What's baking in the oven? A baby, you say? Well, that's a new one." He winked toward me. "I'll have an espresso, a banana spice muffin, a vanilla cupcake for Betsy, and the usual dozen donuts for the crew."

"You know that cow will love you permanently now, don't you?"

"Just doing my job. The mamma needs to stay fed for when she gives birth. You're looking gorgeous today, Jo. Any special occasion?"

"None that I know of. But I do feel like taking a walk this morning, so I'll join you on your way to the firehouse."

"Take your phone with you, Jo." Marge waved the device I was known to forget occasionally.

"Did you eat?" my father asked.

"Oatmeal." I hadn't fainted since the day I found out I was pregnant, and I took extra good care of my body. Still, Marge and my father were always over-protective, and I loved them for their constant care.

We walked side by side. For the first few minutes, both of us were lost to our own thoughts, enjoying the warm breeze. As soon as I smelled manure, I knew that we were closer to Betsy; actually, we heard her long before we approached. Mrs. Gladstone was standing at the cow's side, where Betsy always waited for Carter, smoothing her hand between the Betsy's eyes.

"Good morning," we said at the same time.

"Let's hope it will be." Mrs. Gladstone concentrated on Betsy's midsection.

"What's the matter with Betsy?"

"She's overdue, and the way she's been complaining since dawn, I think the calf could be born today. The vet's on the way."

"Can she still have the cupcake?" Carter asked.

"You can try, but I don't think she'll want it."

"Why not?"

"Because when your stomach's in pain, the last thing you want is to fill yourself with food," I explained. I'd been reading a lot of pregnancy and birthing books.

"Oh, Betsy. Don't cry." Carter stepped toward her from the right side and rubbed her behind her ear before offering her the cupcake. As expected, the cow rejected it.

"Is there anything we can do?" he asked.

"I don't think so. Nature's gotta take its course."

"Thank God I'm not a woman."

"You got that right," I said. "Because a woman with your leg muscles and big arms would be a little difficult to look at."

"Hey!"

"Just kidding, Carter. Don't have a cow."

Mrs. Gladstone finally took her attention away from Betsy and burst out laughing. "You two, the way you bicker you'd think you were married."

What?

"No, Mrs. Gladstone. I assure you, we're just good friends."

It was enough that Doctor Burke had initially assumed that Carter was my baby's father, and he'd fainted, or at least he pretended that he did, and I promised him that one day, I'd get back at him.

"And I gotta go to work if I want to make it on time. I'll stop by afterward to see how Betsy's doing."

"Take care, you two."

We walked toward the firehouse, and once again I remembered the day I'd seen Duke mount Betsy. Nick had been right behind me at the time, thrusting his hips forward.

"So, you're really ready for this?" Carter pointed to my stomach, bringing me out of my thoughts.

"I think so. I have the diaper bag ready, and the room is perfect. All we're missing is..."

"Nick?"

"Yeah." I shook my head. "I don't think he's gotten my letters."

"I'm sorry. But on the bright side, I've got the camera ready. There's no way Nick's missing this. I'll make him watch it first thing he shows up."

How was that a bright side?

"There's no way you're taking a camera to the hospital. In fact, there's no way you will be in the same room as me when the baby's born."

"Jo, it's not like I haven't seen a pussy."

"Carter!"

"What?"

"You're doing it again. Gentleman, remember? If you can be that nice and courteous to Betsy, you can show a little more chivalry toward women."

"Yeah, but you're you."

"Practice on me, then use what you've learned on Molly when she comes home next weekend."

He looked like he was lost in deep thought before his mouth curved up in a sly smile.

"Right, then it's not like I haven't seen a cha cha."

"Cha cha?"

"Isn't that what you girls call it?"

"No, it's not." Sometimes I felt like I was fighting a losing battle with Carter.

"And no matter what you call it, you won't be anywhere near my vagina."

"Aha! Vagina! I feel like I should have known that."

"You know, you never cease to amaze me."

"Which means that I'm doing my job. Except not the firefighting job. Nothing wants to burn."

"And that's a bad thing?"

"No, it's a good thing, but I wish I could practice all those skills with the water hose and all that shiny equipment."

He gestured with his hands, taking a wide stance, pretending to be holding a hose awkwardly in front of him, as if he wanted to pee.

I sighed.

Looking at his arm muscles and remembering the strength with which he had spun me when he lifted me in the air when I found out I was pregnant, I was pretty sure that he had plenty of practice with his own hose.

"I'm pretty sure you know how to handle a hose," I said.

"Wait, was that a joke from Joelle Kagen?"

"Maybe."

"Well, well, well. I guess we are good friends, after all."

I stopped at the sudden sharp pain around my navel.

"You okay?"

"Yeah, the baby just kicked me a bit harder." Which was odd because the baby was usually asleep at this time, no matter how much I walked. I picked up my pace again, my hand remaining over my baby bump, anxiousness swirling through my veins. Was this a good time to pull a fast one on Carter?

"Ahhh!" I screamed, grabbing Carter's hand and squeezing it as tight as I thought a woman in labor would.

"Is it time? Oh, my God! Jo, we gotta get you to the hospital."

"No, Carter. It's coming right now!" I widened my stance, pretending that I was giving birth.

"You want me to catch it?" he asked.

I stood up straight and let go of my stomach, cocking my head to the side.

"Catch it? Why would you even say that? You say, 'Lie down,' or at least ask me to sit." I rested my hands on my hips, somewhat forgetting that I was supposed to be pulling a joke on him.

He carefully looked me over, braced his hand on his hip, and leaned a little to the side.

Busted!

"Ouch?"

"Are you pretending?"

"Well, yeah. But you deserved it. I almost died when you pretended to faint at the clinic."

"Jo, don't ever do that to me again. You almost gave me a heart attack. And I'm serious this time."

"I highly doubt that. I can't believe you wanted to catch my baby."

"I panicked, okay?"

"Panicked? You're not allowed to panic, Carter. What if it was for real?"

"So, were you like testing me to see if I could be in the room?"

"No, I wasn't testing you. Like I said, there's—" A sharp pain tore through my lower abdomen, and I grasped Carter's arm, squeezing my fingers around it.

"Jo, I'm not falling for that again."

I felt my knees shake a little as water dripped down my leg.

"You know, if you wanted to pee we could have stopped at my house."

"Carter," I said between my teeth. "That's not pee, that's amniotic fluid."

"Oh." His brows scrunched together as he took in the scene: me, slightly bent over, trying to concentrate on breathing while not thinking about the next sharp pain coming from my uterus. "Oh! Shit, this is real, isn't it? We've got to get you to the hospital, Jo."

"I... I can't walk."

"Where's your phone?" He reached inside my dress pocket before I replied. Waving my hand at him and catching the next breath before another sharp pain tore through me, I took a few steps to the tree at the side of the road and leaned against it.

"Jo, your battery's dead."

"Then get your phone."

My lungs would only allow short and shallow breaths. Why was this happening so fast? I struggled to suck in more air.

"It's at the fire station."

"What good is it there?"

"Well, yours is here and that doesn't do us any good now, does it?" He cocked his head to the side with a smug smile on his face.

"Never mind. Ahh!" The contractions were coming closer and way too quickly. What happened to the twenty-four-hour labor I'd been warned about? Well, there went my good feeling that the baby would wait until Molly was here.

"Oh, my God! Jo, we gotta get you to the hospital. And why does it feel like I'm repeating myself?"

"Carter, I don't think we have time for the hospital."

"Okay, wait here while I go get Doctor Burke."

I grabbed his shirt near the collar and pulled him to me, hoping the threatening look of a crazy woman in labor was enough to keep him at my side. "Don't you dare leave me."

"Hold it in, Jo."

"That's impossible. I need to push."

"Whoa! Let's get you sitting." He took me under my arm and helped me down. I leaned back against the tree trunk and wiped the sweat off my brow.

"Take my underwear off," I said.

"I've been waiting for you to say that," he winked, but when I threw him a dirty look, he became serious again.

"Once this baby is born, we will never speak of this moment again, do you understand me?" I lifted my skirt up to my knees, bent them, and pointed to my underwear.

"Yes, of course." Carter pulled them off while his gaze darted up to the tree above us.

"It's not going to fall out of a bird's nest, Carter."

"Just trying to give you some dignity."

"Fuck dignity. I want this baby out!" I screamed, and Carter jumped up.

"I heard this happened to women, and I completely understand if you want to take your anger out on me, but Jo, as much as I want to help you, I don't know what to do."

"Catch the baby."

I pushed.

"You said not to catch it."

"That was when I wasn't in labor. Catch the baby, Carter. I swear if you let it fall to the ground, I will kill you."

"Got it. Catch the baby." Carter removed his shirt. I didn't quite know why, but I didn't have time to ask because the next contraction came.

"Ahh!" I was sure that my scream would finally be heard by someone. Carter took a wide stance and held out his arms three feet away as if the baby would somehow fall into his arms.

"You gotta get under my skirt!" I pushed again. The pressure was greater than before. I concentrated on my breathing and on the baby making its way down the birth canal.

He hesitated but finally lifted my skirt and looked between my legs just as I felt the baby's head pop out.

"Jesus, Jo. You look like a truck slammed right between your legs."

"Not what I wanted to hear right now. Ahh!" I pushed again.

"Come on, little baby. Come to Uncle Carter."

"I like that," I said, in between the contractions.

He looked up. "Really? Can I be the uncle?"

"You deliver this baby, and I promise you'll be the number one uncle in this baby's life."

"Cool. Okay, Jo. You can do this. Push."

From far away, I heard Betsy as she let out a long and painful moo. With Carter's better coaching, I pushed again and felt the baby come out, right into Carter's hands. He wrapped it in his shirt and, grateful for his quick thinking, I smiled and made a note to buy him a few extra shirts. It seemed that I had a knack for ruining them.

"What is it?" I asked.

"Congratulations, Mama. You have a beautiful baby girl."

I broke down crying as he passed me the baby with the umbilical cord still attached. Mesmerized by my daughter, I didn't notice when Carter stepped away and waved down a passing car. It was the vet going to Mrs. Gladstone's farm.

"She just gave birth," I heard Carter say. "We need help."

"Okay, let's see."

The vet called for Doctor Burke before tending to the baby and me. He cleaned her up with a few of the sterile supplies he had in his car, and when Doctor Burke arrived, the vet left to help Betsy.

"I've already called the hospital. The ambulance is on its way, but it will take some time."

"Is she going to be okay?"

"Yes, she is." He clamped the cord, made sure that my baby's nose and mouth were cleared, and then said, "I need to get the placenta. Can you give me another push, Joelle? Not too hard."

I nodded before tensing a little.

"Perfect."

"So, what are you going to call her?"

I wasn't sure. I hadn't told anyone that I'd been secretly waiting until the last moment, hoping that Nick would still show up and we could name our baby together. So I hadn't picked a name.

"I always liked the name Mackenzie," Carter whispered under his breath, sort of to himself.

"Did you hear that, Mackenzie? Your Uncle Carter just named you."

"You're serious?"

"Yes. You did a great job, Carter. Thank you."

"Well, I can officially say that we'll never be that close again." He extended his arm and made an imaginary circle with his flat palm. "Especially in that area."

But at this moment I wasn't paying attention to him because my focus was only on my daughter, Mackenzie.

CHAPTER 23

Dear Nicholas,

Three days ago I gave birth to our daughter. Her name is Mackenzie, and everyone tells me that she looks like me, but when I look at her, I see you. Now I have part of you with me at all times. This feeling of motherhood is incredible, and I wish you were here. I don't want to sleep and miss a moment of her precious life, even when she's sleeping.

Mackenzie is feeding well. She's up every two to three hours for her feedings, and of course she poops in between. I love every minute of her beautiful little smile. And then I think how long I still need to wait for you and I want to cry. I miss you so much. I'm taking plenty of pictures and my father even bought a new camera to record Mackenzie so that you can watch her first smile, learn how to say

Mama and Dada, sit, crawl, and walk. I can't wait for your return.

Her christening is next weekend. I've asked Carter and Molly to do the honors. I think you'd approve. They've both been so supportive. As soon as she's back home for the summer, Molly said that she wants to spend as much time with her as possible.
Got to go. Mackenzie's feeding time.
Love you,
Jo

Now I understood what Nick meant by days blending in with the nights, because that's how it was for me. I also understood why the baby had been active at night, trying to keep me up – because she was trying to prepare me for motherhood. Today, my father took Mackenzie out for a walk to see Betsy and her new calf that was born the same day she was. I pumped enough milk for the walk, dressed Mackenzie, and sent them off. Once I hit that couch, my eyes shut and I passed out into deep sleep. I didn't get up until I heard Mackenzie's cute giggle and picked my head up.

"Oh, we woke up Mama," my father said to her.

"You're back already?"

"We've been gone for two hours, honey."

Why did it feel like I only slept for minutes?

"Look who we found wandering around." My father stepped out of the way to reveal Carter standing behind him.

"Uncle Carter to the rescue!" He pulled out a plush cow toy from behind his back.

"Carter, you have to stop buying her toys."

"Well, when I saw this cow one and realized that *my niece* didn't have a stuffed cow yet, I couldn't resist. And Molly helped me pick it."

Molly peeked from behind as well, waving, and then came running to my side.

"You're back?"

"Yes, for the summer. I missed you." She hugged me. "And Mackenzie's gotten so big. How are you doing?"

"I'm in love with that girl."

"As you should be. And how are you feeling?"

"A little tired, but it gets better every day."

"I'd love to watch her sometimes during the summer. Maybe we can take her for a walk too?" She looked back at Carter, who appeared to be lost for words until my father elbowed him in the side.

"Ahm, yes. Mackenzie loves spending time with her uncle."

Carter was still at that proud stage of letting everyone know that he had earned the title of uncle the day he delivered her. I wondered how close he and Molly had gotten while I'd been busy with the baby. When I saw the two of them together, I felt my heart squeeze. I missed Nick so much. This was supposed to be one of the happiest times of my life, and it was, but I couldn't completely let go of the fact that I was missing Nick with all my soul. And he was missing out on so much.

"Anytime you guys want, just come over."

Carter and Molly kept their word for the entire summer. They both helped me out as often as they could, and with more sleep and a new schedule of a mother with a newborn, I was beginning to feel like myself again, as if I could actually do this until the day Nick returned.

* * *

Dear Nicholas,

Mackenzie is growing up so fast. Her first birthday is in a week, and a few months after that, you'll be back home. I'm baking her a cow-shaped cake. Her room now is full of cow toys, because Carter won't stop buying them.

She has my curly hair, although the curls are still short. She looks like a little Shirley Temple but with brown hair, like mine. And she has my freckles. There are only a few for now but I'm sure more will sprinkle her face as she grows up. Oh, and did I mention her cute little teeth? They're adorable. She's adorable.

She now calls me Mama and she can say Dada as well. Apparently that's early for a one-year-old. She babbles a lot and I'm pretty sure that she thinks she's having a conversation with us when she does. I've been showing her your pictures so that she recognizes you when you come back. Carter's frustrated that she can't say his name just yet, but he's been persistent. She definitely knows how to say "moo" but that's probably because we visit Betsy and her calf often. Tank is not so little anymore, but Mackenzie is in love with him. Mrs. Gladstone says that she'll keep him for breeding because he's so big and Duke is getting old.

It feels like Mackenzie's changing every day and growing up so quickly. Dad's been filming her do.... well, pretty much everything. But you'll be back soon to see it for yourself. Sending you Mackenzie's sweet baby kisses. Love always,
Joelle and Mackenzie

For the first of May, the day was perfect. Little did I know, it would be a day I'd remember for the rest of my life. It was Sunday morning, and I'd just gotten Mackenzie into her new dress. She was walking now, no longer wobbly, and she'd even taken a few of her first runs.

"This is the dress you should wear when daddy comes home," I said to myself. "But then again, you'll grow out of it in two months.

"Joelle, give Mackenzie to me." My father was looking out the window.

I stopped combing her hair and looked up to my father's concerned face.

"Dad, she's not done—"

"Honey, give her to me right now. I'm going to take her to the back yard. You stay here with Marge. Come on, sweetheart, let's see if Grandpa can find a special cupcake and a freeze for you."

"Walter? What's going on?" Marge asked, and then she looked out the window. Her face went pale white, and I wondered what she saw that scared the living ghost out of her.

As soon as my father disappeared, tears spilled out of Marge's eyes.

"Marge? What's the matter?"

She didn't say anything, only brought me to her body and squeezed me so hard that I thought she'd break a rib or two. "You need to stay strong for your daughter, do you understand me?" she whispered into my ear.

"Yes, of course. Oh, my God, what's wrong?"

Marge was shaking. She didn't let go of me until the doorbell rang, and then she took me by my shoulders, looked me straight into my eyes, and said, "Remember what I said – stay strong."

At this point she was really scaring me. She held me under my arm as we both walked to the front door. When I opened it, I was a little surprised to see two police officers, not from our town, standing on the front porch. One of them was holding a folded American flag, and Captain Clark was standing behind them. Marge was sobbing before they spoke a word. In the back of my mind, something clicked, but I forced away the disturbing thought that was trying to break through.

"Good morning," I said quietly.

"Ms. Kagen? Mrs. Tuscan? May we come in, please?"

"Yes, of course."

I stepped out of the way, noticing how weak my knees felt. We went to the living room, and Marge forced me to take a seat on the couch. The officers remained standing.

"I'm sorry to have to inform you, but your son" – he looked at Marge first, then at me – "your fiancé has passed away."

One of the officers stepped forward and handed me the folded flag. I refused to cry because I refused to believe it. It couldn't be true. I would have felt it if Nick was gone, and so I only shook my head in disagreement.

"Where is the body?" I whispered.

"Ma'am, I'm very sorry, but Mr. Tuscan died in a battle at sea. His body was never recovered."

No, no, no. I had to see the body; otherwise, I was afraid that I'd never believe it.

"I'm sorry to have to be the one to bring this news to you, but please feel free to call me if I can be of any further assistance."

I just sat there, with my back straight, staring at the wedding picture hanging on the wall across the room, until they left. And then slowly, I felt my heart shatter into millions of pieces, my lungs collapse, and my soul leave my body. As soon as the door closed, I broke down.

* * *

Dear Nicholas,

It can't be true. I refuse to believe it and I won't. You promised me you'd be back. You said we'd be a family. Why did you lie? We had your funeral a month ago. We buried some of your clothes, books you liked to read, and the stones you collected at Pebble Beach. It was weird. One good thing about not burying a body is that you still have hope. I still picture you somewhere out in the country, simply lost, and pray each night that one day you'll find your way back. Any falling star I see, that's my wish as well. That you'll be back.

Mackenzie's doing well. I don't think she understands what happened, just that her Mommy and the rest of the family are sad. I don't want to tell her that you're in heaven. I don't want to steal her hope, either. Without seeing you in that coffin, I don't think I'll ever stop hoping. Please... Nicholas... come back. Come back to our little girl and me. Please...I... I don't want to do this on my own. I can't.
Yours always,
Joelle

This was the first letter of many that I didn't mail; instead, I kept them in an old shoebox under my bed.

* * *

I hadn't thought that birthdays would be the most difficult. I mean, who thinks of those things? For Mackenzie's second birthday, we invited family and closest friends only, including her godparents, Carter and Molly.

This spring had been delayed and we still had snow on the ground. Come to think of it, it had been a very depressing year, but how could it not have been? Nick was gone. Some nights, I had dreams of him coming back home. Other nights, I'd dream that he'd shifted into a Merman and was swimming free in the ocean he passed away in. The only time I got any peace was when I sat on the shore of Pebble Beach. I felt Nick's presence with me then, not on a spiritual level, but connected, as if he were on the other side of the globe, but still alive. It gave me hope.

"Hey, where do you want the balloons?" Carter asked, bringing me out of my thoughts. Molly took Mackenzie for a walk while we decorated the house for her surprise. She was back only for the weekend, for the birthday. Except that the moment my daughter left, I sat in the corner of a couch and didn't move. When Mackenzie was not around, I allowed myself to feel the depth of Nick's passing and what it meant for our family. Those were the times when I pulled open the closet door where his clothes were still hanging, stepped in, and locked the door behind me, losing myself in his scent, pretending he was there with me.

At night, when Mackenzie went to bed, I would go up to the rooftop where we used to watch the night sky. I'd stopped crying, though. At least that was a good thing. But living where he had his entire life was definitely not easy. Every time I turned around, something reminded me of Nick. And it wasn't that I didn't want to remember, I did, but being reminded that the love of my life was dead while reading a happy bed time story to my daughter tore me apart.

At some point, I stopped referring to him when I spoke to Mackenzie. Nick's death didn't seem to affect her as much, but I thought it was because she had never really known him. All she'd ever know of her father was the empty grave we visited. I, on the other hand, merely lived through the motions of each day, the glimmer of light that was my old life only sparked by my daughter. Without her, I was lost and in torment which was slowly turning into anger at the world around me. I wanted to scream that life wasn't fair. I wanted to rip apart anything in my hands. I wanted to go drown in that ocean to be with Nick.

"Earth to Jo." Carter gently tapped my shoulder. "Balloons?"

"Oh, ahm, wherever you put them will be fine."

Carter crouched in front of me. "Jo, you gotta stop this. It's been almost a year."

A year filled with grief, doubt about my future, and constant reminders of Nick, while my memories of him were beginning to blur. I didn't want them fading; I wanted to keep them intact. I needed to remember the color of the shirt he'd worn at graduation, the length and shape of the scar over his left brow, how his hair felt when I combed my fingers through it, and the way he used to look at me when no one else was paying attention.

"I know. I know. It's just… you know, maybe we should have had the birthday elsewhere."

"This is Mackenzie's home," he whispered.

"I want to move on, for her at least, but I can't. Not when everything around here is reminding me of Nick."

"It will get better."

"You know, sometimes I feel like part of me died that first time he left me for his training, but I held on to hope, and Nick came back. We were so happy when he came back. I felt complete."

"Are you still holding onto that hope, Jo?" Carter asked, gently smoothing his hand over my arm, forcing me to join the real world. That would have been fine if the real world was a better place. It used to be. Then I found out that Nick died, and my life had been forever changed.

"The last thing that a human being should lose in life is hope."

He thought about that for a moment, before nodding. "You're right, so long as you're not hurting that beautiful girl of yours."

"I would never hurt Mackenzie."

He turned me toward him and wiped a tear off my cheek.

"I know. That's not what I meant."

By that time, Molly had returned with Mackenzie. I could hear them laughing out in the front yard. I got up, wiped away my tears, and straightened my dress before turning back to Carter.

"Do you really think I may be hurting her?"

"Not on purpose."

"Okay. I think I need a change."

He narrowed his brows but didn't say anything, because the front door opened. We sang *Happy Birthday*, gave Mackenzie lots of kisses and hugs, cut her cow cake, and watched her happily open her gifts — many of them with patches of cow patterns, some black and white, some brown and white.

When she tired out and Marge took her upstairs to shower, I quietly left the house to go for a walk that led me all the way to Pebble Beach, the same spot where I'd made love to Nick for the first time.

Moments later, I heard crunching footsteps over the pebbles, but I didn't turn around. Instead, for that brief moment, I allowed myself to pretend they were Nick's.

"Jo, you can't lock all these emotions you're feeling away. It's wrong." Carter sat down beside me.

"It was wrong for Nick to leave me, and he did." I stood up and walked along the shore, away from Carter.

"Jo, you need to talk to someone." Of course he followed me.

"Leave me alone, Carter."

"You need to tell them how hurt you are."

"I said, just leave me alone!"

"I'm afraid I can't do that, Jo."

"Why? Why can't you just go back to your stupid garage and let me be?"

"Because I made a promise to my best friend that I'd take care of you if something happened. And I'm not going to break that promise."

I turned around to face him.

"Well, fuck you! And fuck Nick and his empty promises!" I punched his chest with my fist. Although my strike was hard, Carter barely flinched. "He left me! He left us, and I'll never forgive him for leaving and dying! His daughter will never get to know her father, and I'll never have the love of my life back!" I was screaming at the top of my lungs, crying big ugly tears, but Carter came closer again, so I punched him again. "I told him not to leave, and he still left!"

"Let it out, Jo. Let it all out!"

"Ahh!" I was slapping him so hard, now using both palms onto his full chest, that my hands were beginning to hurt. He finally grasped my wrists and pulled me into his body, holding tight. My violent sobs continued as he slowly lowered us to the ground, cradling me against him, smoothing my hair and kissing the top of my head.

"I'm sorry, Jo. I'm so sorry for your loss, baby."

"He left me." My words were quieter. I'd just used all the strength I had to let out the anger, and I didn't have an ounce of fight left inside me. My whole body was trembling with loss. He slowly rocked me in his arms, never letting go, and whispering, "I'm sorry."

I don't know how long we sat like this, but I didn't want to get up; yet somehow we ended up at Carter's house. Carter laid me on his couch and covered me with a blanket. He called my father and Marge, and then made me tea.

"I don't want to go back to that house." I sighed. "It hurts too much. Everything reminds me of Nick."

"You can stay here for as long as you want. Both you and Mackenzie."

"Thank you."

"You're welcome."

"I know you know what it feels like to lose someone you love," I whispered.

"I do."

"But with Nick, it was just different. He was my life."

"I know, Jo. I know. You feel like no one understands what you're going through. You feel lost. You don't want to live."

My head flew up, for the first time in a year finding understanding in someone else's eyes.

"But you survived."

"I did, and so will you. I'll make sure you'll survive because that's who you are. You're a survivor, and you have a beautiful girl waiting at home for you."

I smiled. Mackenzie was beautiful. Marge said that she was a mini me.

"Carter? Can you ask my father to bring Mackenzie here?"

"Already did. They'll be here in half an hour."

"Okay. I think I'll close my eyes for a moment."

"Sure. Take as long as you need, Jo. I'll be here. I promise."

I remembered Nick made a promise to me too — that he would come back. He broke it, and he broke my heart. I missed him with my whole body, inside and out. I lost my best friend and the father of my child, who didn't even know that he had a child. I wished he at least had known her. Maybe if he had, he wouldn't have left. Part of me hated him for that and another part would love him forever for the most beautiful gift he'd given me: a daughter.

CHAPTER 24

Days turned into weeks, weeks turned into months and months turned into years: three years, to be exact. It had been three years since, along with Mackenzie, I had moved into Carter's house, and four years since I'd found out about Nick's death. I wish I could say it was easier now, and maybe on some level it was, because of Mackenzie, but when she wasn't around, in the darkest hours of the night, I always felt like I was living a nightmare.

Today was a long day of filling new orders, so I'd been up since four in the morning and missed kissing Mackenzie when she got up. She was spending today with Carter, who had a day off. I didn't leave the bakery until six o'clock, and I usually liked to get home earlier so that I could spend time with my daughter. I mean, she was always over at the bakery, mixing something with Grandma, but it wasn't the same. When it was just the two of us, plus Carter of course, I felt complete.

On my way home, I bumped into my duo at Mrs. Gladstone's ranch. I leaned against the gate and watched Mackenzie ride Tank. Given that we lived right beside Mrs. Gladstone's ranch, Mackenzie and the cows there had become quite close — especially when she fed them my cupcakes over our backyard fence. The bull that had been born on the same day as my daughter was fully grown now.

She squealed and laughed as he paced, led by Carter. Sometimes Tank jumped a little, as if he knew it would make Mackenzie giggle. I waved to her when she saw me, and they came over to the gate.

"Hi, baby. Are you being careful with Tank?" I asked Mackenzie, but I was looking directly at Carter.

She nodded, leaning down to give me a kiss while keeping her upper body firmly on Tank.

"I promise we're being safe," Carter said.

"Because you know that Tank has a temper sometimes." While it had been fun for Mackenzie to ride Betsy's calf when he was younger, I was afraid she'd fall off the beast someday, or worse. In spite of his temper, though, when he was around Mackenzie, he was as gentle as a lamb.

"It's okay, Mamma. Tank and I are buddies."

Maybe it was time to think about pre-school more seriously. Up until now, Mackenzie's days had been spent at the bakery. She was quickly becoming a good baker, too, though she was also sassy with our clients. Her over-confidence and positivity reminded me of Nick. I wondered whether she needed more interaction with kids her own age.

"Will you be long?" I asked.

"Another half hour, maybe."

"I might take a quick nap."

"Take your time. Dinner's in the warming drawer."

"Thank you." I leaned over and kissed Carter on his cheek. Mackenzie leaned down off Tank and gave me a kiss as well, saying, "Come on, Tank. I know you can gallop."

I mouthed *no* to Carter. There was no way that I wanted Mackenzie to be galloping on a bull. He winked at me, understanding my fear.

Tired, I walked home. It smelled like spaghetti and meatballs, but I had no strength to eat. And once I sat down on the couch, I couldn't move. My muscles were aching in all the wrong places. I pulled a blanket on top of me and laid down. I must have dozed off because the next thing I knew I heard happy screams and splashes from the back yard. Carter had a pool installed the year before, and splashing around had quickly become one of Mackenzie's favorite activities. I stood up and wrapped a blanket around my body before stepping outside. Mackenzie was in the shallow end of Carter's pool, squirting water through a bottle right onto Carter's face, while he pretended that he was drowning. She was laughing so hard that her little belly was shaking. Having never met her father, I had no doubt that she'd have a void in her heart for the rest of her life, but at least she'd never feel the loss of such a wonderful man like Nick. Maybe this was better. Perhaps having a positive male role model like Carter was better than mourning someone you loved with your soul.

I stepped over the patio stones and pulled out a chair. It squeaked as I sat down, drawing Mackenzie's attention toward me.

"Mamma, come swim!"

I waved. "It's getting a little late, isn't it? You're going to turn into a raisin."

Mackenzie laughed, completely ignoring me, "Look! I can almost swim." She flapped her arms back and forth over the water while walking on the pool steps. She still wasn't too comfortable in the shallow end on her own. Mackenzie was shorter than most kids her age, which meant that she took her height from my side, not Nick's. "And Uncle Carter told me that he'd teach me how to swim for reals."

Each time I heard her say *for reals*, it reminded me of Nick. Goosebumps covered my arms.

"You're a natural swimmer, Mac. I know you can do it," Carter encouraged, supporting her body above the water.

Just like her father.

"Mamma, come here. Swim with us."

I took the blanket off my shoulders and came closer to the pool. Of all the odd days, I wore shorts today. I wasn't sure where the strange feeling in my gut came from, but something was off — as if the entire atmosphere had shifted. I had that same feeling the night the tornado struck, and so I looked up to the skies, but they were clear. I sat at the ledge and dipped my legs in the water.

"How about I sit and watch as Uncle Carter teaches you for reals?"

"Uncle Carter, teach me how to swim!" she squealed, splashing him. For the next fifteen minutes I watched him give Mackenzie instructions for her first swimming lesson. She was relentless; she wouldn't stop until she could at least float on her back, then on her front, with her face submerged and arms stretched out. By the time they were done, the sun was behind the trees in the back and a shadow covered most of the pool.

"Did you see that, Mamma?"

"I did. You were great, but I think it's time to come out." I gave Carter a knowing look, asking him to help get her out of the pool.

I wrapped the towel around her. "It's bath time."

"Bubbles?"

"Yes, bubbles."

"Did you know that Tank likes bubbles? We showed them to him today."

"I think that maybe it's time to make friends your age, don't you?"

"Tank is my age."

"Human friends, Mackenzie."

I knew that she knew what I meant the first time. My little girl was smarter than she let on. After the bubble bath, Mackenzie had some cereal, brushed her teeth, and I tucked her into bed. After reading her a story, I turned on her night light, said goodnight, and went downstairs.

"A glass of red?" Carter reached out toward me.

"My favorite." I took a sip, swirling the aromatic wine in my mouth.

"How was your day?"

"The same as yesterday?"

"Was that a question?"

"Maybe?"

"Jo, stop that."

"What?"

"Playing your twenty questions game."

"Okay, then how was your day? I'm sorry, this is a genuine question, not a game. Did you hear from Molly?"

"Nope." He shook his head. "I've officially given up."

"Carter, you can't. You two belong together. I thought things were going well. What the heck happened?"

"It's a long story, but to make it shorter, she's with some other guy now. But I want you to know that I'm ready to move on."

"That's good, I guess. Can't say that I'm not sad about it. I just always thought you belonged with Molly."

Molly was working at a hospital fifty miles away from our town. She was renting an apartment there, and I'd visited her once with Mackenzie. Molly definitely looked like she was born to be a nurse. I also knew that Carter could be a chauvinistic pig when he got nervous, especially around Molly, and I had wondered whether I should fix them up on a date. Better yet, lock them away somewhere so that they could find love in each other the way I had found mine with Nick.

"Well, I was thinking that maybe *we* could go out."

Where did that come from?

"Like on a date?"

"Would that be bad?"

"I... I'm not sure I'm ready. And Molly—"

"Molly is dating. I think it's time for me to move on as well."

"I don't know if I want to confuse Mackenzie. We've been doing so well as friends; what if it didn't work out?"

"I hate to tell you this, but it's been working out for three years now, Jo."

He was right on that one. We had been living together for three years – in separate bedrooms of course – as friends, and the arrangement was working out. But how long could this last? I didn't expect him to be single for the rest of his life, and as for me... well, I'd been so busy with Mackenzie that I hadn't had time to think about me. Carter was a handsome man and so good with my daughter. His gentle nature with kids was a quality any woman would die for. He'd changed so much from the boy who first kissed me at our camping trip. But could we be more than friends?

"Carter, I can't give you my whole heart. There will always be a part that belongs to Nick, and I can't ever let that go."

"Jo, if I only have a fraction of it, I'll be the luckiest man alive."

Wow! When Carter was pulling the moves, he definitely could do it with all the right words.

"We may not be compatible."

"Sure we are. Look – you like baking cupcakes, and I like eating them." He winked.

And he was definitely the master of charm.

"We're compatible as friends..."

"Those cupcakes are so delicious, they're worthy of their own quotes." He pointed his finger at me with seriousness, and I burst out laughing.

"It's a good thing you're only my friend, Cupcake, because if you were my woman, I'd teach you a little bit of respect and about not laughing at your elders."

"By seven months only, Carter."

"Still, I'm older, which makes me wiser."

"Gentleman skills, remember?"

He shook his head. "What for? Molly doesn't get me anyways. Not the way you do."

"Carter…"

"You've gone through a lot. You can't expect to be on your own for the rest of your life, and the friendship between us is working so well, I'm sure we'd be great lov…" He stopped before finishing the sentence. "I'm sorry. I didn't mean to push this."

"It's okay, Carter." I reached for his hand. Now that Carter had told me his intentions, the touch seemed to mean so much more. I pulled my hand away in fear that the touch would mislead him. Yet it didn't ease the tight sensation in my stomach that had been gone for years. It felt nice to be wanted again. "You've pulled me through my darkest times and helped me with the business."

"That's what friends are for. You have a beautiful little girl now, and you're the best baker in town. No, scratch that. You're the best baker in the world."

I laughed. "Thanks, but I'm sure you haven't tasted other bakers' goods."

"Well, that's their problem, isn't it? Because yours are the only ones I want to taste."

He was looking at my lips. Were we still talking about cookies and cupcakes?

I cleared my throat and pulled away. "You've gone through a lot too, Carter."

"I know. Sometimes it feels like it will never get easier."

"It does, doesn't it? But friends like you, the lifetime kind, definitely help." What if we truly spent a lifetime together? Would it work? Could it work as more than friends? I felt my thighs clench at the thought. Those long showers I took sometimes seemed not long enough, and I craved one now.

"Is that what we are?" I asked. I wasn't too sure where the question came from. I turned back toward Carter and looked into his eyes. I'd always known that Carter had beautiful eyes, but never knew they were this mesmerizing. Or maybe I had just never given them my full attention before.

"I..."

He didn't finish whatever it was that he wanted to say. Instead, Carter's mouth neared mine and gently touched my lips. I held my breath, shocked yet relieved. They were warm and inviting. It had been six years since a man had kissed me. His mouth slowly let go of mine. We leaned our foreheads against one another and I felt my mouth curve up.

"I like seeing you smile."

"I like smiling. And I liked the kiss."

"You did?"

"Yeah, maybe we can try—"

He seized my lips again before I got a chance to finish. This time, they were more dominant, harder and captivating. I opened my mouth wider for him, kissing him back, waiting patiently for that expectant spark to ignite the half-dead heart inside my chest, but it didn't. It was just... a kiss. I may as well have been kissing Tank, but I wouldn't tell Carter that. We finally pulled away and silently stared at each other.

"Not what you expected?" he asked.

"Don't take it the wrong way, and I might have forgotten what it's like to kiss someone, but I... I didn't feel anything."

I held my breath. The last thing I wanted was to upset Carter and to potentially lose my friend. We'd been so good up until this point, raising Mackenzie together. He was the role model I would have wanted for my daughter — she adored him.

"You too? Thank God! I thought there was something wrong with me. Like I lost my gift." He exhaled in relief.

I laughed. *A gift?* "So it didn't mean anything to you either?"

"I'm pretty sure Betsy gives me a better kiss when she licks me."

"Are you comparing me to a cow again?" He beat me to the punch.

"No, just making sure you understand me."

"I do. So, what does this mean?"

"It means that you're stuck as my friend, Cupcake, for the rest of your life."

That was definitely one friendship I was willing to be stuck in.

CHAPTER 25

When I woke up next morning, I somehow knew it was no ordinary day. If I'd thought yesterday was odd, today felt even more so. It all started with dreams of when the tornado had sucked Daisy out at the fundraiser. I remembered the way she closed her eyes and the blood dripping off the gurney. I could smell the irony scent and taste it in my mouth. When I woke up at one in the morning, drenched in sweat, my bottom lip was swollen and cut, and I realized I must had bitten myself. At that point, sleep was pointless. The last thing I wanted was to go back to nightmares, but I had work to do the next day, and I wasn't a quitter. I went to the kitchen, got a glass of water, took a few sips along with some melatonin, and went back to bed. The next dream was even fiercer.

I was wearing an army camouflage outfit, running through trenches, ones I must have seen in a war movie, screaming for Nick. The labyrinth of passages was confusing and I got lost deeper in the tunnels after each turn, until I hit a dead end. I finally woke up at eight, startled, and realized I'd slept in.

"Jo?" Carter was crouching at my bedside. "Are you not getting up today?"

"Shit, I overslept," I groaned.

He was wearing his sweats, ready for his morning run before work. Except he had the entire week off, so I wasn't sure what he was doing out of bed.

"I'll get breakfast going. You shower."

"Thanks."

"You're welcome, Cupcake."

I stretched my arms out and stepped out of bed half asleep. The shower didn't help much. My eyelids still felt like lead. I remembered passing out on the couch after the glass of wine we shared, and then Carter must have carried me to my bedroom. After a quick brush of my teeth, I got dressed and went to the kitchen. It was in full swing of activities as Carter flipped one pancake, then another.

"Feeling any better?"

"Sort of. Thanks for doing this. I hope you're going back to bed after we leave."

"Anytime, and no, I'm not. I promised Mrs. Gladstone I'd fix the farm gate. She's afraid Tank will see Betsy escape one day and he'll run wild." He slid over the floor in his socks, pulling a Tom Cruise move, and I smiled as he kissed me on my cheek. "Good morning."

"It is now."

He pointed to the table. "Sit and eat."

"I think I'm coming down with something."

"I know a couple are burnt, but the stove's been acting up again."

"I promise it's not your cooking. My stomach's upset."

"Coffee, then?"

Ha! That was like asking an addict if he wanted another drink. I didn't even have to answer him, and Carter already knew that my mood would be better after a strong cup of java.

"Thank you. If I don't leave in the next five minutes, I'll be late."

"Say hello to Marge and your dad for me."

"Will do."

I hugged him, then stilled as he looked at me from above. He had that adoring way of looking at me all the time that I couldn't get enough of. He was truly one of the best friends I'd ever had. "Maybe I'll stop by the bakery later and bring you lunch."

"You're too good to me."

"That's impossible, Jo, and you know that."

"Thank you. I'll see you later?"

"Definitely."

"Mamma, Mamma, look what I found!" Mackenzie ran in from the front door through the living room toward me, carrying something in the palm of her tiny hand. I hoped it wasn't another toad. Last time she'd surprised me with something new that she found, I nearly had a heart attack when the green amphibian jumped on my head. Then there were the spiders she was housing in a jar that had escaped through the holes she'd asked Carter to make in the lid for her creatures. We didn't realize her new pets would include six- and eight-legged critters.

This morning, when she opened her palm, I felt my knees give in. Filling almost her entire hand was a flat stone.

"Where did you get that?" I picked it up with my fingers, certain that it was the same stone I'd given Nick for his birthday. When I turned it over to have a closer look and saw the "N" I inscribed there, I almost fell over. It was impossible for an identical one to exist, wasn't it? Especially one that had an engraved 'N' right in the middle. This one was faded, but it was certainly the same one I'd given Nick.

"It was on the front porch. It's perfect for stone skipping isn't it? Can we go to the lake to skip it?"

Instead of answering my daughter's question, I ran to the front door, swung it open, and looked both ways down the street – no one was there, except for Mrs. Crafton, who owned the general store down the street. She was walking her Yorkie.

Mackenzie pulled on my jeans and I looked down. "What's wrong, Mamma?"

"Honey, is this one of the stones you found down by the lake?"

It was possible that Nick had used it, although I didn't know why he'd do it without me, and it had washed up on shore again.

"No, Mamma. All my good stones are under my bed. Remember, we're waiting for our tournament."

I'd promised Mackenzie we'd go stone skipping again this weekend. It was one of those things I wanted to make sure she knew how to do well, like her father.

"It wasn't there last night and then it was there this morning, like magic."

Goosebumps covered my arms and I shivered as the hairs at the back of my nape stood tall. Despite it being morning, it was already hot outside, and I couldn't shake a nagging feeling that I should be somewhere else at the moment.

"Jo? What's going on?" Carter asked.

"Nothing. At least I don't think it's anything."

"Mac, why don't you get your backpack ready for the bakery? I'm sure Grandma's in a mood for coloring today." Carter pointed to Mackenzie's crafts table.

Marge had partly retired to help me raise Mackenzie while I took care of most of the business. We also hired two bakers last year and the online expansion had made the bakeries quite profitable. While she packed a few of her trinkets, crayons, and coloring books, Carter came up to me.

"You're pale." He pulled his hand along my cheek.

"That stone Mackenzie found on the front porch." I pointed, my finger still shaking. "It's the one I gave Nick for his thirteenth birthday."

"I remember that day. He baked you a cake."

"Yes! Carter, I swear to you, it's the same one. I haven't seen it in years."

"I believe you. Do you think it's possible Mackenzie found it at Marge's house? Maybe Nick hid it somewhere in his room and she got it?"

"It's possible. But why would she say she found it on the porch?"

"I don't know. Kids like to make up stories sometimes, or they just get confused."

"You're right. She must have found it in his room. It's the only reasonable explanation."

"Come here. Have a seat for a moment." He pulled out a chair and I sat down.

"I just wish there was a day that something didn't remind me of him, you know. I thought time heals all wounds and crap, and sometimes it just feels like it's getting harder and harder."

I knew that not being reminded of Nick was impossible. Even if it were, I would never want to forget him, but I did wish that it were easier. Besides, despite being a mini me, Mackenzie was a constant reminder of her father.

"You're doing much better than before, Cupcake. I know it's not easy, Jo, but you have to stay strong for Mac." We both looked at my daughter, who was zipping up her backpack. "Look how organized she is. Just like her mommy."

She was the heart of everything I did. She was the reason that I was still alive, because if it weren't for her and for Carter, I would have been gone the moment I opened that door when the officer came with the news of Nick's death.

"You're right. She must have found it in his room."

"You better get going if you're gonna make it on time." He looked at his watch.

"Thank you for the coffee, and for breakfast."

"Which you didn't touch."

"Coffee is my breakfast" I said with a wink. "See you soon."

He took Mackenzie in his arms and carried her to my car while teasing her about there being more sharks in the pool. She giggled, because it was a game they'd been playing ever since she first jumped into that pool. I loved the bond between them.

When I pulled up to the bakery, a familiar aroma of pastries and fresh breads filled the air. A swirl of emotions from the past lingered with the scent — it always would. I opened Mackenzie's door, and she ran to her waiting grandfather.

"Good morning, munchkin. What did you bring for me today?"

"A rock."

"A rock? Well, then it must be special."

"It has the letter N on it. Daddy's name was Nick. The rock is special."

My father looked from his granddaughter to me and then back to her.

"What is she talking about?" Marge asked.

"Has Mackenzie been to Nick's room recently? Because she found his stone. The one I gave him for his birthday."

"No, not recently. But she does like to stay there sometimes and just flip through her coloring books."

"Grandpa, when am I going to be bigger than a munchkin?"

"You don't like being a munchkin?"

"I want to be big like Mommy, so I can make big cakes."

"Well, we make big cakes now. You help all the time."

"But I want to reach the table on my own, not on a chair."

"Well then, did you have a good big breakfast? I mean, a huge breakfast?" he asked with mischief.

"I did. I did." Mackenzie was excited as if she were going to immediately grow like Alice in Wonderland from having eaten a magical cake. My daughter had always been on the petite side, like me, but I knew she'd hit a growth spurt sooner or later.

A gust of wind blew by, and I sighed with relief.

"Are you okay?" Marge asked, as she flipped the open sign on the front door of the bakery.

"I think this heat is getting to me." I wiped my sweaty forehead as a rumble echoed from the back of the house. "What's going on at the old barn?"

"I think it's being painted." She leaned over the porch and followed my eyes. "Someone's been busy there for a while. We've been hearing a table saw and hammering for a few weeks now."

"Who's doing it?"

"I don't know, sweetheart."

Well, that was odd. The place had been abandoned ever since I was a little girl. It hadn't occurred to me that anyone would touch it, because secretly, I'd had faith that one day that barn would become my house. I didn't know how I'd manage it, but when I thought about a future, that's where I pictured myself with Mackenzie. Now all of a sudden someone was painting my barn? And why did I just say *my*? It might have been a dream at one point, but not anymore.

"Did someone buy it?"

"Looks that way to me."

That made me sad. Having the barn there, just waiting through time, had always given me a sense of hope, albeit a false one. I held on to that weird dream of me and Nick living there one day, decorating the inside the way he'd described on the day he proposed to me, watching our kids run through the corn fields, maybe even splashing in a sprinkler on the front lawn. But now someone else would live there? How did no one in town know about this? Keeping the secret of a new neighbor in a small town definitely took some skill.

"Why is this making you upset, honey?"

"It's where Nick proposed." I sighed. "He said when he came back from the military, we'd buy it and fix it up. I don't know why it's making me so emotional. It's stupid. The day has barely begun, and it's already been weird."

"Weird in what way?"

"Well, first the stone and now this." I pointed to the barn, still perplexed. "It just feels like wherever I turn, I'm reminded of him. It still hurts."

"Honey, there's nothing wrong with remembering him. In fact, it's wonderful. He lived here his entire life, and you've known him since... well, forever. I'm not surprised you're reminded of him so much."

"I know... and I'm usually fine with all the memories and little reminders. But today's different. I don't know why."

"Come inside. Have you had breakfast yet?"

"Carter made Mickey Mouse pancakes this morning."

I, of course, hadn't gotten a chance to sit down and eat, because I'd been running unusually late, and my appetite wasn't ready to wake up. But I didn't want to worry Marge, so I didn't tell her that I was functioning only on a cup of coffee.

"Good. Let's get Mackenzie settled. Maybe you'll feel better in the kitchen."

Baking always picked up my mood. Yet today, the frosting didn't want to stick, the batter came out too runny, and I burnt the first cake I put in the oven.

Lunchtime came and went, and that nagging feeling didn't ease. I tried to concentrate on work, but I couldn't. Each time the front bell rang, distracting me, my head flew up, and I didn't know why. I kept peeking through the back window to check on the painting progress of that barn in the back, but I couldn't see well that far in the distance. Usually, I kept to myself in the back: decorating, mixing, blending, and checking new orders, but today there was something odd in the air. I could almost taste that something wasn't right.

At two o'clock, I removed my apron, had a sip of water, took two boxes of fresh cupcakes and muffins, and headed for the barn. My knees shook underneath me as I steadied my breathing. It had been almost five years since I'd last set foot inside that barn, and the memories flooding my mind were reviving a grief I'd stashed deep in my heart. When I approached the barn, I waved to the men painting its roof. "I've brought some cupcakes, gentlemen."

I didn't recognize any of them, which somewhat confirmed that feeling of weirdness I'd had in my chest that morning. New people in town no one had mentioned were definitely a good enough reason to raise a brow.

I set one box on a round wooden pillar in hope that our new neighbor would appreciate my small gift of welcome. I wondered what he was doing to the inside of that barn, and about his intentions in our town.

Where's the door? I remembered a sliding barn door on this side. I looked at its remembered spot, where a new stone chimney rose in its place, well above the roof. I paced around the corner to where the real front door, with an enclosed glass porch, had been added. I wouldn't have thought glass would match this wooden structure, but in this case, it did.

Fresh roses bloomed all around the front yard and the smell of brand new grass lingered in the air. Whoever had done the landscaping here must have just finished. Four sprinklers were spraying water in a circular motion, one of them right up to the front door. I timed my steps and hurried by just as the water passed the front steps. I knocked on the glass, looking back as the water made its clockwise run. It was almost at the halfway point when I knocked the second time, harder.

No one answered. As the nozzle neared in my direction, I had two options: either run away or step inside. I touched the handle and decided it would be safer to be on the other side of the glass. Thankfully, the door wasn't locked. I turned around to look back at the water streaming down the front glass door, satisfied with my swift escape. When I turned around again to knock on the actual wooden barn door, I bumped into a hard chest.

The smell of him hit me first, confusing me. It triggered a flood of emotions before I even lifted my gaze to meet his. Recognition dawned in slow motion, and I fainted.

CHAPTER 26

My head hurt. I was back in that dream, in the trenches. But instead of it being a war, the trenches were in a dark forest, and a bear was chasing me. I could see its teeth each time I turned, hear its loud growl behind me, and smell the stench of wet fur. And then it was all quiet. I stopped and warily turned around. Nick stood a couple of feet away, holding my hand.

"Nick?" I looked up but met Carter's loving gaze instead.

Is this a dream?

"Hey there, Cupcake. Are you okay?"

"Yeah, I think so."

I shut my eyes closed, desperate to collect my thoughts.

"Carter, I saw him. I saw Nick."

This couldn't have been a dream, could it?

"I know."

"What?"

"I said I know."

I hadn't gone mad? Nick was actually alive? So why wasn't Carter excited? Where was Nick? I sat up and tried to clear my head. My heart was begging to be ripped out of its cage in my chest so it could leap closer to wherever Nick was.

"It's true then? It wasn't just my mind?"

"You fainted, and he called me. At first I thought it was a prank call, but it wasn't. It's true. Nick is alive. You fainted when you saw him, and you've been falling in and out of consciousness." I reached down, wrung some water out of a cloth, and pressed it to my head. Faint memories of Nick holding it over my forehead drifted back, the searing touch of his fingers on my skin generating new heat in the spots I thought he had touched me. I wanted to feel that euphoric again. I wanted to forget the past five years and be back in his arms.

"Where is he?" I tried to sit up, but still felt too dizzy.

"Take it easy, Jo. He's by the garage. Mackenzie's still at the bakery."

My daughter's name singlehandedly brought me back to reality.

"I told Marge you weren't feeling well and that I took you home."

Home.

That's when I noticed that I was lying on a cushioned seat outside. I didn't recognize this furniture, nor the fire pit nearby. "We're still by the barn, Jo."

"Barn?"

"You came here with cupcakes."

That sounded familiar, but concentrating when I knew Nick was somewhere nearby was impossible.

"Have you eaten anything since your coffee?"

I shook my head.

"Here," he said, and passed me one of my funfetti cupcakes that I'd left for the workers. I mean, what better a way to welcome someone to town than with funfetti? I took a bite and my memories began to rush back again.

"Oh, my God. He's actually here? Alive?" My chest was rising and falling more rapidly.

The man I had mourned for the past four years had reappeared out of thin air. The only man I ever truly gave my heart to and the father of my child. How was this possible?

"Did he see her?"

"No. I don't know how much he knows."

I tried to stand, but my legs gave way. "Slow down, Jo. This is a lot to take in. I'm not gonna let you get up until I know that you won't fall back down. Okay? Eat and drink first."

"Okay."

I took the delicious cupcake and ate it slowly, drinking the water from the glass Carter was holding. I was glad that he was holding it, because my hands were trembling. Once the cupcake was gone, I wiped the sweat off my forehead.

"I think I'm okay now. Where is he?"

I slowly sat up, careful not to rush. Or maybe it was just the fear cruising through my veins. I'd never been this afraid in my life, and I wasn't sure why.

"I'll walk with you, then let you two be."

You two. I repeated in my mind. Even that sounded unreal. Nick, in the same room with me again.

"Thank you. Will you stay close?"

"Of course, Cupcake. I'll be here until you need me."

Carter took me under his arm and led me to a frosted glass door in the barn. It slid open as soon as we approached.

"Let me know if you need anything," Carter repeated, worry shadowing his face.

What I really needed right now was for the clock to turn back time. I'd forbid Nick to leave; I'd cuff him down and never let him go. So much time has passed and so much had happened. I opened the door and inhaled deeply. That familiar scent filled me right down to my toes, reviving a plethora of feelings. Joy, fear, anticipation, anger, trust, desire, love – there were so many, I felt lightheaded from their onslaught before I even stepped inside that barn. Desperate for confidence, I took in another deep breath of air, but it didn't do much to steady the nerves. Whom was I kidding? No matter what I did, I was sure that nothing would prepare me to see the man I'd been in love with my entire life, who had been dead to me for almost four long years.

"I will." Carter kissed my forehead and left.

My legs felt like one of the pool noodles Mackenzie liked to use to float around with. I finally crossed the threshold and saw him. My heart leapt. My hands tingled and the cupcake I'd eaten earlier swirled in my stomach. I slowly lifted my gaze, scanning him from the bottom up, appreciating the parts of him that were familiar and intrigued by the new man he had become. He looked different and yet the same. Nick had grown a lumberjack beard and a few extra muscles that would have ripped the shirt and jeans he'd worn when he left home. His hair was overgrown, even longer than when we were teenagers. He snapped the band around his wrist and pulled it all together at the back, into a bun, and I almost drooled. I looked him over once more, acutely aware of the strength behind this new body, both physical and emotional. The definition of his muscles... holy crap. The man standing in front of me had morphed into a head-turning Adonis. He ran his fingers over the beard and took a step closer.

"I'm sorry. I would have shaved if I'd known I'd be running into you."

If he'd known? What did he mean by that? Apprehensive, I crossed my arms over my chest. I didn't trust my hands not to fly right to his chest to feel him. Was this still the same man I loved?

"Jo..." He took another step toward me.

I lifted my hand, palm flat out toward him. "Stop. Don't come any closer. I'm not sure I can take that just yet."

"Okay." He backed up to the spot he was standing in before, by the kitchen counter. That's when the interior finally caught my eye. It was everything Nick had described to me the night he proposed, but I'd never imagined it this beautiful and perfect. He shifted, drawing my gaze back to him.

I took a deep breath in. "How are you alive?"

"I didn't know I was dead."

"What?"

"They made a mistake."

"That's one big mistake, Nick. What happened?" My voice was trembling and I was an inch away from breaking down right there. Nick went to the fridge and took out a bottled water. He set it down on the wooden counter, which was coated with something to make it smooth, and motioned toward it for me to have a drink. I needed a drink, but definitely not water.

"Do you have something stronger?"

His brow rose, but he didn't question my request, and instead reached underneath the counter and poured what looked like bourbon into a glass and then reached for a can of ginger ale.

"Just the ice is fine."

I got another glance at the gorgeous countertop. It was a tree plank, crafted from the middle of what I assumed had been a ginormous tree, with all the rings stretching its length, knots and imperfections adding to the natural look. I turned in a circle, once, then again halfway, mesmerized by the interior; or maybe I was afraid to look at Nick again because my body wanted to run to him to be held by those arms. Just one touch — that's all I craved, to keep me going for the next part of my life. I took a swig of the alcohol and closed my eyes. It flowed through my veins, instantly warming me as well as making my head spin a little. I felt something behind me and jolted up.

"It's just a chair, Jo. You should have a seat."

I nodded, and given that my knees were still shaking, I lowered myself into the chair.

"There was another guy with the same last name in our troop. His first name was Nelson. The papers... they messed them up. They saw N. Tuscan and they got the wrong guy. I never knew you were told that I died. Not until I came back and figured out that things had changed."

"That doesn't make any sense. You were supposed to be gone for two years only. If you were alive, which you obviously were, why didn't you come back when you were supposed to? I wrote letters. So many letters..." I shook my head.

"I had to finish the fight that Nelson began. He saved my life and lost his. There was no time to explain and the decision was quick. It meant another three years of deployment. I wrote you a letter before I was shipped off and gave it to one of my Fleet Commanders. I'd spend the next two years deployed on a submarine. I thought you'd know."

"I never got any letters."

"I figured that when I saw you kneeling by my headstone at the cemetery. I later found out that my Fleet Commander suffered a heart attack just after we were deployed, so I don't think he ever got a chance to send it."

I took another swift sip, feeling the burn in my throat flow into my stomach.

"How long have you been back, Nick?"

"Since January."

"Six months?" I wanted to punch him in his arm –
actually anywhere – but touching him would have been too
painful. "You've been back for six months, and you didn't
bother telling us that you were alive? Jesus, what were you
thinking?"

"I saw you and Carter on New Year's Eve. I wanted to
surprise you, and then I saw you dancing in his arms, and I
really thought that death would have been better for me."

"Nick! You... you... I don't even know what to say." I
was so mad at him that I could feel the rage burning right
out of my eyes. So much had happened. My life had been
flipped upside down since our last goodbye, and I'd thought
I was beginning to grasp my life without Nick, living with
my best friend, Carter. Carter, who'd helped me through
one of the darkest moments of my life, who was there for
me when Mackenzie was born, and when I got the news
about Nick's death. Carter, who had always been there for
me. But Nick wasn't dead. He was back. He was actually
back.

"Do our parents know you're alive?"

"No."

"Well, good luck with that. You may need that
headstone after all."

I was feeling the alcohol ease my anxiety. It was exactly
what I needed.

"I see you haven't lost your sense of humor."

"I'm just not sure what to say or do."

"I love you, Joelle. I never stopped loving you."

"Nick, I never stopped loving you either, but you've been dead to me for over three years now and out of my life for five. I never thought I'd see you again. I still can't believe this isn't some sort of a dream where I'll wake up and you'll be gone."

His face twisted in pain.

"I know it doesn't sound right, but that's the reality I've been living. I had to keep going for my family. I... I didn't know you were out there. My feelings are all jumbled up, and I need time to process this."

I lowered my head to my knees, feeling my pulse rushing too quickly through my veins, then looked up at him again. He pulled another chair and sat across from me, about three feet away. Even from this distance, I could feel the energy buzzing between us.

"I'm back now, and if there's even an ounce of a chance that you'll have me in your life, then I'll take it. I know it's confusing right now, and I know you're with Carter. But I want you to know that I will do everything in my power to prove to you how much I love you. I'm a stupid man who left the only woman he ever loved and who is ready to beg for her forgiveness for the rest of his life. And no matter how much I beg, I know that I don't deserve it. I won't ever deserve you and your love, but I won't stop trying."

He thought I was with Carter? I shook my head, trying to make sense of everything, but I didn't correct him. There was too much going on at this moment. Nick was close enough to me now that I could smell him. The masculine scent I remembered was still intoxicating, even more so than the drink I was holding in my hand.

"It's just... I'm confused. So much has happened." I looked around the renovated barn and tears started falling down my cheeks. This was supposed to be our home, our forever after. We were supposed to get married and live here, and raise our children close to our family.

Mackenzie. Did he know about her? Would he be shocked? Would it change our relationship? I wasn't ready to bring my daughter – our daughter – into this mess of a life I couldn't even understand. I didn't want to confuse her. She'd seen his pictures and photographs, but most of them were from our teenage years, and Nick was a man now.

I knew that it was wrong to keep Mackenzie away from her father. But I was so mad at him, first for leaving us, then for being dead when he wasn't. How was I supposed to tell her that her dead father, whom she knew only as a headstone and a few photographs, was alive? I couldn't. Not yet — at least, not until I was sure that he would be back in our lives permanently. What if this was just another month in town for him? What if he was going to leave tomorrow and was here to tell me his last goodbye because the navy had changed their mind again? I felt a lump form in my throat. I'd never forgive him if he did that.

"Will you be deployed again?"

"No. Agreeing to the last deployment meant that I could return home and work online as a consultant to the navy. I'll go away for a week every few months, but then I'll be home. My plan was to come back, marry you, renovate this place, and have our happily ever after, Jo. Instead, I found you'd moved on."

Moved on? How? He must have been thinking about Carter. Would he really remain in Hope Bay forever? Was this permanent? And if so, how could I live so close to him and have all these feelings bubbling inside of me all the time? Now that Nick was back, he'd fill every second of my spare time, as well as the busy time. How could I stop thinking about him? I never could and never would. The pearl drops of my tears fell to my lap and I wiped them with the back of my hand.

"I'm... It's too much right now."

"I understand, Jo. I won't push you or hurt you ever again, but I also won't stop fighting for you."

"I need time to process this. Is this where you're living now?"

"Yes. The barn is yours and mine."

I felt my brows scrunch together. "Nick, you can't be saying things like that to me. So much has happened. I..."

By now I was sobbing. It was so hard to hear this, to hear him, to see him. And then he touched me, wiping the tear away with his thumb. I jerked back and brought my hand to the searing imprint of his thumb on my skin as my memory flashed back in time to all the times he'd touched me, held me, and loved me.

"Don't cry, Jo. Please."

"I... I can't help it." I wiped my nose with my sleeve. "I don't know what to think."

"I'm almost done with the renovations. I should probably visit Mom before the end of the day and explain things. I've had some time to think about you and me and what a fool I've been. I'm afraid I made the biggest mistake of my life when I left. And I'm even more afraid that there's no chance of fixing it. Tell me there's no chance, Jo. Tell me and I'll turn around and leave and you'll never see me again. But if there's a sliver of hope I can hold onto, then I will until the day I die."

I didn't say anything. I couldn't. I didn't want him to leave, for our daughter's sake, but I needed time to figure things out. If I'd thought that my life was complicated before, then right now it was in the middle of a full out nuclear war.

He smiled at my silence.

"The stone on my porch. That was you, wasn't it?"

"Yes. I saw you with your daughter by the lake. You were teaching her how to skip stones. I just thought she could use that perfect one you gave to me."

"You've seen us?"

"Yes, by accident. I went to Pebble Beach to clear my head, and you two were there. So I stayed hidden. I needed to figure out how to break the news of my mortality to you."

"Her name is Mackenzie."

"She's beautiful, just like her mother. She's got your nose, hair, and eyes. And freckles. She has your freckles as well."

I smiled. While Nick may have seen me in her, I saw him. Her gestures, words, and abilities were all inherited from him.

"I thought I was going crazy when she brought the stone. I thought she'd found it back at the house."

"I'm sorry, Jo. I'm so sorry."

An uncomfortable silence buzzed between us, or maybe it was something else. I looked up, connecting our gazes. My tears were falling, but I couldn't stop staring at the man I'd thought was gone.

"I should go home. This is... no, I'm sorry." I stood up, set the empty bourbon glass aside, and headed for the door. A gentle touch on my hand when I reached for the handle startled me. Heat snaked its way up my arm and through my body, reviving a long forgotten need for a man I loved, forcing my heart on a new stampede and my mind to travel back in time, to when we were still together and life seemed uncomplicated.

I can't do this.

"Please, forgive me."

I exhaled. Forgive him for what? Miscommunication? The awful way in which Fate had torn us apart? The only forgiveness I could give was for his first decision to leave, and I'd made peace with that a long time ago.

"I'm at the bakery every day."

"I know."

He knew. Of course he knew. He'd known all about my life for the past six months when I thought he was six feet under. Well, technically I'd known he wasn't there, because we never got a body back, but that's where I'd thought him to be, at peace. I turned around before I left and looked at him once again.

"You need to tell your mother what happened. Do it before tomorrow because I won't be able to keep this secret even for a second."

"I will, I p—"

"Don't promise. Please don't promise."

That may have been a direct stab to the heart, but how could I believe another one of his promises? The last one he'd made, to come back safely after two years, he broke. Still, deep inside, I knew that he meant it. It wasn't his fault that he couldn't fulfill it.

I gave him a weak smile and left. I didn't even turn around to see whether he closed the door behind me, because I knew that he didn't. He was watching me, the heat of his stare burning into my skin. I was afraid that if I turned, I'd run back into his arms and never let go. But I had others to think about: Mackenzie and Carter. They both deserved an explanation, except that I didn't know what the right explanation was.

Carter drove us home in silence. When I finally closed the door, blocking out the world, I leaned my back against it and slowly lowered my body to the ground, sobbing.

"Shh, it's okay, Jo. Everything's going to be okay."

"How can you be so sure?"

"I don't know; but I do know that whatever happens, you'll have my full support."

Was he saying what I thought he was saying? That I was free to make a decision, any decision, and he wouldn't object? He wouldn't fight for me? Did I want him to? I sort of did, even though we were only best friends.

"I'm so confused."

"I know, Cupcake. I know. But we'll figure it out. You have a beautiful girl, a successful business, and a best friend that will forever have your back."

"Thank you, Carter. For everything."

As I sat there, I thought how difficult it had been to come to terms with Nick's death, and wondered whether it'd be even harder to accept his new life.

CHAPTER 27

That afternoon, as Mackenzie frolicked in the pool with Carter, feeling a need for normalcy, or maybe to clear my head, I took my purse and walked to the grocery store. The shock of seeing Nick a few hours ago was still messing with me. I felt like I'd stepped out of a dream. Believing that he was alive would definitely take more convincing. At one point, I wanted to run back to that barn, throw my arms around his neck, and never let him go. A memory of that gentle touch of his fingers rushed through me, setting the hairs on my arms on full alert.

As I approached Mrs. Crafton's store, I stopped and held my breath. There he was, in the middle of our street, loading up his truck with evergreens from the nursery by the general store. I sucked air in through my nose and, feeling anger burst, I marched over to him, pushing him on the arm.

"What the hell are you doing here?" I pushed him to the side where the truck would cover him somewhat. I didn't mean to be so rough; but then again, maybe it was just an excuse to touch him to make sure he was real.

"Jo, I'm just getting a few supplies."

I looked back to the store and grabbed his thick arm, pulling him out of direct view, yearning for that slight touch again. It would take a long time to convince me that he was real, and I wanted as much convincing as possible.

"What if someone recognized you? Have you told your mother?"

I finally let go of him. He scratched his long beard with his hand. His hair was still up in a bun.

"Not yet."

"Do you know what would happen if she ran into you?"

I was close enough to smell him, and my head thrummed when his scent infiltrated my lungs, sending memories of the past deep into my lungs with one inhale. It was an intoxicating blend of the man I used to know and someone new - someone adventurous and exciting. I got a tightening feeling in my chest and my stomach tingled in a funny way.

"Jo, I doubt she'd recognize me with this beard and hair."

Concentrating with him so close to me, the heat of him enveloping my body, was difficult, but I shook it off.

"Any mother would recognize her child, no matter how many years have passed. Trust me."

"I guess you should know. Ahm, congratulations."

"For what?"

"Your daughter. She's beautiful. Old Mr. Grafton's house looks good too."

He wasn't saying what we were both thinking, except he was wrong. I could see the assumption of me living with Carter swirl in his mind, and I thought about correcting him, but I couldn't. It would take a long time to explain everything that had happened, and I wanted to – just under different circumstances. This was the first time I truly felt guilty for not telling him the truth as soon as I found out that he was alive. But how could I have? I was in shock. And now, well, I just had to find the right time.

"Listen, Nick. After you talk to your mom, we should probably talk as well."

"I was hoping you'd say that."

"Pebble Beach. Meet me there tomorrow afternoon, but only after you speak with your mom."

"I promise to be there, Jo."

"Good, okay then. Bye." I twirled on my foot and left the captivating aura of his aroma behind.

It was still with me when I returned home. Carter was sitting on the couch, watching the news. A long drought had sparked fires in the north. Many firefighters from larger cities were called out to assist, and Carter was getting antsy, waiting for his opportunity to help. Captain Clark said they had to remain in Hope Bay, because let's face it, we only had one firehouse. Come to think of it, I didn't remember the last time it had rained in Hope Bay.

"Hey, how did shopping go?" Carter asked.

"Shopping?"

Oh, my God! I totally forgot about shopping after I ran into Nick, and I knew that Carter could see it all over my face. I looked around the room for Mackenzie, careful not to bring up her father's return in front of her before I figured out how to tell her the truth.

"I ran into him by the store," I started. "And then I sort of forgot about the groceries." I felt my cheeks heat with the foolishness of the situation. What was coming over me?

"You'll figure it all out, Jo. You know, I've never seen love as strong as the one the two of you have."

"Have?"

"I wouldn't expect you not to love Nick, just like I know I would love Daisy if she came back."

"Carter, I'm so sorry. I know it must feel unfair."

"Don't be sorry. Be grateful because Mackenzie will get to know her father."

"What would you do if you were me? I'm so confused."

He sighed and finally looked up from the floor to meet my gaze. "Jo, I know you still love him, and he obviously loves you. It will take time, but you gotta give him a chance. My only worry is that... well, what if he decides he wants another adventure? What if they call on him again? And he may *say* they won't, but how do you know that? Imagine telling that little girl upstairs that the father she thought was dead her entire life and just met has to go away again, and you can't tell her if or when he'll come back. Can you picture Mackenzie opening that front door to receive the flag?"

My heart almost stopped. He was right. How could I have let my heart be fluttering with possibilities of a reunion when there was way more to consider? This wouldn't be an easy decision, no matter how much I loved Nick.

"I just don't want to see you hurt again," he added.

I sat on the couch beside Carter, hugging him. "I couldn't have gone through the past five years without you. You mean so much to Mackenzie and me. I know we're just friends, but I do love you, Carter—"

"I love you too, Cupcake, but I also know that you love Nick. You never stopped loving him, and I would never expect you to. Whatever happens, know that I'll still be here. After all, I am an uncle." He grinned. "And you were there for me too. If it weren't for you, I'm pretty sure I couldn't have pulled through after Daisy died. No one's pressuring you to do anything. I'm a grown man. I will support any decision you make, but whatever that is, I promise that I will not let you out of my life."

I threw my arms around his neck again, squeezing harder. How did he always know the right thing to say?

"Take your time, Jo, with whatever it is that you need to work out. Also, you should tell him about Mac."

"I know. I told him to meet me at Pebble Beach tomorrow after work."

"That's good. And Jo, I know he's my best friend, your first love, and Mac's father, but that won't stop me from protecting the two of you."

"I wouldn't expect anything less, Carter."

"Good. Now, what do you say we watch a movie?" He flicked the channel before I got a chance to answer him. It was a comedy, or maybe a superhero movie. I don't quite remember, because all I could think about was the new man in town who had never left my heart.

* * *

The next morning, when I stepped into the bakery, I could tell the atmosphere had shifted. As soon as I laid my eyes on Marge, I knew that she knew. I ran to her, hugging her tightly.

"I found out yesterday," I said.

"He came last night," Marge confirmed. "I wanted him to stay, but he wouldn't. He lives there now." She pointed to the back of the bakery. Even though there was a wall there, I knew she meant the barn Nick had renovated beyond the field.

"I can't believe this is actually happening." I felt Marge's tears on my shoulder.

"And I can't believe he's been so close for six months and didn't say anything."

My father came up from behind, smoothing his hand over Marge's shoulder, while using his other hand to pull a stool closer to her. She sat down and I joined her. "Nick is a good man. The situation is complicated for everyone, but I'm certain Nick would have never hurt you, or hurt any of us, intentionally."

"He thinks I'm with Carter, and I'm pretty sure he thinks that Mackenzie is Carter's."

Thank God my daughter had stayed at home with Carter. I couldn't have had this conversation in front of her.

"What if he leaves us again? I'm not going to put Mackenzie through potentially losing her father. I don't know what to do."

"One way or another, he has the right to know," my father said.

"I know, I know." I lowered my head into my hands, shaking it. I should have been happy, but instead, I was so terrified of losing him again, I wasn't willing to even try to reconcile. I didn't want to give him another chance because if I did, I'd hang on to it like it was the only lifeline I had left.

"Joelle, honey. Do you love him?" Marge smoothed her hand over my cheek.

"Of course I do. I never stopped loving him. I'll love him for the rest of my life."

She smiled at my answer before exhaling. Was she hoping for that answer? As a mother, I knew she'd always hoped that her son would have a complete family. It seemed like we had all the ingredients: hope, fear, will, love; all that was missing was a guaranteed future of Nick staying in town.

But I did trust Nick. On some level, I always had. He would never have hurt us on purpose. He would have been here after those first two years, if he could.

"Then talk to him. Jo, this could be the chance you've been praying for."

I'd wished for Nick's return on every falling star I saw, even when I thought he was gone. Marge's words... *a chance...* they stuck with me until it was time to meet Nick at the beach.

* * *

I was sitting on Pebble Beach watching Mackenzie skip stones when I heard his footsteps crunch behind me. I didn't have to turn to know it was him; I felt him before the first sound of rolling pebbles reached me. He sat down beside me. While I wished he wasn't this close to me, because it was difficult to think, I was grateful that he was. It only confirmed that this wasn't a dream.

"I saw Carter by the car," he said.

"Yeah, he's pretty protective. He thinks you'll leave again."

"I won't."

"You've said that before."

"This time I won't."

My heart raced. I tried to steady my breath, but inhaling him was a mistake. Instead, I tried to focus on what mattered: Mackenzie. As if reading my thoughts, he said, "She's good at skipping stones. Just like her mother."

"We've been coming here since she was born. It's peaceful, and it reminded me of you. I always thought this was our special place."

"I remember every minute. And it was a special place to me as well."

Mackenzie kept busy searching for flat stones, picking and choosing between them. She'd kept Nick's in her pocket ever since she found it on the porch.

"How old is she?" Nick asked.

"Five. She was born nine months after you left."

I turned to the side and watched his face react in slow motion as he probably double-checked the math in his mind. The truth was slowly seeping into his mind. He blinked once, then again, slightly shaking his head.

"Wait, I thought she was Carter's."

"She does look a little young for her age." I shrugged.

I heard him swallow through his throat.

"Dammit, Jo, are you telling me that this beautiful" – His voice broke in between the words, as emotions rolled over him – "this beautiful girl is my daughter?"

"Yes, Nick. She's yours and mine."

"How? I mean, I know how... is this really true?" He wiped away the first few tears that fell down his cheeks. I never thought I'd see Nick cry.

"I wouldn't lie about something like this, but I'm afraid to tell her about you. She's only known you from a few graduation pictures, and if you leave—"

"— not in this lifetime, Jo. Not ever," he whispered. "I won't ever abandon you again. Either one of you."

Unfortunately the emotional trauma of losing Nick forced me to keep my guard up. I wouldn't allow Mackenzie to go through that pain.

"You didn't abandon me. You didn't know. Nick, I want her to know you, but I'm not sure how to do it. I don't know how to tell her that the father she thought was dead is here. I don't know how to protect her if you—"

"—I won't leave," he repeated.

As if sensing me, Mackenzie turned around. She leaned her head to the side a little, taking in the scene of Nick and me sitting together. There was a moment of recognition on her face, but it passed — or at least I thought it did. She let go of the stones she'd been holding in her tiny fist. They tumbled to the ground and she ran toward me, nearly tripping. I shot to my feet and moved toward her as fast as I could, stopping her. I crouched down to the ground before she got too close and recognized him on her own, although with that beard, I doubted she could.

"Are you done stone skipping?"

"Mommy, who is that?" she whispered, looking over my shoulder, captivated by Nick and completely ignoring my question.

"Why don't you come over and say hello?"

She took my hand and, hiding halfway behind my body, walked with me toward him. Nick didn't get up, which was probably better because his sheer size could have scared her. He was a stranger to Mackenzie, and strangers weren't frequent in Hope Bay.

What if his beard scares her?

"Hi Mackenzie," he said.

"Hi." She stepped out from behind me a little.

"You're good at stone skipping."

"Mommy's better. And my daddy was even better than her. Mommy says I've got his strong arm. Are you from Hope Bay?"

"Yes."

"Why didn't I see you here before?"

"I've been away for a while and just moved back."

"Are you my daddy?"

What?!

I looked to Nick, then back to Mackenzie. Nick's gaze connected with mine, his eyes searching mine for the answer he should give her, but he didn't even have to. She threw her tiny hands around his neck before either one of us confirmed speculation. "I knew it! I knew you'd be back because I told Tank a secret and he mooed and I knew he told me you'd be back because I wished on every single falling star my whole entire life that you'd come and you did, Daddy!"

My heart split open when I heard her call Nick *Daddy*.

She was squeezing him so tightly, I thought he'd choke. And Nick, well, now he was crying like a baby and so was I. He was actually sobbing. When Mackenzie let him go, she asked, "Why are you crying?"

"These are happy tears, baby. I'm happy that I get to finally meet you."

She grasped his face between her small hands, then closed in and kissed him on his forehead. "I'm happy that I get to meet you too, but you look like a bushman." She lowered her hands and tugged on his beard, then looked behind Nick and screamed, "Uncle Carter, Daddy's here!"

She pulled out of Nick's embrace and ran to Carter, jumping up into his arms.

I saw a pinch of guilt and jealousy run over Nick's face.

"It will take time for her to adjust to the idea of another man in her life," I said, secretly wondering whether I was talking about Mackenzie or myself.

"Will you allow me to spend time with her?"

"Of course. She's your daughter."

"My daughter..." Nick appeared dazed, as fatherhood was beginning to hit him. Carter set Mackenzie down, but she held on to his hand.

"I'm sorry. I didn't mean to interrupt, but Mackenzie's bedtime is soon."

"Uncle Carter?"

"I earned that title when I delivered her," Carter said with pride, catching Nick off guard. The moment only confirmed to me how much Nick had missed, and I wondered whether we could truly catch up on the past five years of our lives. The sun dipped beyond the horizon and I got up off the ground.

"We should go," I said.

"Will Daddy come?" she asked.

"Not today sweetheart, but soon. Maybe Sunday?"

"I love Sundays. Daddy, will you come to our family dinner?"

Nick looked from me to Carter, then back to me, a little confused as to what the appropriate answer should be. Since Mackenzie had taken to him so quickly, I nodded gently. After all, I wanted Nick in her life, didn't I?

"I would love to."

"This will be the best dinner ever. Uncle Carter, we have to barbecue. But no Tank meat."

"She means no beef," I whispered to Nick. "Mackenzie says it hurts Betsy's and Tank's feelings."

"Anything you wish," Carter replied.

That was how easily Mackenzie warmed up to Nick. To her, it was as if he had always been part of her life. Never gone and never forgotten. Could I make that leap as easily as she had? I wanted to – I really wanted to – but five years was a long time for relationship dynamics to shift, and my biggest fear was that ours had changed forever.

"Do you girls mind if I have a word with Nick?" Carter asked.

I stepped back, a little surprised at Carter's tone, but nodded and took Mackenzie back to the car. She showed me the new stones she'd collected, but when I heard Carter and Nick's voices rise, I asked her to wait for me and went back to the beach. I could hear their argument long before they came into view.

"You don't know that, Carter. I couldn't let them think that I was dead forever."

"All I know is that we were happy. We were finally settling down and could have been a happy family. And now you're coming back and confusing them both!"

"She would never be happy with you, and you know it. No matter what may have happened between you two, she loves me. She always has and always will."

"Ha!" Carter laughed and motioned me closer when he saw me. "Come on, Jo! Tell him. Who's the first boy you ever kissed?"

Oh, my God! This wasn't really happening to me, was it? Why were they arguing now? And what kind of a question was that? They were both my firsts. Carter was a *first* first, but Nick was my first adult kiss. How was I supposed to explain to them that each one meant something different to me? Wait, why was I supposed to explain anything?

"Jo?" Nick asked, confusion shadowing his face.

"You can see it in her eyes, can't you? She could have moved on without you, and you know it."

"Stop it! Just stop it both of you!" I cried out, then pointed back to the car. "There's a little girl in that car who's hoping to have a nice dinner with her uncle and her father this weekend, and I swear that if you two can't behave like adults, there will be no dinner for anyone. Do. You. Understand?"

They each nodded.

"Shit happens in life. It doesn't matter who I kissed first, second, or third." Although there'd never been a third. "What matters is that we can figure out this second chance we've been given in a calm manner that does not scare the living crap out of me or Mackenzie."

"I'm sorry, Cupcake." Carter lowered his head. "I'm just afraid that he'll leave again. I don't want you hurting. I want you happy."

"And I love you for the way you've always cared for us both. I always will, Carter, but no matter what Nick's plans are for the future, I cannot deny Mackenzie her father." I took his hand into mine. "We'll figure it out. If there's anyone I can do this with, it's you."

Nick shifted uncomfortably from one foot to another, doubt filling his eyes. I didn't have the time or nerve to explain the inner workings of mine and Carter's relationship at this moment, and I felt bad for allowing him to think that we were together, but I saw Mackenzie approach from behind the hill.

That conversation will have to wait.

"We'll see you on Sunday?" I asked.

"Yes, I'll be there."

"Good."

As I headed toward Mackenzie and saw her wave at Nick, calling out, "Bye, Daddy," my heart skipped a beat. If there was anyone who had the right idea about reuniting, it was my little girl.

CHAPTER 28

Saturday afternoon I knocked on the wooden door to Nick's barn, thinking that I should stop referring to his house as a 'barn' in my head. It had been two days since I'd last seen him at the beach, and Mackenzie wouldn't stop talking about him. When she found out where he lived, she kept peeking into the back yard behind her grandparents' house. In fact, she packed a little suitcase with some of her clothes so that she could one day have a sleepover at Daddy's house. For me, the past two nights had been restless. I tossed and turned. My mind wandered through all the times we'd spent together. And once I was done with those, my imagination spiraled into new possibilities. My body ached for him. I craved his touch, wondering whether he'd be as gentle as he was five years ago, or maybe a little rougher. A much more intimate reunion with Nick was definitely at the forefront of my thoughts all night and all day.

Standing on the glassed in front porch, I secretly knew exactly why I came here. It was the hormones. The stupid twirling in my stomach that wouldn't stop combined with my drenched panties that I had to throw into the laundry each morning. It was the way Nick had looked at me by the general store and when I first saw him last week. That sinful new body of his drew me in as I wondered whether his skin would feel the same underneath my palms. He still made my heart go pitter-patter, forcing me to tense in the most delectable ways. My nerves trembled through my limbs as I shifted from one foot to another, wondering whether it was stupid of me to wear a matching set of undergarments. What was I thinking?

I wasn't. Today, my body was doing the thinking for me, fighting to claim what it had been denied for five long years. It didn't matter how many times I told myself that I had to take it slow. My hormones let out a mocking laugh and pushed my feet forward until I ended up here.

He opened the front door. Dressed in ripped jeans and a washed-out shirt, so unlike the Nick I knew, he leaned against the doorframe with a crooked smile on his face. The confidence in his eyes shook me awake and twirled a new wave of need through my body. Was he expecting me? There was no surprise on his face, only a spark of desire in his eyes, mixed with the look of a man who'd just gotten what he wanted.

"Hi," I said.

"Hi, I—"

"I know I should have called first, but I don't even have your phone number."

"Jo, my home is your home. Always. Come in, please." He stepped to the side, opening the door further. I brushed past him, my arm inadvertently grazing against his, and the most pleasant chills swept through my body. A flicker of impatience sparked in my chest because all my body wanted was to press against him. All I needed was to be in his arms. I wanted him to remind me what it felt like to be held, cared for, and loved.

The delicious aroma of a home-cooked meal filled the room. I looked around the pristine home, immediately welcomed by its warmth.

"I brought something." I passed him the box of letters I'd written over the past three years, and never sent, the compilation of my grief, heartache, Mackenzie's milestones, and wishes for his return that I'd made on the falling stars. The ones I'd never sent because I thought he was dead. "I thought you might want to read some of these before you come over tomorrow."

Caught off guard, he reached for the box and opened the lid. "Letters?"

What? Was he actually waiting for me to do the spread eagle for him as soon as I walked in? Yeah, it appeared that I wasn't the only one expecting more than a spark of excitement from my visit. Instead of that spark, I'd entered into an inferno of lust and desire the moment I stepped over that threshold. A bead of sweat dripped down my back.

"I wrote them after they told me you died. I didn't want to believe it. They kept me somewhat sane."

"Do you talk about Carter in these?"

"Yes."

He looked at me, confused. "Jo, I'm not sure I want to know those parts."

"What parts?"

"About you and Carter. I mean, I understand, because you thought I was dead and you have needs and Carter's a good-looking man and..."

"Whoa, hold on there. Nick, I've never... we've never... Carter's just a friend. You're the only man I've ever been with."

"What?"

"Why does that surprise you?"

"He's not with Molly."

"So? He's a good friend."

"So you two have been living in his house as friends?"

"Yes. I couldn't move on after they told me about you. Believe me, I tried, but your home reminded me of you, and I couldn't stand it. I couldn't breathe when each time I looked around, I saw a memory of you; of us. Knowing that you were gone and would never come back hurt me every minute I was there. I broke down after the first year and moved in with Carter."

"And you two have never—"

I shook my head. He breathed out in relief and rested his hands on the chair in front of him. "Thank God."

I tried to put myself in Nick's shoes, wondering how I'd feel if he moved in with another woman, even if she were my best friend. I didn't think I'd like the idea.

"Anyways, I'll leave these here for you." My voice shook. "I should go. Mackenzie's been cleaning her room for two days now, and I promised her we'd make a special cake for tomorrow."

He let go of the chair, stepped closer, and took me by my hips. The heat of his touch seared through my dress, and more beads of sweat instantly formed on my spine, slowly trickling down. I didn't expect him to be holding me for this long. I wanted him to, but I didn't think he would. Heck, I hadn't expected him to touch me like this at all. Now that he had, I couldn't pull away.

"Join me for dinner," he pleaded, his voice deeper than before and full of need; or maybe it was just me.

"They're expecting me back." That was a lie, of course. I'd already told Carter that I might be out for a while. He'd wanted to high five me, but I refused, once again denying to myself the real reason for coming over.

"Then call Carter. We have a lot to catch up on. He'll understand."

I removed my phone from my purse and texted Carter that we might need to postpone the cake baking until tomorrow morning. He replied immediately with three kiss emojis plus a thumbs up, and I turned the volume on my phone off. Knowing Carter, he'd be teasing me for the next few hours.

"You cooked?" I asked.

"Yes, I'm starving."

His tone made the goosebumps on my arms dance. I shook them off, feeling that it was too early to give my body what it wanted – and it definitely wanted it all. It wanted him like a thirsty survivor who'd crossed the Sahara.

"Have a seat, Jo. Let's talk over dinner." He pulled out a chair for me. I took my seat, feeling his gaze on me the whole time. Nick took a tray of baby baked potatoes, grilled asparagus, and chicken breast out of the oven. It looked like the food had been waiting there for this specific moment, as if he'd been expecting me to come over this evening.

"You cooked for an army."

"Well, I was hoping I'd have company over; I just didn't realize it would take you two full days to stop by." His voice was teasing and flirtatious.

"I wanted to drop by yesterday, but I didn't know if I should."

"I'm glad you're here. Wine?" he asked.

I nodded. Some alcohol right now would definitely ease my nerves. I downed half a glass in a few swift gulps and wiped my mouth with the back of my hand. Nick appeared amused.

"What?"

"I've never seen you like this."

"Like how?"

"You've always been beautiful, Jo. But now you're this breathtaking woman, and I can't keep my eyes off you. You're different."

"Don't flirt."

Despite what I said, I wanted him to, and he knew it.

"Just stating the obvious." He reached for the chicken and plated some for me, along with the veggies and potatoes. Instead of eating, I reached for my wine glass again and emptied it."

"If you don't eat, that wine will get to your head much quicker."

"I sort of want it to. It makes me think less."

It makes me want to do things I'm not sure I'm ready for. It was giving me some much-needed courage.

Desperate to not give into my needs, I asked. "Where are the sheep rugs?"

"You said you didn't think they would match."

"When we came here the first time?"

He nodded. I didn't think that he'd remember that. It was true. Everything he described that day was here, except for the rugs, and I loved it. This house was beautiful.

I finally took a forkful of veggies and looked around his beautiful home. "I can't believe you did all this."

"Not on my own."

"It's breath-taking." Exactly the way he'd described, with the deer antler chandelier and a spiral wooden staircase leading to the second level, where his bedroom must have been. The thought of his bed and Nick sleeping there, naked perhaps, made my head spin. Or maybe it was the good old wine working itself through my system.

"You're the one that's breathtaking, Jo. You always have been."

Emotions swarmed through me at his compliment. The heat from my cheeks snaked to the core of my body, and I jabbed my fork into the chicken, wanting to concentrate on something other than the desire emanating from his deep voice.

"This house will always feel empty without you. It will never be a home unless you're here; it will just be a house."

I shook my head, not wanting to say no to him, but also not wanting to lead him on. I couldn't just leave Carter's and move here. I couldn't uproot Mackenzie. The time that had passed between us forged mountains of uncertainty. And since I didn't know how to reply, I changed the topic once again.

"How did no one know you were working on this?"

"I don't need much to survive. And I made Mrs. Crafton promise when I did groceries. I cleaned up her yard in exchange and fixed the shingles on her old shed."

"Well, that was sneaky."

"You gotta do what you gotta do. The Navy compensated me for the whole *telling my family I died* mistake. They would have compensated you as well, if you were my wife."

My attention was drawn to the ringless finger on my left hand. Yeah, he might have gotten compensated, but I felt like I'd lost most of my heart the past three and a half years that I thought he was gone. My heart and my soul. If it hadn't been for Mackenzie, I wouldn't have been able to survive.

"I'm sorry. I couldn't wear it. I thought—"

"You don't have to explain yourself, Jo. I understand. You thought I was dead, and I'm sorry. I'm so sorry that you had to go through all that pain. If the situation was reversed, if it were me mourning my love, I... I couldn't have been as strong as you. If I could turn back time, I would."

Time – we had it now, but I didn't know how to use it best. I didn't know how to take down those mountains, or at least, cross them.

An awkward silence filled the room. It wasn't that I was uncomfortable, but more confused.

"Nick—"

"You're going to tell me you can't live here, and I understand. But I can't hear it now. Please don't let me hear it, because the hope that I'll one day have you back in my life is the only thing I can hang on to, no matter how impossible that sounds."

Why did he think it was impossible?

"I need time. All this just feels like a dream. A happy dream, and since I haven't had too many of those the past few years, it will take some getting used to." I smiled.

So much had happened and so much had changed. And honestly, all I wanted to do was to be held by him. I wanted that connection I knew we still had, but I didn't know how to break through that five-year wall built between us. He didn't say anything else. We both must have been lost to our thoughts, or at least I was, because the next thing I knew, dinner was done.

"Why don't you read some of those? And I'll wash the dishes." I pointed to the box of letters and pushed my chair away from the table.

"All right."

He helped me clear the table before sitting down on his sofa. I turned on the faucet and poured soap onto the sponge, keeping my mind on the task so that I wouldn't join him on the cushioned seat he sank into. There was a window by the sink, with a view of the back of our bakery and Nick's old house. I wondered how many times Nick had seen me while he worked on the barn. I wanted to know about his life in the navy, what happened when he was deployed and whether he had any regrets.

As I pulled the sponge over the plates and glasses, a feeling of calmness swept over me. This was how it would feel if we lived together; sharing dinners, talking, joking and enjoying each other's company, and then cleaning up afterwards. Mackenzie could play outside. She'd wanted a pet bunny for a while now. Here, we could have a special bunny house right by the barn. Being here felt easy — in fact, the more time I spent here, the more the barn felt like home.

I felt him behind me before he even touched me, and I froze. The water flowed from the faucet, and while I should have been washing the last plate, I couldn't. He was too close. I closed my eyes and the hum of the running water brought back memories of when we had gotten lost on the camping trip, and kissed for the first time by the river.

His front pressed against my back as his hands slid over my forearms to my palms, twining his fingers over the slick soap. The touch sent a new stampede of emotions rushing through my body. I leaned my head to the side and felt his hot breath feathering over my neck and then his lips skimmed my skin as he murmured, "God, how much I've missed you."

Nick slowly turned me around to face him. I was afraid to open my eyes and face reality. I still feared this wasn't real.

"I missed you too. You don't want to read the letters?" I asked.

"I do, but there's something else I'd much rather do than read right now." His wet hands grazed up my arms to my face. He took it between his hands, his thumb running over my bottom lip, his gaze concentrating on my mouth and mine trying to find his underneath that mustache and beard. When he kissed me, I giggled, pulling away.

"That's not the reaction I was expecting," he said against my lips.

"I'm sorry. It just tickles."

"I'll shave it right now if it means I can kiss you."

I bit my lip, wanting to jump on the offer. "Why don't you let me shave it?"

He lowered his hands and gave me a bemused smile before stepping back. When Nick went up the spiral staircase to get what I assumed was his shaving kit, I finished washing the last plate and dried my hands. By the time I'd pulled one of the chairs away from the table and brought it closer to the sink, Nick had returned.

"It hasn't been used in a while." He passed me the razor.

"I promise to be gentle. You sure you want to part with this?" I tugged at his beard playfully.

"Yeah, it looks like I may be getting a new start in life, so it only fits that I shave it."

A new start... could we, please?

"Well, I don't know about shaving. I have to cut it first."
I reached for the scissors. "Were you planning on becoming
a bear?"

"I wasn't planning. But I was hoping that maybe one
day, I could become yours again."

I gasped.

Mine?

I knew the words were difficult for Nick to say. It was
always his rooftop, his bakery, his stone skipping records,
his need to run missions for the navy, and his decisions.
And here he was, that strong man who'd completed one of
the most difficult trainings of a lifetime, who fought for our
country and freedom, offering himself to me — a simple
country girl.

I couldn't reply to him. Instead, I took the scissors and
slowly cut away at the growth on his face, careful not to
touch his skin too much because, after all, I needed to
concentrate. Once the hair was less than an inch long, I
lathered him and gently pulled the razor over the bristles.
He sat with his eyes closed, waiting for me to finish,
trusting me with the sharp blade in my hand. I took my
time, gently scraping the foam off. It was easier to be this
close to him now, and as the hair came off, I slowly started
seeing my Nick. I leaned over to the other side, felt his
breath near my chest, and I stilled. If I inched any closer,
his lips would touch my skin. I cleaned him with the kitchen
towel, and when I pulled my hand away to set it aside, he
opened his eyes and took hold of my wrist.

I stared into his eyes, captivated.

"I am not a man without you, Joelle. If you'll still have me, know that I'm yours. All I'm asking for is a chance."

I was his. I always would be. Instead of pulling away and wasting precious minutes, giving time another chance to add a new mountain, I hiked my dress just above my knees, swung one foot over his legs, and straddled him, taking his freshly shaven face between my hands.

"We have a lot to catch up on and a lot to talk about, but I do love you Nicholas. I never stopped loving you, and I never will."

That moment I'd craved for years finally came as our mouths and bodies collided. His strong arms wound around me, pulling me against him until I couldn't breathe. The air we shared was enough, though. His lips overpowered all my senses, taking me into his world. They were old yet new, soft yet demanding, warm and full of desire.

My soul must have left my body and my insides melted. The intensity of our kiss increased with each passing second, hands searching for new places to touch, bodies yearning for a greater connection and mouths performing some sort of a dance. Even if I wanted to stop, I couldn't. His hands roamed over my arms, back and forth, uncertain which part of me to grasp first, until they settled on my hips, scrunching my dress up as fresh air cooled my thighs. I reached down to his belt buckle. He shimmied out of his pants while pushing my panties to the side with his free hand. Definitely a new multitasking talent I'd just witnessed. Nick had no underwear and was ready for me. My mind flooding with new appetite, I lifted myself and slid over him, feeling my essence coat his thickness in one long slide down.

And I stilled.

I wanted to savor this moment.

The penetration was as thick and filling as I remembered, and I felt a tear sneak out of my eye, grateful that my memories hadn't faded before Nick's return. I needed to feel our connection and remember it forever, just in case this was the last time I had him. These thoughts would have never crossed my mind before. We had all the time in the world – time I hadn't fully appreciated until now.

His next kiss was gentle, and he leaned his forehead against mine. I closed my eyes and slowly began to rock my hips over him, the movement felt new and exquisite, as the momentum increased. His fingers swiftly unfastened the buttons of my dress and lowered my bra beneath my breasts, sealing my nipples with his lips.

It felt amazing to have his mouth on me and him inside me.

My need for more flourished. As if reading my mind, Nick's hold on my hips strengthened and I began riding him until I was bouncing, my ass slapping against his thighs. The only other sounds in the room were his grunts, my moans, and mutual heavy breathing. He was firm and slick, hot and thick – the perfection of a man I thought had died.

The friction increased with each pump. His thrusts became rougher, my gallop more desperate to reach the finale. He seized my mouth with passion and I trembled, the shakes of my orgasm spreading through my body as I bit his lip and felt him grunt one last time as he spilled inside me.

I was out of breath.

Nick wrapped his arms around me, tightening his hold. We sat connected until the beating of our hearts calmed and the world came back in focus.

"Now that's the welcome I was hoping for." He grinned with cockiness, and I chuckled.

"I missed you. I missed you so much."

"I'm here now, baby. And I'm never leaving again."

"I don't think I'd let you leave." I stood up slowly, feeling his seed trickle down my thighs. Nick reached for the paper towel beside the sink and wiped me clean.

"I wanted to do this somewhere else, but I couldn't pull away."

"Somewhere else?" I asked.

"You can't see it from here, but there's a ladder going up to a rooftop terrace from our bedroom."

"Our?"

"Yes. Yours and mine. It's on the east side, so you can wish upon all the stars that cross the night sky."

My side? Should I have told him that all my wishes had come true? That he was back and I was in his arms again? But I didn't say anything. Instead, I kissed his lips once more, admiring his cleanly shaved face.

For the second round of catching up, we moved to his bedroom where Nick tested the limits of his king sized bed. I couldn't get enough and if it weren't for the urgent knock on the front door, we would have gone for seconds and thirds.

The pounding on the door shook me awake as a feeling of dread replaced the euphoria in my chest.

CHAPTER 29

Nick put on his jeans and opened the door.

"Carter? What's the matter?" he asked. The words jolted me out of my delirious state of arousal as I jumped back into mommy mode.

"It's Mackenzie. She's missing," I heard him say.

"What?"

I almost ran naked downstairs, but managed to put on my underwear. Instead of zipping up my dress, I pulled Nick's t-shirt over my head and rushed down.

"What are you talking about, missing?"

"Jo, we've checked everywhere."

"You couldn't have, because if you checked everywhere, you would have found her."

While Mackenzie was an adventurous child, I was sure that Carter hadn't looked for her thoroughly enough. She once fell asleep on top of Tank in a barn. The bull was younger back then, but still, much larger than Mackenzie. We found them cuddled together. If Tank had shifted, he could have easily crushed her, but the two of them had always gotten along so well that sometimes I thought they were meant to be best friends.

"How did you let my daughter get lost?" Nick accused.

"Wow, hold it right there, Navy boy. No one 'let' her get lost."

"I didn't mean it that way."

"Which way did you mean it, then? I've been more like a father to that little girl than you have."

"She's still my daughter."

"And she's my niece."

They were almost nose to nose, testosterone pouring out of their ears.

"Okay, you two. Tone it down. I know you both love her, and I'm sure she's somewhere."

Carter looked me up and down, and Nick stepped in front to cover me somewhat, at which point Carter frowned.

"What did she say?" I asked. "The last thing you can remember."

"She mentioned getting decorations for the special cake."

"The only decorations she keeps are the stones in the attic. Did you check the attic?"

"No, I didn't. Shit, I'm sorry. I didn't mean to interrupt you two."

I didn't remember the last time I'd been so calm about Mackenzie wandering off, but life was finally working out for me, and nothing could get me in a bad mood, except for the awful feeling I got in my stomach. Carter's phone rang, and then mine. He picked it up, his face going pale.

"Dad?" I asked through my receiver.

"Thank God you're all right. We were so worried when we heard Carter's house caught fire."

What?

I dropped the phone and bolted out the door. They yelled after me, but I barely heard them. Only muffles and sounds squeezed past all the dreadful thoughts that were rummaging through my mind. I ran until my legs ached and my feet bled. I ran like the ground was the only connection I had to Mackenzie, because without it, I couldn't get there. I ran when I wished I could fly. Carter's truck pulled in beside me as I was sprinting down the road, in a pair of panties and a t-shirt.

"Get in, Jo." Nick jumped out of the passenger seat and opened the back door for me. "And put on a pair of pants."

"Mackenzie?" I asked, pushing my feet through what looked like Nick's sweats: way too long and way too big, but they'd have to do. I rolled the top band down and the pant legs up.

"No word yet."

I prayed that she was safe. She was my life, and I'd die if anything happened to her. We weren't that far from our house, and the way Carter was driving, we'd be there in half a minute.

The sight of smoke billowing from our house stopped my pulse. "No, no, no."

"Shit!" Carter said, pressing his foot harder on the gas. The engine roared, and I was so grateful that Carter was a mechanic as well as a firefighter and had always kept the truck in pristine condition.

The smoke plumes got higher the closer we got, and I could see fire spewing out the front windows.

"God, please no." I covered my mouth with my hand.

"We'll get her, Jo. I promise."

Carter was focused on the destination, his nerves as calm as I'd ever seen, but I knew that he must have been dying on the inside. If anything had happened to Mackenzie... no, she *had* to be okay.

Captain Clark was running toward the house just as we pulled up. The half a minute it took us to get here felt like a lifetime. A few other firefighters wearing their full suits were affixing the hoses they'd carried on their backs, or maybe drove over in another car, to the fire hydrant.

Neither Carter nor Nick waited for instructions as Captain Clark called out to them as if they were part of the crew. I rushed behind them toward the house.

"Jo, stay back." Carter stopped me.

"She's my daughter."

"And I love her like she's mine as well. If she's in there, I promise to get her out." By that time, Nick was next to me, holding my arms. I was ready to bust through that fire without looking back.

"You can't go in there," Nick said. "Not without me."

"Wait, you can't both go in." I looked from Nick and then to Carter, and before I got a chance to protest, Nick took ahold of my hands. "You need to stay here for

Mackenzie. If something happens, our daughter will need you."

"Nick..."

"I love you." He kissed me quickly, and they both headed for the front door before Captain Clark was able to stop them. I doubted that a hundred men could have stopped them.

"Where is the fire truck?" I asked.

"It's being serviced," Captain Clark answered, then called out to his crew. "Joe, Andrew – my stupid heroic son just went in. You better get that water going."

But as they turned the hydrant on, air hissed out, along with a few stray drops.

"Shit! Carter! Nick! Get out of there!"

"Two minutes later, Nick came outside, carrying Mackenzie's limp body in his arms."

"Oh, my God!"

We quickly moved away from the house, and he set her on the ground. "Carter found her hiding in the attic. She was still conscious."

I knelt next to her, checking for any sign of breathing, but she I couldn't find any, and so I gave her mouth-to-mouth and began chest compressions.

"Come on, baby. Breathe!" A window burst in our direction with only a crackle of the glass as a warning when the cooler air with it before it shattered.

Nick was panting from exertion himself, but I couldn't look at him now. As I blew the next breath into Mackenzie, her eyes fluttered a little and she took a breath.

She coughed out a lungful and my heart soared with happiness. "I wanted to bake a cake for Daddy," she gasped.

"My son?" I heard Captain Clark ask.

"Baby, you're okay now. You're okay."

"Daddy? Where's Uncle Carter?" she asked, and we both looked to the burning house, just before Nick dashed back through the front door. As soon as he disappeared, flames swallowed the entrance. I pressed Mackenzie's head to my chest, blocking her eyes. If God forbid something happened, I didn't want her to remember this scene.

"Stay still, Mackenzie. We're going to give you some special air, okay?" Captain Clark placed an oxygen mask over her face just as Doctor Burke's car pulled up. "Will somebody please get my son out of that house!" he screamed.

"Mommy?" Mackenzie asked through the mask. "Is Uncle Carter okay?"

"Yes, Daddy went to get him. They'll be out in a moment." I wanted to believe my words, but looking at the flames spitting through the roof and a house that resembled a burnt skeleton with every passing minute, it was difficult. The next few seconds happened in slow motion. When Andrew, one of the firefighters, heard the first crack, he stepped away from the front door. He must have sensed it — Carter had told me that all firefighters sensed that moment. The trusses burned through and collapsed, then the walls and our home turned into a dragon's never-closing mouth. The flames and the heat pushed Andrew face down to the ground, and I felt it burn my lungs as I gasped in a breath of despair.

"No!" I stood up screaming, holding Mackenzie tightly against my body, away from the billowing flames. "No!"

Fire was everywhere, consuming the air I was trying to breathe, burning away my hopes and dreams. I fell to my knees as my father ran down the street. Marge was close behind him, out of breath. She froze when she saw me collapse.

"No," I sobbed, rocking Mackenzie back and forth in my arms. Just when I thought I had them both back in my life, they were taken away from me. I looked at the horrid black smoke taking away our precious memories when a familiar silhouette broke through the grey cloud: Nick was carrying Carter's lifeless body around the side of the house, where Carter's garage used to be. He was still within the flames' reach, and heat seared at them both. Nick's body, including his face and hair, were covered in soot. His pants and shirt were burnt through in random spots, showing red gashes of burnt flesh underneath.

Someone helped him with Carter's body, laying it in the shade.

"Honey, stay with Grandma and Grandpa. I'm going to check on Daddy and Carter." I left Mackenzie with Marge and my father.

I dashed to Nick and Carter and when I saw them up close, I froze. Carter's shirt was completely gone, burnt right off his body, and the left side of his torso was blistered in red, blood spewing from the skin that was nowhere to be found. Black, crispy spots dotted his face. Nick looked up at me, fear covering his eyes: a fear that he was too late.

I shook my head. Nick stood up and walked right into me. My body pressed to his and my arms would around him as I hid in his embrace, denying the possibility that I could lose Carter.

"I'm sorry, Jo. I really tried. He got trapped after he passed me Mackenzie from the attic."

"He saved Mackenzie?"

"We wouldn't have found her without him."

"Is he going to... " I couldn't even say it without the word getting stuck in my throat full of sorrow.

"I don't know. I don't know."

I saw Molly's car pull up. She jumped out and rushed to Carter's side, helping Doctor Burke to revive him.

"We need to get him to the hospital," I heard one of them say.

They didn't see me watching their expressions. The fear and desperation to work faster when they were already doing everything in their power said it all. I knew that he wouldn't make it. It felt like everyone in town was here now, and most were gathered around Carter. Mrs. Gladstone made the sign of a cross in the air over him. No one was fighting the blaze as it consumed the remainder of what used to be our home. The buckets full of water I'd seen some neighbors carrying were being thrown at the side of the house so that the flames wouldn't jump to Mrs. Gladstone's farm.

Andrew brought over what looked like a surfboard, except it had holes for handles at the sides. They carefully rolled Carter on top of it and then carried him to Doctor Burke's van. I ran back to Mackenzie, who was sitting with

Marge and my father, the oxygen mask over her face. I felt Nick right behind me.

"Mommy?" Mackenzie's eyes were full of tears.

"Yes, honey?"

"I wanted to bake a beach cake like the one you showed me in the picture when Daddy baked one for you, and I told Uncle Carter I needed special decorations and I went to the attic and when I came down Uncle Carter left and I smelled smoke but the door was locked."

He must have thought that Mackenzie had left the house to get the decorations. I took her in my arms and held her close. "It's okay, baby. Everything's going to be okay."

"But our home is gone." She gently laid her head on my shoulder and pulled in a sniffle.

"You know what, this town is our home."

Nick crouched beside us, smoothing his hand over her back. "Uncle Carter is a strong man, probably one of the strongest men I know."

"Where will I sleep now? My room is gone."

"If you'd like, and if it's okay with your Mommy, you can stay at our house."

Mackenzie may not have caught the "our", but I did. I set Mackenzie down and my father took her hand, saying, "Let's go get some cupcakes for the firefighters."

"We should take her into the hospital, just in case," Marge said.

I nodded. "Yeah, that's a good idea."

Besides, I wanted to be close to Carter. I needed him to know that we were praying for him.

"You're hurt." I touched Nick's face. He leaned into me, whispering, "I'll be fine, but if something happens to Carter... I'll never forgive myself."

For the first time since Nick's return, I felt like we truly needed each other to survive.

"The stove. It was acting up before. This wasn't your fault."

"I should have been quicker. I could have been, but the flames..." Nick appeared to be lost in his thoughts, as if his mind had traveled to something in the past I wasn't aware of.

"We need to take Mac to the hospital. We can get an update then."

Everyone drove down the one road leading out of our town toward the city. And all the way there, I couldn't help but wonder whether I'd lose another friend.

Molly was pacing the hall as Mackenzie and Nick got checked in. They'd go for chest x-rays to make sure there was no damage to their lungs. Mackenzie was sitting in her gown, right beside Nick's gurney, sucking on a Popsicle and smiling, playing a hand game with her father. The doctor said she should be fine since she didn't seem to be coughing or spitting up soot.

"How's Carter?" I asked Molly, once both Mackenzie and Nick settled in. Captain Clark sat in a corner, pulling his fingers through his hair, the way Carter always did, while trying to comfort Mrs. Clark. Molly pulled me away, out of earshot.

"He's still in surgery. He didn't regain consciousness, and the burns... they're pretty bad."

I took her hand into mine. "Carter's a fighter, Molly. He's got this. I know he does."

He has to.

"I'm worried, Jo. They won't tell me much because I'm not technically family, just a friend, so I can't get any info, but they haven't updated them either." She looked back to Mrs. Clark, whose eyes were so puffed up from crying she had difficulty opening them. She was holding a rosary in her hands, rolling the beads between her fingers after each Hail Mary.

"Come to x-ray with us. It will take your mind off Carter."

She released a breath and nodded. We spent the next hour wheeling Mackenzie around on a gurney and then a wheelchair until she was cleared by the doctors, along with Nick, before we returned to the waiting area. When the doctor came through the door, everyone stood up.

"He's in intensive care right now. The surgery went well, but with the third-degree burns he sustained, we had to remove a lot of dead tissue. There's a lot of skin missing, and the chances of infection are high."

"Is he breathing on his own?" Captain Clark asked.

"Yes, his lungs will recover. He'll need skin grafts soon. We'll get started on that as soon as his vital signs improve. His body is still in shock. There was a lot of fluid loss and we'll be monitoring him for edema, but if he does improve, we'll go ahead with the grafting as soon as possible."

"That's good news, isn't it?" Mrs. Clark asked. From the look on Molly's face, though, it didn't sound like so.

"Transplanting larger areas of skin could cause shock to his body."

"What if you had a matching donor?" Nick asked.

"Yes, that would help."

"Take me, then."

What?

"If I'm a match, take whatever skin you need to help Carter."

Mackenzie must have overheard us and raised her hand calling out from where she was sitting with Dad and Marge. "Me too. I want to help Uncle Carter too."

I smiled. Knowing there were so many people here praying for Carter gave me hope, and hope had brought Nick back into my life. If there was anyone who could pull through this, it was Carter.

CHAPTER 30

It didn't hit me that we were homeless until we returned to Hope Bay. The first two nights, I stayed at Dad and Marge's house. On the third night, Nick was released from the hospital. He was a match for Carter after all, so the doctors transplanted skin from Nick's thigh and buttock to his friend. It only made sense for me to take care of him, so I moved to the barn house with Mackenzie to take care of her father while he recovered. Days turned into weeks, weeks turned into months, and somewhere along the line we became a family again. I couldn't pinpoint the exact moment, but I knew the first time I stepped over that threshold with Mackenzie that we were home.

"How's my favorite woman?" Nick snaked his arms around my waist from behind, kissing the side of my neck.

"Perfect now." I turned around and met his lips, certain that no matter how much I kissed him, I couldn't get enough. They were tender, and over the past few months I'd grown to need them every day.

"And how is our little one?" He rubbed my belly, then crouched, kissing it though my dress. The baby kicked, and he smiled.

"He's up."

This baby was the exact opposite of Mackenzie. He'd started kicking two weeks ago and slept during the night, for which I was grateful, and was more active during the day. I dated our conception to the day of the fire, when I first made love to Nick after his return. He'd been excited about the pregnancy since we first found out. Actually, Nick was over the moon in love with my belly — he wanted to feel the baby's every kick and had fulfilled every single one of my pickle cravings. We had jars of these, courtesy of Mrs. Clark, who could not stop thanking Nick for saving Carter. If he could have, he'd have gotten up in the middle of the night to pee for me as well.

I in turn would never be able to express my gratitude enough to Carter, who had saved our daughter.

I kissed Nick's expectant lips when he stood back up, then pulled my finger over Mackenzie's *Welcome Home* drawing. She was now adding finishing touches on the flowers and butterflies she'd drawn. Carter was coming home today, and we'd planned a huge "welcome back" party at the Clark house. I'd had a special wooden plaque made for him from the only piece of unburnt wood that I'd found in the rubble, inscribed, "No fire can burn hot enough to destroy our family."

"Do you think he'll like it?" I asked Nick, pointing to the package.

"He'll love it. And I found something else in the rubble as well." Nick pulled out a rock from his pocket: his rock, with the scratched out "N."

"What? How?"

"I went back after the investigation. It took a while to find it, but I did." He set it on the table in front of Mackenzie.

"Daddy, this is our rock."

"Yes, it is."

"We should frame it."

"I have a better idea. Why don't we go to Pebble Beach and skip it? I think it's time for this little stone to hit some new records."

I couldn't remember the last time we went stone skipping, and with the few days that we had left of this beautiful fall weather, I was looking forward to making use of it before the party.

"Maybe I should change out of this dress. It feels too fancy," I said. Last week, I'd gone shopping in the city with Marge, and she'd insisted on buying the white summer dress for me. It had beautiful white floral patterns and right now, at least, it fit perfectly.

"You look beautiful, and it's a special occasion, isn't it? Carter's finally coming back."

"Yes, you're right. It is special."

"And if he wants to move in here for a while, he's very welcome to. Our home is his home."

"Thank you for saying that, but last I heard, Molly was taking him into her house. She finished her residency."

"Is she really giving up the hospital for him?" After becoming a nurse, Molly had decided to be a doctor.

"She said she's gaining much more by moving back. And Doctor Burke will be retiring soon, so she'll be the only other doctor in town."

"Come on, Mackenzie, put your dress on as well." Nick winked to her and she winked back. I'd never seen them do that before. Nick then leaned into me, whispering, "I hope you don't mind, but I bought a special dress for her as well."

"You bought a dress?"

"Yes. Mom helped."

On any normal day, I would have questioned the gesture, but given that we'd lost all of our possessions in the fire, we'd been slowly catching up each week with clothes, toys and other items that we still needed for the house.

When Mackenzie came downstairs, she was glowing. Her smile stretched wide, just like her father's when he smiled.

"Looks like Daddy is good at picking dresses. Uncle Carter's not going to recognize this big girl."

"It's a special dress."

"Yes, it is. Come on, let's get going."

"Daddy, can I pick some flowers for Uncle Carter?" Mackenzie asked, and winked at him again. It looked like this was a new thing between the two of them. Seeing thei growing bond fused the broken pieces of my heart like crazy glue.

"Of course."

Fifteen minutes later, we were in the car, on our way to Pebble Beach. "You think we'll make it? The party starts in fifteen minutes." I looked nervously at my watch, but Nick was as calm as ever.

"We'll make it."

We pulled up over the grass, and I took Mackenzie's hand. "Mommy, can you hold these for me?" she asked, passing me her bouquet of beautiful daisies.

"Of course."

Nick took her other hand and we headed over the hill toward the lake. As soon as we passed the top, I froze. Right by the water, a floral arch with flowing white fabric at the sides had been set up. Chairs were lined to the left and to the right, with an aisle down the middle, and our entire family, friends, and pretty much the whole town was waiting. Near the head of the aisle, Carter was sitting in a wheelchair, waiting with Molly, smiling. We walked toward them with Mackenzie between us. It didn't hit me until I felt everyone's eyes on Nick and me that this was not a welcome back party for Carter.

"Nick?"

But he was already down on one knee in front of me, looking up. "I want to spend the rest of my life with you. You are my love. You are my everything, and I would not only give up my life for you, but also for anyone here. We were meant to live in this town and nowhere else, and I promise to spend the remainder of my life here, with you, our children, and one day, our grandchildren. I know we're technically still engaged, but since so much has happened,

I'd like to ask you in front of our family and friends: will you marry me, Joelle Kagen? Will you marry me today?"

Mackenzie urgently tugged on my hand. "Say yes, Mommy. Say yes!" Her eyes were filled with joy, the kind that soared through her and filled the hearts of all the guests.

I laughed, feeling my happy tears trickle over my cheeks, and slowly drew my gaze from our daughter to Nick.

Molly passed me a handkerchief.

"Yes, I'll marry you today."

Mackenzie squealed, Marge cried, and everyone cheered.

"Are you the best man?" I asked Carter. He stood up from his wheelchair, his legs a little wobbly, but Molly took him under her arm, steadying him. "I'm so happy you're doing better.

The right side of his face was still bandaged to protect the healing wounds.

"You can't get rid of me, Cupcake. I'm like glitter."

"How do you know about glitter?"

"Mac."

I laughed.

"Molly, will you—"

"Of course. It would be my honor."

And so the five of us slowly walked down the aisle toward the arch where Father Sinclair was waiting. The scene was out of this world. When I woke up that morning, I didn't expect that I'd be married by the end of the day, yet here we were, a husband and wife, sharing a kiss that sealed our vows. Mackenzie clapped with happiness, and everyone cheered.

"Is it time, Daddy?" she asked.

"Yes, I think it's time."

He reached into his pocket for the stone I'd given him for his thirteenth birthday. I removed Mackenzie's sandals, then mine. Nick rolled up his pants and left his shoes and socks on the shore. The three of us stepped into the shallows of Stone Lake, and Nick handed Mackenzie the special stone. She swung her arm like a professional, lunging the stone forward. It skipped further than I'd ever seen her throw, gliding over the glassy water until its heart shape sank to the bottom.

The sound of applause and laughter echoed around us. Dad and Marge cried, Molly leaned over to Carter and kissed him, and for the first time in my life I knew that I didn't need another falling star to wish upon, because all my dreams had come true. The world ceased to be his and mine, and became ours.

Dear Reader,

I hope you enjoyed reading Yours and Mine. If you have time, I would love for you to leave an honest review for the novel.

Do you love Carter and Molly as much as I do? Well, Carter's been talking to m e day and night and has been persistent. Especially when he talks dirty. It's a whole new ball game for this dude when he wants to woo a lady, but his mouth gets away from him. So the good news is that Carter and Molly will get their own book! When? Most likely before the end of the year (2016), though if he keeps talking so much, it may be earlier.

Happy Reading!

Lacey Silks

To be the first to know about new releases visit my website www.laceysilks.com to sign up for email alerts. I don't spam and only send information when I have something important to share with you.

About the Author

Lacey is a USA Today Bestselling Author who enjoys writing Erotic and Contemporary Romances, with a touch of suspense. Her stories come from her life, dreams and fantasies. She's a happily married wife with two kids. Lacey likes to make her readers blush and experience the story as if they were the characters. Drawing on the reader's most sensitive emotions through realistic stories satisfies her more than... ...ok not really, but you get the point;) She likes a pinkish shade on a woman's cheeks, men with large feet and sexy lingerie – especially when it's torn off the body. Her favorite piece of clothing is a birthday suit.

If you enjoyed Yours and Mine, please consider leaving a review. All authors depend on the support of their readers to find an audience.

Also by Lacey Silks

Dazzled by Silver (prequel to the Layers Trilogy)
Layers Deep (Book 1)
Layers Peeled (Book 2)
Layers Off (Book 3)

Crossed (prequel to the Crossed Series)
Layers Crossed (Book 1)
Double Crossed (Book 2)
Crossed Off (Book 3)

When Things Go Wrong (short prequel)
Cheaters Anonymous (Book 1)
Loyal Cheaters (Book 2)
Broken Cheaters (Book 3)
Chloe (Book 4)

Perfectly Equipped (0.5 short prequel)
Perfectly Seduced (Book 1)
Perfectly Kissed (1.5 short prequel)
Perfectly Loved (Book 2)

Standalone, Friends to Lovers Series
My First, My Last: an erotic romance novel
Yours and Mine

Connect with Me Online:
https://www.facebook.com/LaceySilksAuthor
http://laceysilks.com/

Acknowledgments

Yours and Mine came to be for three reasons:

1. I wanted dot tell a story of friends who became lovers and fought through life's obstacles to stay together.

2. My First, My Last is probably one of my favourite novels that I wrote, and so I wanted to create a similar feeling (though the two are completely different).

3. A bunch of great ladies decided we would all write a Friends with Benefits series, with a Friends to Lovers trope, and release them within days of each other. And so that's how the Friends with benefits Series came to be.

This novel was different than what I usually write as it didn't have the suspense and some violence, that's in the other series. Okay, maybe there is some suspense, but it's different kind. I wanted to show the strength of love, perseverance and family. I needed to keep hope present throughout and I "hope" I accomplished that.

To my AA (not what you're thinking) group: I've learned so much from everyone there, thank you, thank you, thank you.

To the LOL Ladies: you're the funniest and most supportive chicks ever!

To the Bimbos: I wouldn't be where I am today without you.

To my readers: I love your emails and adore your excitement. You make me want to write more. There's nothing better than knowing you've enjoyed my work.

To anyone who took a chance on my books – thank you!

To my family, I could not do what I love without you. Mom, your go getter attitude has rubbed off on me. Dad, your humour is infectious. Mike, "all you need is love" (thank you for doing all the chores when I can't). Maya and Alex, you are who I live for. You are my life.

I am grateful to my editors, beta readers and friends for their invaluable input, critique, support and love.

Made in the USA
Charleston, SC
04 September 2016